Poor Creatures

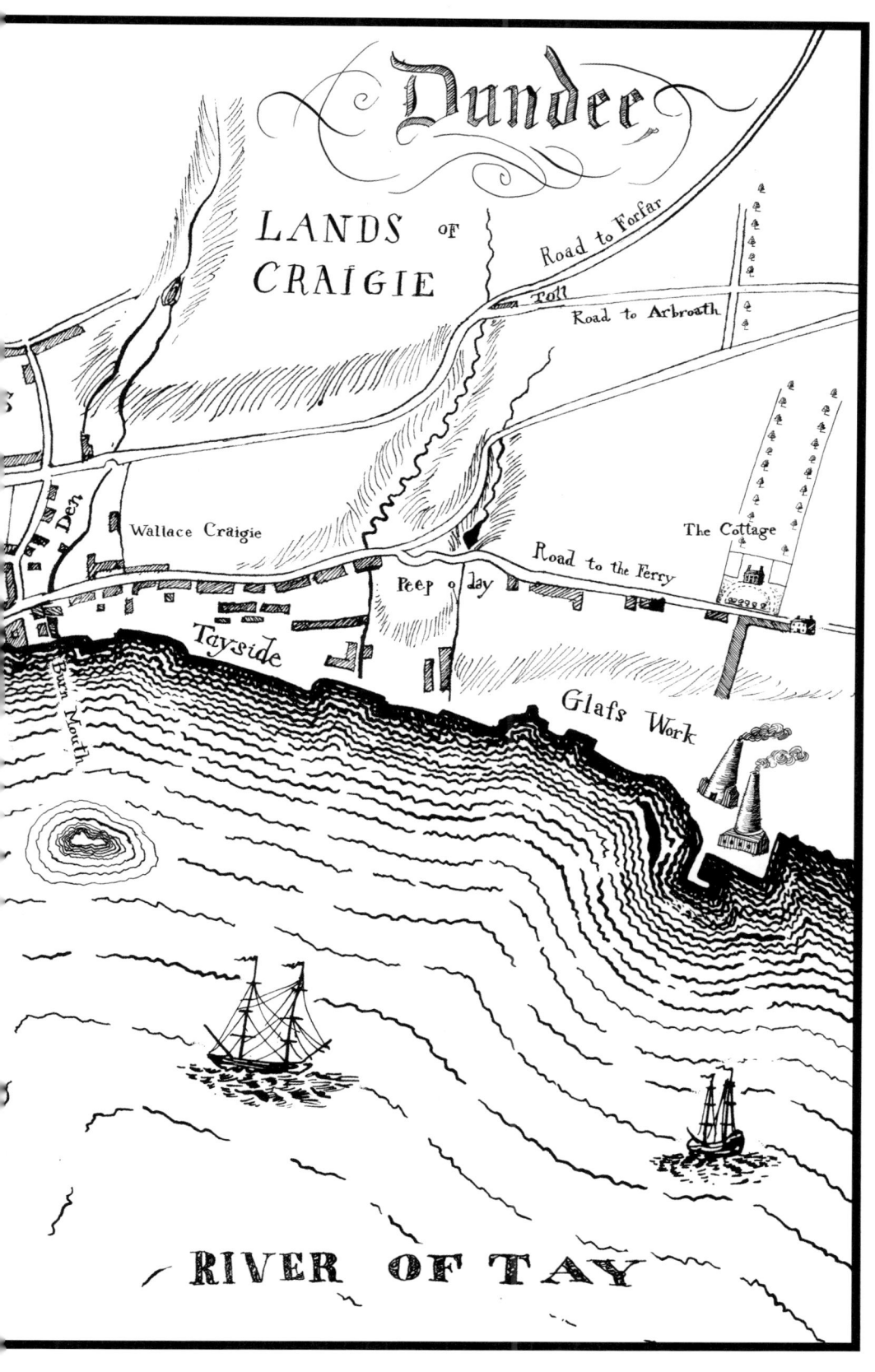

Poor Creatures

MAIRI KIDD

Black&White

First published in the UK in 2025 by Black & White Publishing
An imprint of Bonnier Books UK
5th Floor, HYLO, 105 Bunhill Row,
London, EC1Y 8LZ

Copyright © Mairi Kidd 2025

All rights reserved.
No part of this publication may be reproduced,
stored or transmitted in any form by any means, electronic,
mechanical, photocopying or otherwise, without the
prior written permission of the publisher.

The right of Mairi Kidd to be identified as Author of this
work has been asserted by her in accordance with the
Copyright, Designs and Patents Act, 1988.

This is a work of fiction. Whilst inspired by true events, names, places, events and incidents are either the products of the author's imagination or used fictitiously.

Endpaper illustrated map © Tom Morgan-Jones.

A CIP catalogue record for this book is available from the British Library.

ISBN (HBK): 978 1 78530 648 8
ISBN (TPBK): 978 1 785301 649 5

1 3 5 7 9 10 8 6 4 2

Typeset by IDSUK (Data Connection) Ltd
Printed and bound in Great Britain by Clays Ltd, Elcograf S.p.A.

The authorised representative in the EEA is
Bonnier Books UK (Ireland) Limited.
Registered office address: Floor 3, Block 3, Miesian Plaza,
Dublin 2, D02 Y754, Ireland
compliance@bonnierbooks.ie
www.bonnierbooks.co.uk

To Ged and Adele

'Everything one sees on Earth
Is dolls' stuff, and nothing else.
All that man encounters
He plays with like a child.
Ardently he loves for a short while
What he discards so easily thereafter.
Thus man is, one finds,
Not only once but always a child.'

Poem from the lying-in room of Sara Ploos Van Amstel-Rothé's cabinet house, Netherlands c.1700

Cast of characters

Prologue
Margaret Nicholson, c.1750–1828. A seamstress, later a subject of P. B. Shelley's poetry.

Our protagonists
Mary Wollstonecraft Godwin, later Mary Shelley, 1797–1851.

Isabella 'Isabel' Baxter, later Isabella Booth, 1795–1863.

Mary's parents (London)
William Godwin, 1756–1836. Radical political philosopher, journalist and novelist.

Mary Wollstonecraft, 1759–1797. Philosopher and writer. Died of post-partum complications after Mary's birth.

Isabel's parents (Dundee)
William Thomas 'Thomas' Baxter, c.1764–1842. Sailmaker and political radical.

Isabella Doig, 1771–1811.

Mary's birth family
Half-sister *Frances 'Fanny' Imlay*, also known as Godwin and Wollstonecraft, 1794–1816. Illegitimate daughter of Mary Wollstonecraft, raised by William Godwin.

Mary Jane Godwin, née Vial, aka Mrs Clairmont (assumed name), 1768–1841. Translator, publisher and bookseller, and William Godwin's second wife from 1801.

Mary Jane's children, *Clara Mary Jane 'Claire' Clairmont*, *Charles Clairmont*, and William and Mary Jane's son, *William Godwin* the younger.

Eliza Bishop, née Wollstonecraft, and *Everina Wollstonecraft*, Mary Wollstonecraft's sisters. Governesses and teachers.

Isabel's birth family
Siblings *Margaret*, *Jessie*, *Elizabeth*, *Christina 'Christy'*, *Robert*, *John Cowley*.

David Booth, 1766–1846. Self-taught brewer, teacher and scholar. Margaret's husband and father of their children *William* and *Isabella 'Izy'* (in *Poor Creatures*, 'Tibby').

Mary's wider circle
Percy Bysshe Shelley, 1792–1822, heir to the Shelley Baronetcy of Castle Goring, poet, dramatist and political radical.

Harriet Shelley, née Westbrook, 1795–1816. Shelley's first wife.

Prologue

London, 1786

MARGARET HAD DRESSED CAREFULLY FOR the momentous occasion of meeting the King. She had chosen a pretty overdress with sprigs of red flowers on a pink ground, cut in the fashion they called *à l'Anglaise* to show the paler underdress with its flounces at sleeve and hem. She was plumper of form than she had been as a younger woman, but her neck was slim enough still, and the skin of her bosom unblemished. She tied a blue velvet ribbon around her throat, and tucked a fichu of fine lace into her bosom. Over all she wore a black silk cloak of magnificently generous cut, with a great bonnet in the same silk, muffin-topped with a ruched brim and veil behind. She styled her red hair carefully below her under-cap of lace, and she made her face up neatly with powder and rouge and eyebrow soot. The clothes were all the work of her own needle and she looked every inch the respectable wife – high, but not too high, and elegant, if not quite of the first order of fashion.

The weather was fine after showers of rain, and beads of sweat ran down Margaret's back as she made her careful way along the mile and a half of cobbled streets between Marylebone and St James's Palace, her scroll clutched in her gloved hand.

All across the land, they said, the harvest would be a rich one. Farmer George – for so they called the King – would be pleased, and his people pleased with him in turn.

There was already a small crowd gathered outside the palace gate when she arrived, and Margaret took her place in the back, out of the sun. Another woman tried to catch her eye, hoping to trade stories of hardship, no doubt, but Margaret bent her head so the wide brim of her hat hid her face, and the woman took the hint and turned away. In a few moments she had found a new target and Margaret heard her expounding on a property she was owed by the Crown; she said she had petitioned the King twenty times or more on the matter, but to no avail.

Around midday, a great sound of jingling and creaking was heard further down the street, the pounding of horses and the shouts of guards. The gates swung open and the petitioners began to press forward, and Margaret was pushed between two men and into the heart of the crowd. It was hopeless, she would never get to the front. But then the carriage turned in, the crowd parted and she was in exactly the right place, no more than two feet from where they were unfolding the steps so King George might climb down among them. His leg appeared first, in white hose and silk breeches, and then he was out, a tall man, quite stout, with a ruddy face and a large nose. He wore a blue velvet coat with silver buttons and braid, and a sunburst embroidered on the left breast in thread of gold, so he fairly blazed in the bright sun and hurt Margaret's eyes.

She reached out then, with the scroll in her hand, and the King took it in his, and then she took the knife from its hiding place behind the busk of her bodice. It cut her breast as she drew it out, but she barely noticed; it felt no more consequential than the sting of a bee. She stabbed the knife at his chest, remembering what they said, the skin is tougher than you think, thick as the skin on an orange, you need to put some strength behind the knife to get it in. But it didn't work, the blade skittered off something hard – a button or embroidery or perhaps a rib – and her arm jarred with the impact, so she almost dropped the knife. She pulled it back and tried again, only somehow he had got his arm up and this time the knife caught in the thick cuff of his sleeve. For a second it seemed all was frozen, the King's protruding blue eyes wide with shock, staring wetly into her own. She drew her hand back to try again, harder, but by then two yeomen were on her, pulling her arm upwards so she dropped the knife, lifting her away bodily while she struggled and fought.

'I am well,' the King shouted, 'there is no harm.'

The crowd had caught up with events, now, and they pressed forward in fury, screaming for Margaret's blood until it seemed they might lynch her, right there in the stableyard. It was all the guards could do to hold them back, they threw punches and horseshit and spat at her, until the King bellowed for calm.

'The poor creature is mad! Do not hurt her! She has not hurt me!'

The crowd calmed at that, a little. More guards ran from the palace, and Margaret and the King were jostled inside. No one knew what to do with Margaret then, so they left her in a room inside, taking her ribbon and her hat, with its strings, and her fichu, and even her stockings, so she could not choke the life from herself. The room was grand, not in the servants' quarters, or the guards', but a real room for royalty, all soft gilding and velvet drapes and dusty air. Like a good servant, Margaret did not like to sit, so she stood in the centre of the room and closed her eyes. They had taken her cloak, but the smell of horseshit still clung to her clothes and hair.

At length, she was taken to another room where eight or nine men in powdered wigs sat around a table covered with green baize. She stood on one side, although by now she was worn out and wobbled so that they had to give her a chair to hold, else she would have fallen. They asked her question after question, her name, her place of residence, her birthplace and her parents, her trade. She answered all, though her voice was faint; her name was Margaret Nicholson, she lived here in London in Wigmore Street, she was born in Stockton in the north country, her parents George, a barber, and Anne, and she had been a maid but now was in her own employ as a mantua maker. Then they showed her the knife and asked if it was hers and she said yes, she had had it from Lord Coventry's butler when she was in service there, it was a fruit knife, the handle made of ivory, but she used it for fish and meat too.

They looked at one another as she spoke and then one of them said he had a very serious question to ask her and she must answer truthfully – had she meant to kill the King?

She said she did not know; she thought perhaps she had only meant to give him a scare.

The men looked at one another then, and one of them said it might be true – after all, a fruit knife was no weapon for killing.

'Do you have a grievance against His Majesty King George?' another asked.

Margaret thought of the woman outside. 'I petitioned him upwards of twenty times,' she said. 'About a property I should have had from the Crown.'

The men looked at each other, and the one that seemed to be the head man said they would have to look into that. They scribbled down a few more notes with their quills and then they said she would be taken to the Bethlehem Hospital while they made up their minds what to do with her. This was not a punishment, they kept saying, just a place where she would be safe for now, for she must have seen how angry the crowd had been – they had been like to tear her limb from limb. A woman brought back her cloak, brushed down, and then she was taken outside and put in a carriage with two guards, and she fell into sleep as they swung and swayed and rattled through the dark streets.

She woke as the carriage halted outside a forbidding building, and then she was lifted down by the guards and rushed in a great door that clanged shut behind her like the gates of Hell. Inside, two women stripped her of all her fine garments and gave her a rough linen shift to dress herself in instead. They must have been woken from sleep, for they yawned and complained as they marched her down corridor after corridor, each lined with tall metal doors behind which Margaret could hear all manner of strange clanking and crying. They stopped at one door, and opened it with a great key. Inside was a room with six iron bedsteads bolted to the floor, and they chained Margaret by the hand to the furthest of these and left her there with five other women, all likewise restrained.

So much Margaret saw before she turned her face into the straw mattress of the bed. She had her blood, and they had given her no rags, so she lay there curled up in her shame and tried to ignore the distant sounds of clanking and screaming that seemed to fill the very air, so she could taste the misery of the place on her lips. The other women in the room appeared to be asleep, at first, but then one awoke and began to pace to and fro on the end of a chain that bound her by the foot, sniffing the air and whining like a dog.

'Blood,' she whined, 'blood.'

'Don't mind her,' a voice said, and Margaret turned her head to see a small, birdlike woman watching her from the next bed. 'She thinks she's a werewolf.'

'A what?' Margaret asked.

The woman laughed. 'She believes she can turn into a wolf by moonlight,' she said. 'You'll understand soon enough. She'll growl at you and show you her teeth. Perfectly normal teeth, good even, but she believes these ones . . .' the woman gestured to her eye teeth with her fingers, 'she believes they're fangs. She asks for raw meat to eat, and twice she has bitten an orderly, drawing blood.'

'Has she bitten you?' Margaret asked, horrified.

The woman laughed. 'No.' She lifted her wrist and rattled the chain that bound her. 'None of us can reach the others. The orderlies have to come close enough to feed her, though, and when her madness is upon her, she snaps and snarls at them. Once they put her in a sort of bodice that bound her arms behind her, but that was no use; she ran straight for them and leaped on them, and by the time they had her under control, one of them had lost the fleshy part of his nose. Sometimes she shits on the floor, like a dog. What's your name?'

Margaret didn't register the question, still too horrified at the image of the woman opposite biting the nose off a man, and so the woman asked again.

'Margaret,' Margaret said. 'Margaret Nicholson.'

The woman seemed thrilled. 'You're the one that tried to kill the King!' she said. 'It was all the orderlies could talk of yesterday. They say he spoke for you, he said you did not hurt him.'

'I didn't,' Margaret said. 'The knife wouldn't go in.' She mimed the motion of stabbing again, into the air, still unsure whether it had been a button or a rib she had hit. 'Anyway, I only meant to scare him. I think. I can't remember, really. I'm so tired, they yabbered and jabbered on at me for hours until I thought I should go mad.'

The woman smiled at that, a crooked smile, but she didn't say any more.

'What's your name?' Margaret asked.

'Grace,' the woman said. 'Grace Abney.'

'And why are you here?' Margaret asked. 'You don't seem mad to me. You don't show any signs of thinking you're a beast.'

The woman laughed. 'Not on Thursdays.'

'It's Wednesday,' Margaret said. She remembered that. When she got dressed and left her lodging, it had been Wednesday morning.

'It's Thursday now,' Grace said. 'They brought you here after midnight.'

'So what did you do?' Margaret asked again.

'Nothing,' said Grace, 'and yet here I am. The two at the other end are Mabel and Polly, they're no bother. Mabel's just old, she lost the thread of her mind and kept pleasuring herself on the street, so they sent her here to live out her days pleasuring herself whenever she pleases. Polly's harmless, but she isn't right, so she can't fend for herself. She was born like that and when her mother died she had no one to look after her, so she ended up here. She trusts everyone, and I worry Eliza might get her teeth in her one day. In the middle, that's Ada. Her son died and something cut adrift in her head. She weeps and weeps and cannot stop. They brought her here when she tried to slit her own throat. A bad job she made of it, she's a lady, you see, not used to gutting fish or the like, and she made a dreadful scar but missed all the important veins completely.'

'And then there's you,' said Margaret.

'And then there's me,' Grace said, 'and you. It's not so bad, you'll see. Now, let's try to get some rest while Eliza's wolf is sleeping.'

Margaret found out what Grace had done a day or so later, when Eliza turned back from a wolf to a woman – by her own lights – and told her. It seemed Grace had killed her children, several of them, or perhaps they were born dead, or just died of illness or hunger. Whatever had done for them, Grace was found in her house with all of their little bodies under the floor and one in a basket, although it had been dead perhaps two years.

'She'll never talk of it,' said Eliza, who was quite a wise woman when she wasn't in the grip of her madness. 'She can't. It's like her mind has just folded it all away. It was all anyone could speak about when she was discovered. The scandal sheets were full of it.'

Now, though, it seemed the scandal sheets were full of nothing but Margaret herself; she was quite infamous. Over the next days, they had so many visits from orderlies keen to see her that their room was like Covent Garden on a Friday night in June. They brought the broadsheets for her to see, and then the chapbooks – less than a week after she had tried to stab the King, a whole publication was for sale about Margaret and her life, fifty pages long, and many more followed along. These were full of the strangest mishmash of facts and nonsense, getting her homeplace wrong, unable to decide whether she had been a dutiful maid or a bold strumpet, inventing fanciful stories of seductions and Swiss valets and starvation.

Margaret couldn't make up her mind whether to be affronted or amused, but at least the orderlies brought coffee, and snuff, sweetmeats, and sometimes gin, and they treated her with more kindness than the others said was their wont. Margaret made them small articles with her needle in return, handkerchiefs and needle cases, embroidered with her initials, and they took them out to sell for an enormous price, the mania for Margaret being so wild. Grace and the other women helped with the hemming and other plain work, so they fairly had a little industry going, and everyone benefited from the arrangement and seemed much cheered by it. Margaret was even invited to dine with the hospital steward and some other fine people. They gave her clothes back to her for the purpose, and very polite the other guests were to her too, although they goggled at her when they thought she wasn't looking.

In this way, Margaret settled in, and found herself quite content. It was to be her home, after all – a few days after she arrived, she had been examined by the Privy Council and they said they had found many strange writings in her lodgings, letters that said she was the rightful heir to the throne and all sorts of fanciful things like that. She didn't remember writing those things, perhaps she had done so in gin, and they spoke very high and agitated her, so when she tried to unravel it all, she found she tied herself in worse knots and somehow ended up saying it was a mystery, her grievance, she knew she had one but it was one she could not relate, and then she buttoned her lip and would say no more.

After that they had her speak with a man called Monroe, over long hours, and he said she was mad and should live out her life at Bedlam. He said this was a kindness, the penalty otherwise for a woman guilty of treason was burning – they knew she was a woman, and not a man disguised, because so many had suggested the latter that the court had felt obliged to bring in some elderly midwives to check. She should be thankful to the King, Monroe said, for still he would not see her harmed. He insisted she had done him no damage and should be cared for kindly.

And so Margaret came back to Grace and the others and took up her needle again, quite calm and peaceful and content. She expected that her infamy would soon dim and she would be left in peace, but it was not to be. Her crime had fairly gripped the public imagination, and the orderlies told her she was being talked of in France and even in America, she was famous across the whole world as a lunatic murderess, a scheming swindler, or a romantic heroine abused at the hands of rich men.

Two years later, or so, they heard that Farmer George himself had taken leave of his senses. It was an orderly that told them, a woman called Smith who was as lazy as the day was long and was forever idling in their room talking to anyone who would listen. Mabel was gone by then, having pleasured herself to a ripe old age, and Ada had made a recovery of sorts and been taken home by her sister. Mabel's bed had been taken by another girl like Polly, with the same button face and easy smile, and the two of them were as happy as larks together, singing songs and clapping until anyone not already gone mad would find themselves so. Ada's bed had been taken by Lucy, who had been sent there for low morals, although she argued vehemently that the low morals in the case more properly belonged to the uncle who had got her with child when she was just thirteen.

She was mad for politics, was Lucy, and soon she had Margaret embroidering for the abolition of slavery, copying a pattern for a man in chains, and slogans like 'Am I not your Brother?' and 'Thou God seest me' onto needle cases and watch pockets and all sorts. Lucy asked Margaret to teach her embroidery, too, although she had little patience for it and was forever twisting her thread and pricking her finger so it bled onto the cloth.

Lucy didn't mind, though. 'In this way our needles will prick the conscience of those who would deny the humanity of their brethren,' she said piously.

Eliza had become quite a skilled sewer in her own right, when she reckoned herself a woman and not a wolf, and she stitched alongside them while Grace helped trace the patterns onto the cloth. Eliza still had her times of trial, and she was under the care of Monroe the mad-doctor, who had attended Margaret before her trial, and who – as Smith told them – now also had the care of Farmer George. As Smith chattered away to Eliza and Lucy, Margaret remembered the cut on her breast from the orange knife, the day she had attacked the King. Had her blood mingled with his own as she plunged the blade in, leaving its taint of madness in his veins? Had she truly killed him after all?

By then, of course, it was no matter; her old life was packed up, the tangled threads all snipped and neatly tied off here in Bethlehem, where she would end her days.

Part I

Dundee, 1812

1

A WARM WIND FROM THE WEST carried the ghost of burnt sugar and oranges from the jams Mrs Keiller cooked up in the small factory beside her family provisions shop on the Seagate in Dundee. It stole into the house through every open window and tickled Isabel Baxter's nose in the secret place where she sat, curled up with her book on a wide windowsill in Father's library, hidden by a heavy velvet curtain that was never opened for fear of fading the volumes on the shelving on the adjacent wall.

Isabel was too old for hide-and-seek, of course, being seventeen and second oldest of the Baxter children to remain at home. The habit had come about the year before, when Mother had died. Isabel had done little of the nursing; Mother had insisted they had had a trained woman in so Isabel and her older sister Christy could continue with their studies, but Mother had liked to have Isabel sit with her and read to her in the afternoons. It had been a hot summer, and they had stifled with the windows closed – Mother couldn't stand to have the sickly scent of the Keiller woman's boilings in her room. It wasn't the taste, for bitter marmalade was one of the few things she could stomach in her last months; she said it helped the saliva flow, so she could swallow a corner of toast or a crumb of cake without choking. Still, she found the smell impossible to bear.

She could eat nothing, by the end, of course, Mother, and neither could anyone else, the nerves of their stomachs were so shot through. The night she died, Isabel went to cover a mirror and caught sight of herself in the glass. She scarcely recognised the red-eyed creature looking back. She had lost weight, her once rosy cheeks were thin and pale, and her wavy black hair seemed to have lost its gloss. For many nights she had fallen into bed exhausted, only to lie awake through the long hours till dawn.

That night, Isabel had a terrifying dream. She had always had a fascination for the second sight and suchlike things, and once even she thought she had experienced it, seeing her friend Jemima walk towards her on the sands when Isabel knew the poor lass had been sewn into her shroud three nights before. Now Isabel dreamed she walked again on the same stretch of shoreline, but this time it was Father who had gone, and Father who walked past her as though he could not see her or hear her, no matter how she called or waved. She became afraid it was a premonition, and she could not rest when he was out of her sight. That was when she found her hidey-hole, and had taken to spending her days there, unseen, able to breathe more easily listening to him go about the business of his day. It was easy enough to slip out the window, when she heard Cookie call her, and stroll in through the door as though she had been outside taking the air or picking flowers for the parlour all the while. Opening the window caused a noise, of course, but fortunately Father had a weak bladder, and left regularly to use the pot.

The fear had dulled, in time, as Father showed no signs of failing, but by then Isabel had grown used to having a place of her own, where she might have a little respite from Christy's dullness and her little brother John Cowley's demands that she play with him, and so she would take herself there on warm days with a book and curl up like a cat in the sun. This was how she came to be trapped there, when her sister Margaret arrived unannounced from her home across the River Tay in Fife.

Any visit from Margaret was a rare happening, and a surprise one quite unheard of. She was the eldest of the Baxter siblings, and had survived consumption as a child. It had left her frail, if lovely, touching her blonde good looks with a sort of frantic brilliance of lip and eye. She had suffered regular episodes of illness ever after, and no one had expected her to marry or to leave home. During Isabel's childhood, it had seemed the house was run to suit Margaret, the rest of the siblings shushed and scolded whenever they looked set to disturb her peace. Their next eldest sisters, Jessie and Elizabeth, had both married young and gone to live far from home, and Isabel suspected they had done so to escape her. They could have saved themselves some trouble for, in the end, Margaret had surprised them all by announcing that she was to marry David Booth, a widowed friend of Father's. He was twenty years her senior, and lived in a strange stone house in Fife he had carved out from one end of the great complex of barns where he carried out his trade of brewing. Margaret had been installed there after the wedding, and had rarely stirred forth since. Two children had followed and her brilliant good looks had dimmed, but she had lost none of her expectations that her illness should be uppermost in her family's minds at all times.

It was a little after the dinner hour when their carriage turned into the drive, and there was immediate consternation among the servants. Isabel heard it all through the open window, the fuss as a maid was called to bring in the baby, and then sent back to set out a chair inside the door, so Margaret might sit to remove her cloak and bonnet once David had lifted her from the carriage. A manservant was called to help, and Margaret shouted that she needed David's arm again, and Father's, to get her into the house and settled. Isabel expected that they would go to the parlour, and was opening the study window wider to slip out when the door swung open and Father came in, calling for a blanket and a glass for a measure Margaret was to take. David directed Margaret to the sofa and Isabel was well cornered, for there was no way she could open the window further while they were all there without being discovered.

For a time all speech was of Margaret's needs and comforts after the hardships of the road and the ferry crossing. Father was solicitous and David practical, and Margaret acknowledged their attentions in a flat and colourless voice. Eventually, she said she was well enough, but they knew that Father had had a letter from William Godwin in London, and they wanted to hear it. Father demurred, saying Margaret should rest herself, but David added his voice to his wife's. He said they had come to hear Godwin's news and would be much obliged if Father would read his letter to them. Father couldn't say much to that, and Isabel heard him riffling for the letter among the papers on his desk.

'Godwin sends his daughter Mary north to spend some weeks with us,' Father said, evidently having found the letter. 'He writes ... let me see ... he writes that he intends to send her on the packet *Osnaburgh*. In fact, although I say "intends", she will be on her way by now. The ship left London on the eighth of June and she should be with us on the thirteenth.'

'Alone?' Margaret said, sounding as close to animated as Isabel had heard her since her marriage. 'A fourteen-year-old girl, travelling from London to Dundee on her own?'

'Indeed,' Father said, 'I would not always act as Godwin does. He says his Mary is a bold creature, somewhat imperious, though without vice. He thinks she has considerable intellect. We spoke much of education when we met.'

'I do not understand your loyalty to the man,' Margaret said. 'Either of you.'

There was silence for a moment and Isabel almost laughed, picturing their faces. William Godwin was a great man in London, a famous man, a political radical reckoned by many as one of the great thinkers of the age. David, on the other hand, was the child of plain people, a man with almost no schooling who had become learned through the force of his own will. She knew David had courted William Godwin's attention, and counted himself beyond fortunate to have gained it. Father had been introduced to Godwin by David as a fellow radical, and liked him well enough, but David treasured his friendship above all things.

Margaret had evidently seen there was no chance of dissuading either of them, since she changed tack back to the daughter. 'I can't think the girl can be so bold as to seek to travel alone on a mail packet,' she grumbled. 'Why has he not sent a servant with her?'

'He has not two pennies to rub together,' David said. Isabel was surprised that he would speak so bluntly of Godwin's affairs, but perhaps he saw this as a mark of closeness to the family. 'There has been some trouble at home, you see,' he continued. 'Mary Godwin and her stepmother do not live together comfortably, as I understand the case.'

'Mercy,' said Margaret waspishly.

'Godwin says there is to be no preferential treatment,' Father said. 'Indeed, he suggests we make a sort of trial of the first few weeks of the visit. He says, "I am quite confounded to think what trouble I am bringing on you and your family, and to what degree I may be said to have taken you in when I took you at your word in your invitation upon so slight an acquaintance".'

'Well, I agree it is an impertinence!' said Margaret. 'And unwise, Father, after that business of Christy's last year. The last thing we need is a scandal.' She sounded almost animated, and Isabel knew she would be sitting bolt upright, bright spots burning on her pale cheeks and her dress hanging loose on her tiny frame although lines of stitching showed under the arms where it had been taken in again and again. She stopped, choking, before beginning again in a lower voice. 'I know you have a fondness for Mr Godwin, Father, and you too, Husband, but you know he does not always have a mind to propriety. That scandalous book he wrote ... For pity's sake he exposed his own wife's daughter as a bastard!'

'Steady, now, Margaret,' Father said gently. 'You will make yourself ill again. Try not to distress yourself. That book of Godwin's was written long ago. I agree it was published in error, but it was done in the full force of his grief when Mary Wollstonecraft died. He has paid for the mistake in full. For a time no door in London was open to him. But he has published much since that is rational and sensible. In essentials, I believe our beliefs are as one.'

'He is an *atheist*!' Margaret hissed.

'Yes,' said Father, 'and in that I cannot support him. But we share a commitment to reason, and the same causes are dear to our hearts.'

'What your father says is true, Margaret,' David said, 'and William Godwin has been a good friend to me for many years, and encouraged and supported me in my work. You should not speak ill of him. But, William' – his tone was firm as he addressed Father – 'Margaret is right to speak of Christy. Mary

Godwin is a headstrong creature as far as I can tell, and full to the brim of romantic ideas. She has a tendency to drama, like her late mother. I am by no means persuaded that Godwin's wife is the devil she is painted by the girl. Or perhaps I should say Mary is no less a devil! Godwin knows it, William, and he seeks respite by passing her on to you.'

Father chuckled. 'You would know more than me on such matters, David. There are plenty hereabouts who maintain you sold your soul to Auld Nick long syne!'

'Father!' Margaret snapped, clearly irritated at the teasing. Isabel knew that local people in Fife said that David was in thrall to the Devil because of all of his studying and cleverness, although she couldn't imagine why, unless it was his brewing they objected to.

Margaret coughed for a moment, but began again as soon as she had caught her breath. 'That business with Christy and the German tutor hastened Mother's end, I'm sure it did. And now you plan to take in a girl whose conduct has been such that she must be sent away from home to live among strangers. And you will have her bed in with Christy, no less!'

'It is good of you to worry about your sister,' Father said, 'but I think you concern yourself overmuch. Mary Godwin is only fourteen, and Christy is nineteen. Five years older! I shouldn't think Christy likely to be influenced unduly by a girl so many years her junior. They met in London last year without disaster. And really, I think Godwin is hard on Mary. I have met her more than once and she struck me as clever, certainly, but quiet in her way. She spends much time alone, and she has been very unwell. I cannot countenance sending her back, she needs rest and clean air and we can offer more of both than Godwin can. But if it soothes you, Margaret, I will have Isabel take Mary into her room instead. They are closer in age, after all, and Isabel's a sensible girl, you know she went straight to your mother when she discovered that business of Christy's.'

Isabel's ears burned at that. She had had no idea that Margaret knew she'd gone to her mother on her sickbed and told her Christy's friends were tattling that Christy and their German tutor had fallen in love. In fact, Isabel had had no idea anyone but Mother knew. She put that out of her mind, though, too interested in the prospect of the visitor who was to share her room.

It seemed Margaret had been mollified by Father's proposal, and she fussed a bit but said nothing much more of substance. Father said they should go into the parlour, it was cooler there with a breath of air, and David said he would fetch a cold compress for Margaret's head. Then there was all the fuss of getting Margaret on her feet, and out they went.

Isabel was just about to step into the room when she heard a cough on the other side of the velvet curtain concealing her hiding place. David had not left with Father and Margaret after all, and he seemed to be standing just inches from Isabel's hiding place, so close she thought she smelled the spicy green scent of the angelica he was always chewing. She held her breath, feeling her heart beat wildly once, twice, quite out of rhythm. Did he know she was there? What would she do if he pulled back the curtain and discovered her? What would *he* do?

A minute passed, then thirty seconds more, the air so thick with tension Isabel felt she could taste it, until at last she heard footsteps retreat and the door open and close.

Abandoning all thought of escaping through the house, Isabel lifted the sash and slipped out of the window and onto the grass outside. She ran round the back and then walked more slowly round the far side of the house. As she came in the front door, she met David, who gave her a strange smile. Feeling her cheeks flame, Isabel dropped her head and hurried into the parlour, calling out to Margaret as if in surprise.

Margaret and David did not stay long after that, Margaret telling Father that she should not be able to attend on the Godwin girl; she could not bear the disturbance of the journey only to arrive at an overcrowded house. Should her sisters and Mary Godwin find themselves at leisure, she said, perhaps they might stir themselves to visit her in Fife. Isabel crossed her eyes at Christy behind Margaret's back, and Christy looked sternly at her, although Isabel knew she bore little more love for their sister than Isabel did herself.

It seemed all was bustle, then, as the household readied itself for the visitor's arrival. Isabel found herself almost panicked. To share her room with any guest was nerve-wracking, but Mary Godwin was the daughter of not one, but two great thinkers of the age. Isabel was a devoted admirer of Mary Wollstonecraft and her *A Vindication of the Rights of Woman*. True, she knew she should have been discomfited by the woman's unorthodox lifestyle – before she married William Godwin, she had had an affair with a married man and borne a child out of wedlock – but really, she found it exciting. She deeply wished to have a friend; Mother was dead, Elizabeth and Jessie far away, Margaret unbearable and Christy often ill-tempered since her great disappointment of the previous year. Brother Robert visited from Edinburgh now and then and there was little John Cowley, but it was female companionship of her own age she craved.

It seemed that Mary was a reader, like Isabel, and a thinker, but Isabel worried that Mary might prove too intellectual, too sophisticated, and Isabel herself too childish, too countrified, too dull. She tore through her room like a whirlwind, removing all traces of childhood. The poorly worked sampler and clumsy watercolours went into the attic with various little trinkets, and Father gave her a silhouette of Mother, a large plaster intaglio with a scene of Greek goddesses, and a pretty print in a pressed brass frame to hang in their place. A little wooden box printed with Britannia and containing a library of tales for children went to John Cowley, and Isabel was allowed to take damask bedcovers from the linen press to replace the patchworks that had always been on the beds.

Christy pouted at first, for the look of the thing, but Isabel knew she did not really wish to share her room – she had been delighted when Jessie and then Elizabeth married and at last she and Isabel had each a room of their own. In the end she came to help choose the bedding and decide which of the beds Mary should have. They knew she had an injured or infected arm, although no one seemed to know the cause of the issue, and so they gave her the bed closest the fire, as the house could be cold at night. It was Christy who stopped Isabel from putting Madame Pretender in the attic; she said Mother's great old doll in her fine antique clothes was not a child's plaything but a woman's treasure and Isabel should be glad to have it on display. Isabel initially planned to pack away her own little doll, Elspeth, who was half the size of Madame Pretender and nowhere near as fine, having lost her wooden arms and legs after too much cuddling. Mother had replaced them with much fatter stuffed cloth versions, so she looked plump and jolly. In the end, though, Isabel felt sorry for the small doll and let her sit at the feet of the fine historic lady in her specially carved miniature chair.

The day before Mary's expected arrival, David reappeared, looking somewhat travel-worn after riding from Newburgh and crossing the Tay in one afternoon. It transpired he was to spend the night with them and, on the morrow, meet Mary from the boat and escort her to The Cottage. Isabel and Christy begged to be allowed to go, but David said it would be too much for Mary, she would be tired from her journey and they would do much better to stay at home and ready themselves to receive her. Father agreed, and so there was nothing for it but to straighten bedclothes already straightened twenty times, and check again there was space for the trunk, and chatter excitedly about Mary. Christy said there was a rumour she had written a poem her father had published when she was ten years old, did Isabel really believe it? Isabel didn't know. Christy yammered on for a bit about the time she'd met Mary in London, although she had nothing much of interest to say as it seemed there had been a great crowd of young people in the Godwin house and Christy had not taken enough notice to be quite sure which one Mary had been. At last they fell into silence, looking at the oatcakes and cheese and fancy pieces Cookie had laid out on the table in the parlour in readiness and wishing David would hurry up.

As it happened, Cookie's efforts went to waste. When the carriage at last pulled up, David leaped down and called for help, and Father's manservant, John, rushed out and fairly had to heave Mary Godwin out of the carriage like a sack of tatties. David called out to Father that Mary would need an apothecary and a nurse, she was so ill as to be set nearly to expire. Isabel and Christy had only the barest glimpse of red-gold hair and a slim form as Mary was carried up the stairs. Once she was deposited in the bed Isabel and Christy had made ready, Father dispatched John to Dundee to find an apothecary and bring him immediately. The maid toiled up and down the stairs with bowls and bedwarmers and kettles of hot water, while Christy and Isabel seemed constantly in the way until Father told them to go into the parlour and pray for their poor visitor's relief.

At last the apothecary arrived and was a long time in the room with Mary while Cookie served as chaperone. The man emerged looking grave, speaking quietly to Father and David while Christy and Isabel did their best to eavesdrop. It seemed Mary had been grievously sick on the boat, and her arm was worse than ever, so it seemed that between the pain of that and the effect of the sickness on her stomach, she was in real danger.

'She has a pressing need of water,' the apothecary said, 'but she cannot keep it down. Have you someone able to nurse her?' Father said yes, John had already gone back to the town to fetch Nanny Chisolm. The apothecary said very good, he would help Cookie feed Mary sips of water until Nanny came, and he would stay until the immediate danger had passed. He did not say '*if* it passed', but the words hung in the air nonetheless.

Father said that they should all eat, it was long past the hour, but no one had any appetite, and though they served themselves from the dishes Cookie had laid out, they could manage little of it. Father said that Isabel would have to sleep in Christy's room until Mary was better. Nanny Chisolm would sleep with her charge.

As though in answer to her name, at that very moment they heard the carriage carrying Nanny arrive, and John carried in her box, Nanny following behind with her comfortable figure swathed in a great woollen cloak, far too warm for the weather, worn with a hideous green bonnet. She patted Isabel on her cheek and squeezed Christy's hand as she passed, and then she was puffing up the stairs and disappearing into Isabel's room at the top. Isabel became aware of a lessening of the pressure that had been like an iron ring around her breast since the carriage first arrived. Nothing could be so bad now Nanny Chisolm was here.

Nanny Chisolm had seen to the raising of all of the Baxter children, only leaving once little John Cowley was in long trousers. She lived with her sister in the Murraygate in Dundee, in the two rooms her parents had taken in the second half of the last century, when they had been cleared from the land they farmed in the north country to make way for great flocks of sheep. Duncan Chisolm had been told he should shift with his family to the coast to join the kelp industry or the fishing. With only a wife and two daughters to help win a living, he had decided he would rather take his chances in the south, and so they had made their way as far as Dundee. There had been some hard years as Duncan sought work in the town, and his wife and daughters took in plain sewing. Hunger had first introduced them to the Baxter family, for Grandfather and Grandmother Baxter worshipped at the Glasite Meeting House, where good Scotch broth was served every Sunday between sermons. The Glasites believed no man could worship God if he was starving, and they welcomed the hungry as their Saviour had done before them. Those who looked down on the Nonconformists laughed behind their hands and called it the 'Kail Kirk', but for many in need in those hard days the Glasite church was a blessing. The Chisolms soon became stalwarts of the congregation, and in the end Duncan came to work for Grandfather and then Father in the mill, and his daughter to care for the Baxter children as babes.

Isabel and Christy saw no more of Nanny that night, although they heard her call for Cookie once or twice. In the end, Father came from his study, where he had been closeted with David, to tell them they had better get to their beds, the next day was the Sabbath and they would be more use to Mary praying for her recovery in the Meeting House than sitting up late and yawning through the morning service.

In their room, Christy tied on her nightcap, said an ostentatious prayer and then snored half the night. Isabel lay awake fearing she would go distracted, but in the morning she found she wasn't tired, she was still too nervous for that. Over breakfast, Cookie told them Mary was a little better, Nanny had got a goodly draught of water into her overnight and some tea, and she thought she would get some honey into her later, and perhaps even some broth. The poor creature had been so in need of water that her eyes had seemed sunken into her head.

David thanked the Lord for Nanny's success, and Isabel wondered how he could show such concern for Mary Godwin while leaving Margaret at home in Newburgh by herself. Perhaps that was mean-spirited, though, for just then David said to Father he would come to the morning service but then he would set out for home. There would be no boats crossing the Tay on the Sabbath and he would take the long way round, by Perth. That way, if he had to break the journey, he would have a shorter ride in the morning and be home to Margaret all the faster.

In the normal way of things, Isabel enjoyed going to services on a Sunday. She liked to ride out in the carriage with Father and Christy and John Cowley, along the Ferry Road towards the Seagate as the gulls wheeled and jeered overhead, then into the clamour and bustle of Dundee city proper, up the Queen's Road to the Cowgate and onto the Kingsgate where the strange, octagonal Meeting House stood. She generally enjoyed the sermons, when any member who had an edifying message to deliver was free to speak, but her favourite part of the day was the meal in the refectory between the services, when the young women could sit together and exchange their news freely enough so long as it was decorously done.

Today, however, Isabel could not sit still, and it seemed to her that the sermons and readings dragged on and on forever. She had only half an ear for her friend Teenie's chatter over the feast, although there was plenty of it. Poor Teenie had come many miles to attend – her family lived halfway to Forfar, and she saw barely a soul from one Sunday to the next, so she had little news of her own to report but much appetite for discussing other people's. Isabel told her the bare facts of Mary Godwin's arrival, but then she left it to Christy to tell her more; all she could think of was getting home to see whether the girl lived and thrived or – Heaven forbid – had taken a turn for the worse. She was so caught up in the awful thought of losing this longed-for friend that she barely noticed David bidding them all farewell after the meal.

At length the services were over and they were on the road home. Father vexed Isabel greatly by suggesting they drive out the Kingsgate and onto the Arbroath Road. It would add barely half an hour to their journey but would give them all the chance of some country air on the way. She bit her lip and tried her best to sit still and join in the family chatter, but the carriage had barely stopped outside The Cottage when she was up out of her seat and running in, tearing up the stairs before anyone could stop her. She knocked on the door of her bedroom and heard Nanny's heavy steps as she came to answer.

'Good Lord, Miss Isabel,' Nanny said. 'You've still your cloak on!'

'Miss Mary is not worse?' Isabel asked, her heart pounding in her chest.

Nanny looked back over her shoulder, and then she stepped into the hallway.

'Her stomach is on the mend,' she said, 'and I have got her some sheep's wool grease to soothe her mouth, the skin all around had cracked with want of water. Her arm troubles her greatly, and I believe it will take some nursing to set it right. But something else is upsetting her, Miss Isabel, and she won't tell me what it is. She seems unable to take her rest, and without rest she cannot heal.'

'Can I see her?' Isabel asked, pulling off her cloak. Behind her, she heard the commotion as the rest of the family traipsed in from the carriage.

Nanny shook her head. 'I must be daft,' she said, but she stepped back to let Isabel enter, taking the cloak as it fell from her shoulders.

The room was dark, the curtains closed and only a low lamp burning on the table by the bed. Mary lay facing away, and Isabel walked round till she could see her face. There was a chair there, where Nanny had been sitting by the fire – her needlework basket was on the floor below, the needle neatly stuck through where she had laid off her sewing. Isabel sat, and looked at the pallid, tear-stained face on the pillow. The girl was the sickly yellow colour of bone, almost as pale as the vast white nightgown that enveloped her, with great circles under her dark eyes.

'Mary?' she said shyly. 'I'm Isabel Baxter. You met my sister Christy, I think, in London last year.'

'Pleased to meet you, Miss Baxter,' Mary mumbled. Her voice was hoarse, and Isabel winced to see those raw cracks in the skin of her lips.

'Please call me Isabel,' she said. 'And tell me, is Nanny looking after you well? She looked after all of us as children. She says she thinks you are a little better.'

'Yes, thank you,' said Mary, 'everyone has been very kind.' But still tears spilled from her eyes.

Isabel took a deep breath. 'Nanny thinks something else is upsetting you,' she said. 'Can you not tell me what it is?'

Mary half rose, staring at the bedcover, and Isabel had her first taste of a strange power the other girl had to somehow cripple a room with her shyness. Embarrassment rose off her, like a haar from the sea, only hot, and Isabel found herself fixed in place, her face flaming, and her tongue tied so that she could not speak. They sat in red-faced silence until at last Mary broke the spell.

'I am afraid you will think me a fool,' she said. 'And my family reckless fools moreover.'

'Hush, now,' Isabel said, relieved to find her voice still worked. 'No one will think any such thing. I was afraid you would think *me* a fool. I am two years older than you, almost, and look! I still have a poppet in my room!' She stood up and fetched Elspeth from the high shelf where she sat beside Mother's fine lady doll. 'This is Elspeth,' she said. 'I have had her since I was a little girl. I meant to put her away so you wouldn't think me a child, but when I picked her up I felt her eyes on me, so reproachful, and I worried she would be lonely in a box in the attic.'

Mary began to cry again. 'I never saw a baby so nice,' she said. 'May I have her, in bed with me?'

'Of course,' Isabel said, although it gave her a small pang to see Mary take the doll and tuck her under the covers.

'I was robbed,' Mary blurted out suddenly. 'On the boat. Everything I had was taken from me while I lay in my sickness. And so, you see, I cannot bear it. What a fool I must seem to you, and how shameful, coming here as a pauper to be dependent on your father's charity!' She buried her face in the doll's plump belly and began to cry again.

Isabel felt her heart lighten in relief. 'Is that all?' she said. 'But, Mary, Father won't mind that at all! None of us ever have money, he provides anything we need. If ever we want anything, we can order it on his account. You can do the same. He said you are to be treated as though you were another sister, exactly the same as us. We never expected you to have money of your own.'

'But I was travelling alone!' Mary wailed. 'I knew I should not, but there was no one to come with me. Father knew it was wrong, but his wife would not listen.' Her voice hardened and she sat up a little straighter. '*She* told Father it would be fine,' she said. 'They would ask a woman travelling alone or with daughters to take charge of me. That is the sort of thing my stepmamma does, she believes she knows best of everyone and she is endlessly looking for opportunities to boast to us of how she was a woman alone before she married Father, and how well she managed. She is a poisonous creature. She didn't even come to see me off, but she instructed Father to find a woman he liked the look of, on the dock, and bargain with her for my care as though I were a cow to be driven to market. Oh, the woman was very kind, and she promised to see me right, but one of her daughters was poorly too, and she could not be in two places at once. And so I was robbed, and now I am here imposing on you all.' She dissolved into tears again.

'No, no! You are our guest,' Isabel said, 'and we have all been looking forward to meeting you so much. I want to hear all about your life in London and your family and the books you read. We can come with you, perhaps, when you do at last go back to London. I have never been and I do so wish to see it. I am sorry you were treated so horribly, but the money really doesn't matter, Mary, I promise you.'

'That's right, Miss Mary,' said Nanny, who had come up behind Isabel to take the kettle from the fire. 'Mr Baxter is a fell godly man, and you will find him far from grand. He will be most happy to share what he has with you.' She began to pour hot water into a cup with a spout. 'Now, off you go down to your family, Miss Isabel,' she said, 'and leave Miss Mary to her rest. She will sleep better now she has unburdened herself, you'll see.'

Mary reached out and took Isabel's hand as she rose. 'Please don't say anything,' she said. 'I would rather tell your father myself.'

'Very well,' said Isabel. 'I won't say a word. But in return you must promise me you won't be upset any more.'

'And you must try to eat,' Nanny said. 'Cookie has made you a marvellous pudding.' She took the cover off a bowl and the scent of oranges filled the room.

'I'll try,' said Mary, and she pulled herself up a little more in the bed, clumsily, so that Isabel saw how one arm was so swathed in bandages it looked as though it belonged to someone else entirely, someone much larger than Mary. With her good hand, she settled the doll beside her, and she gave Isabel a watery smile.

'May I come and see you tomorrow?' Isabel asked, suddenly shy again. 'May I, Nanny?'

'I don't see why not,' said Nanny, 'if you don't stay too long and tire Miss Mary out. But now you had better get downstairs to your father.'

Isabel picked up her cloak and left the room, closing the door as softly as she could. Christy was waiting outside, clearly dying to know what had happened.

'Well?' she said. 'Did you speak to her? What did she say?'

'Nothing,' said Isabel. 'Only that she would try to eat.' She felt an unusual sense of power, knowing something Christy did not, and the next was out of her mouth before she knew it. 'She has been very ill, Christy. You mustn't expect too much from her.'

Christy's face was a picture, but after a second she turned and went back down the stairs. Isabel poked her tongue out at her departing back.

2

THE WALNUT WAS POLISHED AND shiny, dark with handling and far heavier than a nut should be. A band of gilt metal joined its two hemispheres, and when Isabel pressed on a tiny catch, it swung open to reveal a velvet lining to one half and to the other, gold, with slots holding miniature scissors and needles, a bodkin and a thimble, and a tiny crystal scent bottle no larger than the top of Isabel's little finger. Mother's etui, and one of her treasures, hidden among Christy's linens in her dresser where Isabel had found it quite by accident while looking for a handkerchief.

Isabel sat a while with the etui in her hand, feeling her colour rise, and then she placed it carefully on the table beside her bed and began to search the room in earnest. She was free to do so, for Christy had taken herself off to stay with her friend Agnes at Perth for a fortnight or three weeks, frustrated by the fuss and bother of Mary's illness at home.

Once it had been clear that Mary was out of danger, it had seemed that The Cottage let out a breath no one had known it had been holding. Father took himself off to the peace of his study, where he dashed off a letter to William Godwin to let him know Mary had been very ill on the journey but was now on the mend and in the care of a most competent nurse, and then he settled in with his account books and papers. John Cowley's friends began to visit again and set up their usual mischief and commotion, while the servants ran after them bellowing and Cookie spoke darkly of no pudding at teatime. They all knew this to be an empty threat, for a steady stream of sweet treats and pastries issued from the kitchen as Nanny and Cookie waged their personal campaign to tempt Mary to eat. Isabel was still required to bed in with Christy, and Christy was forever jumping when she came in, and rushing to hide away her letters and diaries. Isabel had been glad when she had gone to Agnes.

Isabel was reading the memoirs of the Girondin Madame Roland for the third time, written when the woman was awaiting execution in the Terror. She was fascinated by Manon Roland, who had hosted a salon where great men discussed business and affairs of state. She had sat smiling over her embroidery, the picture of feminine demureness, while in reality, she was a most able spy, every stitch helping her commit to memory any and all intelligence that might be of use to her cause.

Now Isabel herself turned spy, systematically searching Christy's room. Soon she had found a veritable treasure trove of Mother's things hidden in cunning places – a garnet brooch pinned into the inner lining of a cloak, a pearl ring and a tortoiseshell hair comb hidden inside a pair of thick winter boots. In Christy's work bag she found a pair of evening gloves and an ivory fan, along with the book Mother had been reading when she died. This last Isabel picked up and brought to her nose, in hope some of Mother's scent would cling to it, but it smelled of wool instead. She blinked the tears from her eyes and laid all out on the bed.

Emboldened now by resentment, Isabel wiggled the etui bodkin into the lock of Christy's desk until it sprung open and took out her diary from the previous year. It was full of dull stuff, almost deliberately so, it seemed, appointments and accounts of meals eaten and garden tasks completed, games lost and won between friends. There were letters between Christy and her circle, tied up in ribbons, but again there was nothing of interest and much that was earnest and dull. It all suggested Christy had no inner life at all, and no secrets, but Isabel knew this to be untrue. She put everything back in the desk, then stepped back and looked over the room once more. The only place left to search was the bed.

When she lifted the mattress, Isabel saw that her instincts had been correct. Tied into the springs below was a small silk bag, the sort of notion little girls made to hold lavender. Inside it, Isabel found a tiny, flat folder, barely as long as her thumb. It was an exquisite thing, covered in pale grey silk and embroidered in silver threads, with tiny sequins and moonstones decorating it, a pearl to hold a twined silk clasp, and a central motif in silver she could not make out but thought was perhaps supposed to be Cupid. Inside the folder was a letter, in minuscule script on the most fragile of papers, and another piece of tissue, with so many holes cut out of it that it appeared almost like lace.

Isabel put all else back to rights and then sat before the mirror at the dressing table with the letter. At first she could make nothing out – it was in English, but the words were jumbled, made no sense, and half of them were nothing more than a letter and a dash. But then she looked more closely at the lacy paper and saw tiny spots of ink here and there. She laid it over the letter with the sides aligned, and saw how it revealed the words in order and then, if she moved it to align with some small marks on the top and bottom of the paper, more words in order again. She fetched a pen, and paper, and began to transcribe. It took an age, and she had to fill out the dashed words as she went, but their meaning became clear enough as she worked.

My dearest,

I am full of rapture when I think on our last kiss and our precious vow – 'eternally yours'.

All those long months spent together, bent over our books, never looking, never raising our gaze, our eyes unlit candles, no love to light us – yet.

I think often of the first touch of our hands. You reached for my pen as I reached for yours – as if by mistake – and our fingers touched. Did we speak? I do not remember speaking. Speech is an untrustworthy messenger for love. And then I took you in my arms and kissed you, and it seemed the very earth shook, the sun blazed out, all the birds sang as one in the heavens.

You and I, I and you. There is nothing else in the world. They tell me I must go from this place, and see you no more and it seems to me the most awful heresy, when I have been blest by the holiest of loves.

If I can find a way, my love, I will return. Until then, farewell, a thousand times farewell. My heart is breaking.

Eternally yours, F

As she worked, some of the anger Isabel had felt at Christy for purloining Mother's things dissipated, replaced by shock at what she had learned. She had known Christy and the German tutor had admired one another, but she had no idea there had been a real love affair. Her sister had kissed a man! He had touched her and held her and kissed her – things Isabel had barely thought of, but now she did, she found them interesting, in a slightly disturbing way. She sat staring into the mirror, not seeing her own face, but rather Christy and the German tutor. She replayed the times she had seen them together, wondering what she had missed, and how. She brushed her hand over her breast, and found she could make herself shiver. She ran her hand down her body, pressing harder, imagining the tutor's fingers woven through her own. She thought of Manon Roland, who had had a lover, and then she thought of Margaret and David, and that confused her. She jumped to her feet and smoothed down her clothes, folded the transcribed letter into her Bible, placed it in one pocket and the etui in the other, and took herself next door to see Mary and Nanny Chisolm.

Mary was fully better now of the sickness and the vomiting and recovering from the weakness that followed, and Isabel was able to visit her more often and for longer. Nanny Chisolm welcomed these visits, saying that it helped Mary's spirits to have Isabel's company. Her arm still proved a mystery, some days paining her so that she would cry out if she placed her weight on it, and other times so numb that Mary said she could not feel it at all. Mary said the first symptoms had been a terrible blistering of the skin, but according to Nanny there was no sign of that now, only scratches where Mary had attacked herself in her distress. Now Nanny had bandaged Mary's hands so she couldn't scratch herself in her sleep, and had dressed the arm with onion and garlic and goose grease.

Once Isabel was settled in a chair, Nanny produced a plate of shortbread made by Cookie for them to share, and then she said she would go down to see Father about some items she needed from the apothecary, leaving them together to chat a while in peace. Mary was still shy of Isabel, apologising for the fact she smelled like a soup pot after Nanny's ministrations.

'I like soup,' Isabel said. 'My favourite is cock-a-leekie. What is the book you are reading?'

'It's called *The Daughter of St. Omar*,' Mary said. 'Your father sent it up for me. It's a Scottish book, or at least a book by a Scottish lady. I have other new books, too. My father sent them in a parcel just this morning. He is very kind. Do you know, I was fearful ill as a baby. My mother had died in giving birth to me, and my father's grief was so great that he placed me in the care of a kindly woman friend while he took care of Mother's burial. I almost died in that house, but as soon as I was home again with my father, I became well.'

'I'm sorry you lost your mother so young,' Isabel said. 'Mine died last year.'

'Perhaps that's harder to bear,' said Mary. 'I have no memory of my mother, although I feel I know her.'

'I . . .' Isabel felt her cheeks flush with shyness. 'I feel a little as though I know your mother, too. Because I have read her books. I . . . admire her work greatly. But I know it is different for you.'

Mary seemed pleased at that. 'My father has always loved her,' she said. 'He always kept her portrait above the fire, in our old home. And now, since we moved into the city, he has it hanging in his study, above the shop. We used to visit her grave together. I learned my letters from the carvings on her tomb. And so, you see, we are a pair, he and I. He said it was a charm that saved me when I was a baby, but I know different. It was being with my father.'

'I was almost lost as a little girl too,' said Isabel, seeing they might become less shy with one another if they had this in common. 'I had the putrid sore throat and I seemed like to die, and even after I was out of the first danger, I had terrible tremblings and tremors all over me for weeks. Often it appeared they would carry me off. I remember it well, for all I was younger then. My father says they had given up all hope of me.'

'I'm glad you understand how it is to be so afflicted,' Mary said. 'Sometimes I fear my stepmother looks down on me for my weakness. My arm, you see.' She cradled the offending appendage. 'She is a strong, robust sort of woman, and she despises weaknesses in others. Claire would be kind to me, and Fanny. They are my sisters – well, Claire is my stepsister and Fanny my half-sister – but my stepmother sent me away. I was at Ramsgate before I came here. For my arm.' She looked determinedly at Isabel, her cheeks a little flushed.

'I'm glad she sent you to us,' Isabel said. 'And I hope I can be like a sister to you while you are here. I'm sure you will be well now. Nanny is here to care for you, and she saved my life when I was so ill. Whatever the trouble is, she will discover it, you will see.'

'Trouble?' Mary said. Her cheeks flushed darker and her voice was high. 'Do you mean that someone has said—'

'It's just a manner of speaking,' Isabel said. 'Illness is a sort of trouble, I mean. And Nanny Chisolm always says she's not a woman to be defeated by sickness or strife.'

Mary sighed. 'I don't know how to get well,' she said.

Isabel bit her lip and then she took her Bible from her pocket. 'Do you ... Mary, do you believe in divination?'

'Divination? I – I don't know.'

'I do,' Isabel said. 'I believe in visions and guidance from elsewhere. I like to open the Bible at any place, and read the words written there. Then I try to interpret them. Often I believe the message is sent to help me. Shall we try, and see if there is any help for you?'

Mary seemed uncomfortable, biting at her bottom lip. 'What if the message is a bad one?' she asked.

'Then it is wrong,' Isabel said. 'But don't be afraid, Mary. The Bible is full of hope, you know.'

Mary smiled. 'We didn't have a lot to do with the Bible at home. But let's try.'

Isabel had Mary sit up, then close her eyes, take the Bible in both hands and open it at whatever page felt right in the moment. Then Mary handed it back to Isabel, and she read.

'The Gospel of Mark, chapter five, verses one to twenty,' she said. 'Our Lord goes to the country of the Gadarenes, and meets a man who is possessed of a spirit. The spirit says, "My name is Legion; for we are many." The man had been cutting himself to attack the demons, and he would let no one near except Our Lord. Oh, Mary, do you see? It has worked, the message is meant for you! You scratch at your arm to bring yourself peace from your torment, but all it does is prolong it.'

Mary looked a little perturbed, but then her mouth set in a determined line.

'And was the man cured?' she asked.

'Wait,' said Isabel, and she read on. 'Yes! Our Lord cast the spirits into a herd of swine, and then the swine ran into the water and were drowned.'

'That doesn't seem a lot of help,' said Mary. 'It would be unfair to cast my pain into little John Cowley and have him cast himself into the Tay.'

Isabel laughed. 'You are reading it too closely,' she said. 'I think it means you are to let go of whatever troubles you. Those are your tormenting spirits. Then, when you have done so, your arm will be healed. Can you tell me what troubles you, Mary? It's not the money again, is it? You know that does not matter.'

Mary bit her lip. 'Only my stepmamma's meanness,' she said. 'She has such sway over my father that he disapproves of me too, for my illness. Her name is Mary Jane Vial, and I call her Mary Jane *Vile*.'

'I'm not surprised you have such a scunner against her,' Isabel said. 'She sounds a horrid woman. But you mustn't let her make you unwell. I can see how it would happen – the pain of the flesh is a useful distraction from the pain of the soul. Now you are here with us, you must forget her and let us bring you to happiness again. Let's start with the parcel of books your father has sent. Is that not proof he loves you, and thinks of you? Come, let us look at them now – and perhaps we may choose one to read together.'

Isabel took the Bible from Mary and lifted the parcel of books onto the bed instead. They cut the string together and took the volumes out one by one, Mary reading the letter her father had enclosed with them. There was a volume of *Sicilian Mysteries*, called *The Fortress del Vecchio* by Anne of Swansea, and Isabel and Mary were agreed that they would read that first. Both had a hankering to travel in Europe, where Mary's mother and Isabel's beloved Madame Roland had lived. They set to right away, Isabel reading aloud in the chair by the fire while Mary lay back on the pillow and listened with her eyes closed.

In the coming days, Isabel and Mary scarcely parted for longer than the time they were asleep. They read, and they talked, Mary asking about Mother and Father and how it was to live with so many siblings, and what happened in the Glasite church, and Isabel spinning Mary's own story out of her, her early life with her beloved Marguerite, who had been her mother's devoted maid, and Louisa, a friend of her aunt's chosen by her father to tend to her needs. It seemed Mary's early life had been one of romps and running free, working in the garden with the gardener and learning lessons selected by her doting father. They had worshipped too, it seemed, in their own way, although William Godwin was an atheist. It had all gone wrong, of course, when Mary was four and William Godwin remarried, but Mary said she did not want to speak of that any more, she had taken Isabel's advice after the divination and had put her stepmother from her mind. The progress of her arm was remarkable and Nanny Chisolm was taking full credit for it with her soup mix.

Mary spoke of her siblings, of course, her half-sister Fanny, who was dull and morose, and her bubbly, silly stepsister Claire, who was spoiled and indulged with music lessons and other attentions. Her stepbrother Charles was nice enough, and the baby, William, barely registered. She spoke of her first home outside London, and the challenges of moving to the busy and stinking streets of Holborn, the boredom of working behind the counter in the bookshop her father owned with his wife. She would say not a word about her time in Ramsgate, claiming she had been too unwell to appreciate it, and that she was glad to be here in Dundee and never think of it again.

'But what of the other girls at school?' Isabel asked.

'I did not like them,' was the most Isabel got out of her. 'Nasty girls living in a nasty, damp place. A cold sea and even colder company.'

It was not difficult to persuade Mary to speak of her broader connections – in fact, it would have been harder to stop her. Her family had such a wide circle that any book they picked up reminded Mary of this happening, or that link. Anne of Swansea, they had discovered, was the sister of a very grand actress named Sarah Siddons, and Sarah Siddons had slighted the Godwins after Mary Wollstonecraft's death, through fear of being contaminated by their reputation even though she had been a friend of William Godwin's of many years' standing. The last book in Godwin's clutch was *Tales of Fashionable Life* by Maria Edgeworth, which, he wrote, had a marvellous story of Ireland called 'The Absentee'. Mary said she felt she should have a kinship with the author, who was known to have read Mary's own father's writings, but she disliked Miss Edgeworth's tendency to have the freest thinking of her heroines come to no good. Mary had met Coleridge, and Crabb Robinson, and Lord Byron, and Charles and Mary Lamb, and many more luminaries besides, and she did not stint in her descriptions of their admiration of her wit and cleverness, even from babyhood.

Isabel was a little jealous of the closeness of Mary's connections with such people, but Mary mollified her a little by speaking of her great passion for the works of Walter Scott and her desire to know more of Scotland, which gave Isabel a chance to share her own store of precious knowledge too. Mary said she was fascinated by folk tales and fairy lore, and Isabel carefully chose the stories she shared, thinking of the threads that would most catch Mary's interest and bind her to Isabel as a friend.

She told the story of the cruel stepmother who would have had the king kill his own daughter for jealousy of her, and so slaughtered his hound and his cattle and his mare and smeared the hands and face of the sleeping girl with their blood, until the king had no choice but to instruct his huntsman to put the girl to death. The girl was bonny, and the huntsman soft-hearted, and in the end they cut off only the girl's little finger and took that to the king with the lung and liver of a lamb as evidence that she was dead. The girl said the pain from the finger was nothing to the loss of her father's love. She outwitted her stepmother in the end, of course, taking herself off to the lands of the Norsemen where the stepmother pursued her with a gift of cursed hailstones – the girl seemed struck down dead but was only asleep, and came back to life in time to tell her father of his new wife's crimes.

She told of the changeling children who were placed by the fairies in the cradles of healthy babes, only to wither and sicken while the real child lived with the fairies in the dark places of the earth, and of the poor dead mothers who appeared to living girls in the moonlight to sing of the mistreatment of their babes by the new wives of their poor widowers. Mary seemed especially moved by those stories and often tears would glint in her eyes as Isabel spoke of mothers' voices borne on the wind.

Being from the northlands and understanding Gaelic moreover, Nanny Chisolm was a fine storyteller – in fact, most of Isabel's stories had come from her great store. Isabel begged of her the tale of the jealous woman who wove her sister's hair into the seaweed on the shore to drown her, and of the man who fell asleep waiting to ford a river to fetch a midwife for his wife and woke to find the tide gone and come back again, while a fairy washerwoman sang a lament as she readied the poor wife's shroud. Nanny obliged, and then she told them tales of kelpies and water bulls, fairy hillocks where girls disappeared and were never seen again, and the sad tale of Oisean, the bard of the Fenian warrior band, who crossed into the land of the ever-young and back again, only to discover that one day there was a hundred years here, and he had returned a horror and a terror to all men, so old and hideous he was, his eyes dull and glazed and his yellow skin barely holding together over the bones.

They shivered greatly at that, and Mary said it would make a good story for a book, perhaps her father would pay them if they could write it down and send it to him to publish. But Nanny said no, that wasn't how such stories worked, they didn't belong to one person to pin down on a page and write a name upon them, like a collector of butterflies. Instead they belonged to all the tellers who had tramped the earth with the tales upon their tongues, and they would belong to them until the end of time. The best tellers were the travelling folk, she said, those who fished for pearls in the streams and picked the berries in summer and put their backs to the plough, only to vanish again when the work was done, back into the mist.

'Surely it would hurt no one to write the stories down,' Mary said, persistent, 'or write a new story inspired by the old?'

Nanny set her mouth. 'No, Miss Mary,' she said, 'you may not do that, you must find your own stories to write, from your own heart, if that's what you wish. These stories are like a growing tree, and to choose one would be to chop a part off and kill the living branch. Yes, you might carve a thing from it,' she went on, seeing a glitter in Mary's eyes, 'or you might graft it onto something else and it would grow there, but the tree would be missing its branch forever, and the new growth would not come.'

Perhaps Nanny could see that Mary would not give up on the idea, for then she began another story, this time about a wee doll made of clay called a *corp-crèadha* that could be shaped in the likeness of a person and used to call harm down upon them. She told it in quite a lively fashion, having previously been downstairs with Cookie sharing Dundee gossip and – Isabel suspected – a glass or two of sherry alongside their customary tea and scones. 'Be sure, then, to pay heed to my warnings,' Nanny said, 'or I'll be making a *corp-crèadha* for each of you, and then you'll be lamenting.' Mary laughed and said she had no intention of publishing any of Nanny's stories, and then it was time for Nanny to shoo Isabel back to her own bed and settle Mary down for the night.

3

After her weeks of convalescence, Mary was a little like a character from a fairy tale herself when first she emerged from Isabel's room. She squinted in the sunlight as if stepping out from the darkness of a fairy hill, and peered around her with a troubled frown, as if she could make no sense of her surroundings.

'I thought it was a cottage,' she said, biting her lip.

'Ah,' said Isabel, remembering Mary's shame at arriving penniless at their door. 'Well, it is named so, but it is a jest. It was the dower house of the Countess of Strathmore. Perhaps it seemed a cottage to her. We realise it is quite a grand place, but Father did not like to change the name.'

Still Mary seemed ill at ease, and her strange ability to overwhelm a room with her awkwardness was in evidence again. They were sitting at the midday meal with Father and John Cowley, and all were quiet and unsure, even Father – a grown man with his own business who corresponded with the great men of the age! Nanny had gone home to her sister, saying she would visit now only once or twice a week to check on Mary and change the dressings on her arm – privately, Isabel knew she had told Father the arm was almost healed – and so the rest of them were left to get on as best they could.

'Your childhood home at the Polygon was a handsome place,' Father said to Mary, looking a little desperate. 'I greatly admired the ambition of the building scheme.' He turned to the others. 'Imagine, if you will, a great square to the north of London. Instead of having houses around the sides, as we would build, there is a great building in the centre. At first it appears round, but in fact it has fifteen sides, with two houses per side. There is a garden in the centre, and every second house is four storeys high and the ones in between just two, so the garden and the street have the sun at all hours of the day. Or will do. It was not quite finished when I saw it.'

Isabel could see tears in Mary's eyes, whether from the exertion of getting up and coming downstairs or from Father's praise of her much-missed first home she did not know, but she jumped in in any case, announcing she would tell the tale of Mary Eleanor Bowes, the woman who had commissioned The Cottage. It was bound to please Mary, if not Father.

'She was born a great heiress,' Isabel announced, spearing a piece of chicken and holding it aloft. 'The wealthiest in all of Britain, or perhaps even Europe, they say. She was born in London, and her father doted on her and gave her the best education money could buy. When she was eighteen, she married the Earl of Strathmore. Although they lived much of the time in England, the earl restored the family seat at Glamis Castle – we should take Mary there, Father, she would like it – and Mary Eleanor wrote a drama for the stage and became a botanist. Then the earl died at sea, and by then Mary Eleanor had taken a lover and was with child. She used her botanical knowledge to rid herself of the child, it seems—'

Spluttering, Father tried to interject, and Mary stared, but Isabel continued.

'—then, you will never credit this, she was tricked into marrying again. She had gone back to London, where a man pretended he had fought a duel in her honour, and so she had little choice but to marry him. He was carried to the altar on a stretcher and seemed like to die before he could say his vows. But it was all a ruse and so he made a miraculous recovery. The man was a rogue and his first wife had died through ill treatment, but Mary Eleanor was more canny and had ensured he could not get his hands on her money. When he discovered that, he went quite wild and kidnapped her and took her into the North of England where he treated her most abysmally. She eventually escaped him and tried to divorce him, but she died before it could be completed. She was buried in Westminster Abbey and they say she went into her coffin in her wedding dress, with a silver trumpet. I do not know why.' She popped the chicken in her mouth and chewed.

'Perhaps she was afraid of being buried alive,' John Cowley said. 'A trumpet would be most useful if you were trapped in a coffin and needed to summon help.'

Isabel laughed and Father wiped his brow. Mary offered him a consoling smile and then turned to Isabel.

'It is quite a life,' she said. 'But when did she live here? The Countess?'

'I don't believe she ever did,' Father said. 'It was built for her when the family gave up Castle Lyon, a little east of here. The castle was terribly ruinous, and I suppose they thought she would have need of something better. But ... as Isabel says, she ... er ... remarried.'

Isabel could see that Mary had been excited by the story; there was a shine to her eyes that appeared when she was engaged with a topic, for good or ill. 'I should like to see Glamis

Castle very much,' she said. 'And I have always wanted to learn more of botany. I have a great interest in flowers and plants.'

'That is something you have in common with Isabel here,' said Father. 'And you will find plenty of woods and groves to explore in the neighbourhood.'

'And tombstones,' said John Cowley, who liked gruesome things. 'You should take Mary to Roodyards, Isabel.'

'Oh, yes please,' said Mary. 'I do love exploring graveyards. May we go this afternoon? I would like to be outside in the air.'

'A good thought,' said Father, clearly relieved at the thought of being shot of them. 'The weather looks to stay fine. Finish your meal, and then you can go. Don't keep Mary outside too long, Isabel, and take her upstairs when you return. Cookie can bring you a meal on a tray this evening, make sure we don't tire Mary out.'

Isabel had moved back into her own room upon Nanny's departure, sleeping in the bed closest to the door. She was delighted at the thought of taking a meal there and talking more to Mary instead of making polite chatter downstairs at table.

The walk to the cemetery was slightly delayed by the realisation that Mary's father and stepmother had a somewhat unrealistic idea of Scottish weather in summer and autumn, and consequently Mary had no coat or cloak suitable for the cold winds off the Tay. She was shorter by half a foot than either Isabel or Christy, and nothing they had would suit without alteration.

After another episode of awkwardness, Father called for a maid and said she and Isabel should look in the press in his room for a cloak of Mother's that Mary might use, if the moths had not got to all. The maid looked offended at that, but she went upstairs as instructed with Isabel and they opened the great press. While the maid pulled out this cloak and that and held them up to the light to see which might do, Isabel ran her hands down the familiar fabrics of Mother's frocks, pulling out her favourite tartan dress and burying her face in it. It smelled more of camphor than it did of Mother, but the feel of it brought a wave of loneliness over her. Someday she would ask Father if she could have it, but not yet, it was too soon.

Isabel thought she might be sad to see any of Mother's clothes on anyone but Mother, but she need not have worried, the cloak looked like a different garment on Mary. She was terribly slight after her illness, her skin almost translucent against her red-gold hair, so the velvet that had seemed a cool grey against Mother's dark hair and rosy complexion looked almost green on her, and the cut that had seemed narrow on Mother quite enveloped her. Mary had arrived in a straw bonnet that would look quite wrong with the cloak, and so Isabel loaned her a pretty cap in the jockey style, made from a deep rust-coloured wool that looked well with the rich velvet. Mary's boots, at least, were sturdy, if almost worn through.

'Perhaps you girls can take yourselves to the draper's in Dundee in the week,' Father said, 'and order yourselves some new, er, things for the winter. Christy will be back then too. You girls have had nothing new since your mother died.'

Isabel made a show of crowing in delight, seeing that Mary recognised this for the flannel it was and was ready to paralyse them with embarrassment again – hers was the only genuine need for a new wardrobe. Mary stammered out her own thanks, but Father was already escaping the room, telling them to be off and to take care not to walk too far or stay out too long. Isabel saw him rub his hand across his eyes as he opened the door of his study, and she wondered whether the sight of Mother's cloak had moved him as the tartan dress had moved her.

The trip to Roodyards was a success. Quite apart from her suspicion that Mary would enjoy it, the graveyard was one of Isabel's own favourite places to visit, a small and grassy terrace cut into the slope at a height, overlooking the broad silver sweep of the Tay beyond. The air was clean and alive with birdsong. Isabel told Mary what she knew of the history of the place, from the plague burials of two hundred years before, to the resting places of the Kyd and Guthrie families who had owned all the land hereabouts once upon a time.

'Is your mother here?' Mary asked.

Isabel said no, Mother lay in the Dundee city graveyard, which was called the Howff, a little way away.

'And no body snatchers?' Mary asked. 'I hear there is a dreadful vogue for body snatching here in Scotland, for the anatomy schools?'

Isabel told her there were watches after a new burial, but not so many of those took place here any more. They roamed about, finding the graves of burgesses and babies, citizens and seafarers, many marked with carvings of skulls and crossbones and curious animated skeletons, hourglasses and strange, fat cherubs. Mary sketched a few of them in a little book she had, and wrote down the inscriptions that caught her eye. She was very taken with one that said, 'Death is the Master none may deny, he has lately called from this house persons in great age, in middle years and children full young.' She shivered and said there might be a story in that.

'Do you write stories?' Isabel asked, feeling her heart skip. She had been desperate to start talking to Mary of writing, but had been too afraid of the power of Mary's embarrassment to do so without an introduction from Mary herself.

Mary coloured. 'I do,' she said, 'but my stories are commonplace things by comparison with the works of my father and mother. Even my stepmamma. She is a translator, did you know that? She takes books in French and renders them into beautiful English. She is very good at it. And she can take a poorly written work in English and make it sing. It is a rare skill.'

Isabel was surprised at that. From all Mary had said, she had imagined Mary Jane Vial to be a venal sort of woman, totting up columns in the account books and caring little for the literary value of the work on the page. She squirrelled the thought away for later. 'I wouldn't know where to start,' she said. 'Writing a book, I mean. How does one begin?'

'With an idea, I suppose,' Mary said. 'An image, or a theme. Take that gravestone. It must have been a plague, must it not? To kill all three generations in a house in so short a space of time — it does feel that it was a short space, I think, from the way it is written? Yet someone was left to raise the stone to them. I might ask myself who that could have been, the last one living in a house of death. Did he have the illness, and survive? What would his eyes have opened upon as he woke from his fever? And when he left the house, what did he find?' She raised a hand to her eyes and scanned the coastline. 'Had the plague visited the whole coast? Were all dead but him? What would it be to be the last man standing, as far as the eye can see?'

Then she shivered, drawing Mother's cloak about her, and laughed. 'I wish I had the skill to tell such a story,' she said. 'I am fine at beginning, but I can make no progress once I have begun. Perhaps ... perhaps we could write something together. That way we would have each other's support. Would you like that?'

'Yes,' said Isabel, feeling a thrill in her fingertips. 'But perhaps ... not about a house of plague. I have had enough of sickrooms to last me a while.'

'Well,' said Mary, 'how about that stone we saw before about the good and gracious auntie? The one "packed in Death's portmanty". Would she be a more fitting subject?'

Isabel laughed. 'She sounded too godly a woman to make for a good story to me but ... the story of a woman would be a good thing to tell.'

'Yes,' said Mary. 'And in that way we could pay tribute to our own mothers. We need to think on it. Find a spark of something to inspire us. But now I think the rain is coming.'

Isabel turned to see dark clouds scudding in across the Firth.

'Not yet,' she said, 'tonight I think, but let's not take the chance. I wouldn't like you to have a soaking.'

They made their way back to The Cottage, handed over their cloaks and hats to John to stow away, then looked in on Father before they went upstairs. Father said Mary looked pale and she confessed she was a little fatigued but had enjoyed the outing enormously. Father said he was pleased but now he wished them to get themselves upstairs and rest. This they did, Mary dozing on her bed and Isabel reading until Cookie sent the dinner tray. Mary roused then and they talked a little as they ate, but she was clearly exhausted, and Isabel felt a growing pain in her head. They agreed on an early night and each turned her back while the other dressed in her nightgown before they took turns at the washstand. They agreed to leave the windows ajar and the curtains open a crack; the room seemed like to stifle them otherwise.

Isabel woke in the darkness to hear a whimpering sound. There was a tremendous pressure in the air and an odd smell she could not place, and for a moment she did not recognise her own chamber. Then she heard the sound again, and knew it was Mary, crying in a half-sleep, or in a dream. The room lit up then, suddenly, and Isabel saw that Mary was sitting up in bed, terrified. As a roll of thunder followed, she clambered out of bed and over to Mary, putting her arms around the younger girl as she shook and shivered.

'Hush, Mary,' she said. 'It's only lightning. Just a storm. It will be easier to sleep when it has passed.'

'I thought I saw a woman in the room,' Mary said. Isabel could not tell whether she was awake or dreaming. 'Over there in the shadows. Do you see her? I think it might be my mother. She is angry with me, don't you see? I killed her, Claire. With my birth, I killed her. And I have let her down.'

Isabel followed Mary's finger and saw the thing she had mistaken in her dreaming.

'Hush, Mary,' she said. 'I'm Isabel, not Claire. You are here with me in Scotland. Claire is at home in London. What you are seeing is my mother's old doll. That's all. She means you no harm. Nor does your mother, she rests peacefully in her grave. You have often told me how you visited her there. All is well, Mary, all is well.'

But Mary would not be consoled and continued to cry and whimper and almost climb up the rails of her bed, as if to get herself as far as she possibly could from the doll. Seeing she was truly in the grip of a dream terror, Isabel got up, took the fine old doll from her chair and laid her carefully in a drawer of the mahogany Scotch dresser on her own side of the room. The lightning came again, just as she laid her down, and the doll's face did seem oddly animated by its spark. All was wood and paint, even the jet-black eyes, but its sculptor had captured well the spirit of a high-born woman of the Stuart court of long ago. One eyebrow was raised higher than the other, so she had a look of arch amusement, and the shadows flickered around the well-carved, smirking mouth, lending the whole an impression of life and even humour, but no kindness.

As Isabel closed the drawer, another roll of thunder came, and then the rain began, dropping heavily onto the trees outside the window. Isabel felt the invisible band around her head lift as the pressure was relieved, and she saw that Mary had fallen back into sleep. She clambered into her own bed and closed her eyes.

In the morning, Mary said she had a half-memory of a terror in the night. She seemed disturbed, and Isabel rushed to put her at her ease before she could become embarrassed.

'You had a nightmare, that's all,' she said. 'It was the storm. You were deeply asleep and the lightning feared you.'

'I am not afraid of storms,' Mary said crossly, as though she thought it childish to be so. 'I like them. It is good for the sky to rage sometimes.'

'You have been ill, though,' said Isabel. 'You are still not quite yourself.'

'Did I say anything?' Mary asked. Red spots burned on her cheeks.

'You did,' said Isabel, deciding it was best to be honest. 'You thought my mother's doll had come to life and was watching you. Well, perhaps that's not quite right. You thought there was someone watching you, from the shadows. You seemed afraid it was your mother.'

Mary shook her head slowly. 'Poor Mother,' she said. 'Do you think we can speak to the dead, Isabel? I would so wish to know whether she resents me.'

'I don't know,' said Isabel. 'It is a comforting thought –' an image of her own mother's face flashed in her mind '– but I do not know. I myself have thought I have seen the dead walk, but I have never heard them speak. But why would your mother resent you, Mary? It makes no sense. I am sure she loved you very much and was greatly saddened to leave you.'

Mary looked down and Isabel saw tears sparkling on her lashes. 'But my birth killed her!'

'But you did not ask to be born,' Isabel said. 'This is the chance that women take, when they have babies.'

'Not all babies are a choice,' Mary said. She pulled at a loose thread on her bedcover.

'Perhaps not,' Isabel said. 'But your mother chose to have you, I'm sure. And some women die of it. It is not the fault of the babies. And your mother had no reason to think it would kill her. She had another daughter already, did she not? So she had no reason to think things would go wrong with you.'

'I suppose so,' Mary said. 'She chose to have a female midwife and not a doctor, so some say she brought it on herself.'

'Well,' said Isabel. 'All that proves is that she thought herself perfectly safe.' She was eager to leave the subject behind, since it seemed to be putting Mary in a bad humour, and so she opened the drawer where she had stashed the doll. 'I put the doll in here,' she said. 'She did look a little stern in the storm light, I confess.'

'Poor dolly,' Mary said. 'How silly she must think me. She can come out again, a grand lady like that won't like to be trapped in a drawer with your underthings.'

Isabel laughed and lifted the doll out. Instead of setting her back on her chair, she handed her to Mary. 'She is a fine thing,' she said. 'She was made for James VII, or James II as you say in England. When the Stuarts fell, a family loyal to them was made a gift of her, and she passed down through their descendants until, in the fullness of time, she came to be owned by my mother, whose family had served the last of their kin. Mother was very fond of her.'

'She is a little terrifying even now,' Mary said, laughing to show she didn't really mean it, but not entirely successfully. 'Her expression is quite formidable.'

'I like her patches,' Isabel said, touching the black spots painted on the wooden face. 'I wonder if we are to think she has had the pox and covers her scars, or whether she wears them for fashion.'

'She looks like a woman with a secret,' Mary said. 'She is not a plaything, is she? I mean a toy for a child.'

'No,' Isabel said. 'She is a woman's treasure. That's what Christy said, when we knew you were coming and I wondered whether I should put her away in case you thought me childish. Or perhaps she belonged to a man. She is quite correct, below her bodice and under her skirt.'

Mary pulled the bodice gently away from the doll's bosom so the little carved breasts were revealed. 'Do you think she is meant to be a good woman, or a courtesan?' she asked.

'Were courtesans bad women?' Isabel asked.

'Perhaps not,' Mary said. 'It must have taken much to survive at court in those days. My own mother ... well.' She did not continue on that subject, instead rearranging the doll's bodice and peeking up her skirt. 'She has her underthings on,' she said. 'So she is quite decent.'

Tension relieved, they laughed, but then Mary grew serious again.

'Perhaps we can write her adventures,' she said. 'As though the lightning had brought her to life again, and she could tell us all the stories of her life at court. Like Galvani believed he could do with his experiments. He was wrong of course. We do not have animal electricity in us. Volta proved that. But not before Aldini made some impressive shows. My father's friend Carlisle witnessed one of them. Aldini applied his process to the face of a hanged criminal and the poor creature's jaws began to quiver and his face contort until his eye opened! I still remember how we thrilled and shivered to hear of it, hiding behind the sofa while he told my father all. Fanny and I, I mean.'

'You thought I was your stepsister Claire last night,' Isabel said.

'I like you much better than Claire,' Mary said. 'Claire is a silly baggage.'

Isabel didn't know anything about Galvani or Volta beyond their names and that each had studied electricity, and she knew nothing at all about any Aldini, but she decided not to say so. Mary took many naps still and Isabel could ask Father for a primer on one of those occasions. It was the sort of thing he would follow, always wishing to be informed in scientific advance in case he could learn anything of use to his manufacturing enterprises.

'What would we call her?' she asked instead. 'The doll, I mean. If we were to write about her. Mother said she never had a name of her own, or if she did, it was forgotten long before Mother was born. My grandmother called her Madame Pretender, since she passed down through James III and he was called the Old Pretender, but that was a joke.'

'Countess Strathmore?' Mary said, evidently remembering the story Isabel had told of the builder of The Cottage. 'Or would we have more fun if she were not a real person at all?'

'Yes,' Isabel said, her mind racing. 'She could be a fiction. We could call her Mary Eleanor Gordon. Half for the Countess of Strathmore, and half for the Gordons. They're a great family, with many famous members, and there were many powerful women. And they were Jacobites, originally at least, and very wealthy. They would have been of great importance at the Stuart court.'

'No, not Gordon – or not quite,' Mary said. 'We should call her Lady G–. As if in cypher. She looks as though she might be talented in espionage.'

'Yes,' said Isabel, thinking of Christy's secret letter and thrilling a little.

Mary got out of bed then and placed the doll back in the carved chair on top of the dresser where she lived. The chair itself was a thing of glory, carved in the Jacobean style with snarling snake heads as finials at the end of each of the arms. She crossed the doll's feet neatly, in their pretty slippers embroidered with silver thread. Once seated, the doll looked quite formidable.

'Do you think she is pleased?' Mary said. 'That we shall give her some adventures?'

'I think she wishes us to do her justice,' Isabel replied. 'She would expect us to give a brave account of her.'

'Perhaps we can make her a trunk or a folder,' said Mary, 'so she can keep the stories with her. When they are done.'

'Or hide them about her person,' Isabel said, thinking again of the secret letter of Christy's, written on the finest of paper to fold away to nothing at all. She wondered if she should show it to Mary. Not yet, she decided, but perhaps someday.

'Very well,' said Mary, with a brisk nod, 'but first we need to make our plan. Do you have paper and pens, Isabel? Let's dress ourselves and find a place to work.'

4

THE TALE OF LADY G– was soon underway. Mary and Isabel commandeered a small parlour that Mother had used for her correspondence, and began to cart in paper and notebooks, pens and ink, and any of Father's books they thought might be of use to them. Mary was the leader in the enterprise, deciding that they should make this plan, or that, draw a map or list the members of a royal dynasty. They early settled on the idea that Lady G–'s world should be a fantasy one, but inspired by the French court and the many exiles who had taken shelter there, before the Terror. They called this place Lacunia.

Lady G– had a husband, they decided, but they had separated long ago, Lady G– taking only his title when she left him behind in the Old Country. He would not do her harm, they thought, and perhaps he would do to get her out of any scrapes in which she might find herself should the adventures they created require her to venture home. She had a lover, known only as the Accomplished Peer, and her history wove together elements of Mary's mother's life with that of Aphra Behn, who Mary said was the first woman writer in England to earn a living by her pen, and Anne of Swansea and the rest of the Kemble family.

They decided that Lady G– had been born in a city called Oxenford, at a time of great upheaval, to a family of actors and theatre owners loyal to the Old King. Lady G– had trod the stage in her youth, although it was a scandal for a young woman to do so. Then the family theatre's fortunes had collapsed and she had had to shift for herself. She had spent some time writing for the stage – her early years had equipped her with a formidable intellect – under the pseudonym of Hestia, which they thought witty as she did not intend to spend much time at home by the hearth. That didn't keep her, though, and so she briefly attempted to found a school – as Mary's mother had done – with one of her sisters and a friend. Then she followed in Mary Wollstonecraft's footsteps once again by accepting an engagement as a Lady's Companion in a city called the Spa. In this way she met Lord G–. He was very much older but enchanted by her beauty, and after he married her, he carted her off to the north country where he had a great estate and a history Mary and Isabel designed to the model of the Countess of Strathmore. The marriage was happy for a time and Lady G– produced a son and a daughter – twins – but then a dreadful rogue came to the place, and he schemed and connived to convince Lord G– that Lady G– was playing him false. It was all untrue, of course, and in the end the rogue was exposed, but Lady G– was so wounded by her husband's belief in her supposed deception that she lost faith with him completely and left him.

Around this time the Old King lost his throne, and fled to Lacunia. Lady G– followed him there, and wangled her way into a troupe of performers who were to play for him at a masque. There she so charmed him with her wit and talent for mimicry that he engaged her on the spot to be a spy.

Once this was all written down, and Lady G–'s friends and enemies listed – these were strongly inspired by Mary's feelings towards her own people, dead and alive – they began on the writing in earnest. In the first adventure, Lady G– was required to dress as a man in order to infiltrate a group of noblemen come from the Old Country with the express intention of assassinating the Old King. When it came to describing the dressing, Isabel and Mary were something at a loss, and so they stole into Father's room and took some of his evening clothes to dress themselves in. The style was too modern, of course; Lady G– would have worn a coat with a long skirt, but there were tight breeches and hose of silk, and the waistcoats were embroidered with flower buds – Father must have owned them in his younger days, he would wear nothing so flamboyant now. In their own room, they stripped off and redressed themselves, thrilling at their naughtiness and the freedom of wearing a shirt with nothing underneath, and breeches that let them take great strides across the floor. They had an old wig, too, that had been Mother's father's, and Isabel wore that for good measure.

They playacted as men for a while and then they decided that it should be in this adventure that Lady G– would meet the Accomplished Peer, and so Mary ran her hands up inside Isabel's waistcoat and made a great show of surprise at finding her breasts there. Isabel made as though to slap her, saying no gentleman would do such a thing, and Mary put her hand between Isabel's legs and said she could tell she was no gentleman, what was her game? Isabel protested but Mary tutted at her.

'Remember you are Lady G–,' she said. 'You should kiss me – I mean, kiss the Accomplished Peer – as a means to distract me. I mean, him.'

And so Isabel kissed her, and it was not as she expected, not a peck as she gave Father or her siblings, but instead Mary poked her tongue through Isabel's lips and laughed to see her discomfited.

Mary seemed very pleased with all of their acting, and quickly wrote down an account of the first encounter between Lady G– and the Accomplished Peer. She had Isabel describe the sensations she had felt as Mary touched her. Isabel's face flamed and Mary laughed.

'You are not worldly, Isabel,' she said, and Isabel wondered just when she had become so worldly herself.

Mary wrote on while Isabel sneaked into Father's room to replace the clothes in the press and sit for a few moments feeling her skin prickle and tingle where Mary had touched her. Gradually, her cheeks cooled and she recovered her composure.

They were very pleased with the story in the end. Lady G– foiled the plot, of course, pulling off the man's wig she wore as she ran to the state rooms of the Old King and banged upon the door. The conspirators were all beheaded, but Lady G– spoke for the Accomplished Peer, telling the King that he had never truly been part of the plot at all, only going along with it at all in order to foil it when he had enough evidence to ensure the collaborators' guilt was proven beyond question. To complete this impression, he delivered the cache of arms they had hidden away to the Old King himself. In this way, Mary said, the allegiances of the Accomplished Peer were not entirely clear and there would be much fun to be had with his character in future. They discussed whether he and Lady G– should bed one another, but in the end they decided that he should come to her apartments, and she should meet him in the guise of a serving girl and make advances to him. He would refuse the advances, and in this way she would know he was not a ravisher of women.

They acted this scene out too, Mary playing the Accomplished Peer once more. She said Isabel should try to tempt her to ravish her by pulling down her nightgown to show her bosom. Isabel blushed and refused, but Mary said there was no one to see and so in the end she did, whereupon Mary told her she was a brazen strumpet and should be ashamed. Isabel's cheeks flamed again, and Mary pulled her nose.

'No, no,' she said, 'you are playing a strumpet who would never blush!' Then she kissed Isabel chastely and said, 'You're such an innocent, Isabel, I do love you so,' and Isabel felt young and silly again even though she was two years Mary's senior. Mary wrote it all down again, and very fine they thought it too.

The writing was interrupted for a time then, as Father announced he wished to indulge Mary and Isabel with a ten-day voyage into the Highlands of Perthshire with the carriage, picking up Christy up from Agnes's on the way and taking her along. Mary squealed with delight and immediately began to make her preparations, stuffing paper and pens and blotters into her small trunk with her clothes.

'Great writers must travel, Isabel,' she said. 'It is how they find their inspiration.'

* * *

All trip long, Mary seemed enchanted with her surroundings and with Father. Once they had picked up Christy, they journeyed onwards to Birnam, where they explored the town and the great cathedral of Dunkeld. In the choir, they found a marvellous old chest tomb topped with the effigy of a warrior in full armour, carved in grey marble.

'Who was he?' Mary asked. 'The inscription is in Latin and I cannot read it.'

'The Wolf of Badenoch,' said Father. 'He was a prince, a son of King Robert II. He was a deeply unpopular man, for he was always burning this town or that in his furies. I visited his castle in my youth. A most impressive place it was, on an island in a loch far to the north of here. They called it the Wolf's Lair, isn't that grand?'

Mary's eyes sparkled and she began to scribble in a little notebook.

'I could tell you it all again tonight,' Father said. 'That way you would be more comfortable as you write.'

'Oh no,' Mary said. 'I need to write here, with his bones beside me.'

'Imagine if he came to life, he'd be at least a foot taller than you, Father,' said Christy, who always could be relied upon to make obvious observations. 'Do you think he was so big in real life?'

'Perhaps,' Father said. 'Either way, I shouldn't like to take him on.'

'His face is all chipped,' Christy said. 'And why does he have his feet on a dog?'

'Why not?' asked Father. 'Keep his toes warm.'

But Mary peered more closely and said it wasn't a dog at all, more like a lion, and Father said he thought she was right. Mary scribbled that down too, her eyes shining. She had begun to call Father 'William Thomas' instead of 'Mr Baxter', which Isabel found unsettling, although she couldn't quite decide why.

Once they had finished inspecting the Wolf, they completed their visit to the cathedral and went back to their inn for a good, plain dinner, passing a pleasant evening in front of the fire playing cards. Christy was a dab hand at Commerce and it wasn't long until Father professed himself beaten and left her to beat Mary and Isabel as well. In their room that night,

Mary and Isabel schemed the role the Wolf could play – well, a nobleman known as the Wolf – in the story of Lady G–. Mary said now she realised there was no antagonist in the story, and one was needed. The Wolf, they thought, could be a friend of Lord G–, in Lacunia with the stated intention of persuading Lady G– to come home, but in reality seeking to turn her into a double agent spying on the Old King.

The next day they went to see the great oak that was all that remained of the forest that had marched to Dunsinane in pursuit of Macbeth. Christy had brought paints, and Isabel joined her in capturing its likeness while Mary perched on a fallen trunk nearby and wrote more in her notebook. Father said that William Shakespeare had seen the oak, or so they said, while touring Scotland as a player, and he clowned around shouting lines from Macbeth while Mary howled with laughter. Father seemed much lighter since they had left home, almost boyish, and Isabel remembered with a pang that he had often been so before Mother died and he seemed always stern and formal with them now. She saw other travellers watching him, now and then, and was proud of his handsome face and upright stature.

After that they travelled north to a small place called Grandtully where they saw a strange church that looked quite like a byre from the outside, but inside was painted all over like a jewel casket, and then a fine castle that showed its defensive origins, tall and stout-walled with an old chapel to one side. Father sat and read his newspaper in the carriage while Christy unpacked paper and charcoal and prepared to make a sketch. Mary said it would make a good model for the Wolf's Lair and went off to wander the grounds while Isabel helped Christy set up an easel. Five minutes later, Mary came running back at such a pelt she could not catch her breath at all.

'Goodness, Mary!' Christy said. 'Are you well?'

When at last Mary had recovered, she said she had seen a man with a notebook like her own, sitting writing among the ruins of a building even more ancient than this one, and she would swear on her life it had been Walter Scott.

'Watty Scott?' Father said, appearing out of the carriage. 'Are you sure?'

'I think so,' said Mary. 'I've never seen him in life, but he looked awfully like his engravings.'

'Good Lord,' Christy said under her breath, so only Isabel could hear her. 'A famous writer Mary hasn't met!'

Father said he would go back with Mary to the place she had seen the man; he was a great admirer of Scott's and would be delighted to meet him. But Scott – if Scott it had been – had disappeared and Mary and Father came back directly, speculating about the work he might have been writing, and whether they would recognise the place when the book was published. Mary sighed and said she hoped some of Scott's genius might transfer to her, since they had breathed the same air and taken the same inspiration, and Father laughed and said perhaps the exchange would go the other way and Scott would be a better writer for crossing Mary's path, how would that be?

Christy tore her drawing off the easel then, and said it was no good, she could not draw at all that day. It seemed to Isabel that she was in a cross mood – perhaps she too resented the easy fondness that had developed between Mary and Father.

'We should journey onwards, then,' said Father. 'We'll reach our inn at Aberfeldy tonight and tomorrow we shall walk along a gorge and see a splendid waterfall.'

Christy stalked ahead of them as Father began to recite a poem Robert Burns had written about the gorge. That night she said she had a headache and would take her supper in her room. Isabel didn't mind too much – she and Mary and Father made a jollier party without Christy looking down her nose at them. In the morning she seemed in better spirits, and made some very pretty sketches at the waterfall. She joined them for supper and cards that evening, seeming quite recovered, and Isabel felt a little guilty for judging her harshly when, the next day, they travelled onwards to see the ancient yew tree at Fortingall where, legend had it, Pontius Pilate had been born.

'The people of Abyssinia venerate Pilate as a saint,' Christy said. 'Because he was reluctant to execute our Lord and died full of regret.'

Her face was pained, and Isabel suddenly saw how she regretted the German tutor, and felt sorry for her own part in bringing the business to an end. She decided she would make more of an effort to be kind to her sister during the last days of the trip. In truth, it was not too hard, as this leg proved the best of all, with carved stones and stone circles, lochs and mountains and, at the furthest reach of the journey, the fairytale castle at Glamis, where they terrified themselves with tales of ghosts and hauntings.

On the way home they stayed the night in an inn at Perth so the girls could order new frocks from a draper there. While Isabel and Mary pored over glowing satins and pretty sprigged prints, Christy tried to order herself a simple frock in grey and another in brown, with a plain spencer jacket in brown velvet.

'No, Christy!' Isabel said. 'Those will not do at all! I will let you have the spencer, but you must have prettier frocks to wear with it, not those widow's weeds! Here ...' And she pulled a pretty muslin off the shelf, a deep cream ground with a delicate print of rose trees in green and red. 'This would look very fine with the spencer, it would set off the richness of the velvet very well.'

'That's a good choice,' the shop woman said. 'I have another that would also look very fine.' She scurried off and returned with a sturdy printed cotton striped in cream and yellowish green, with tiny leaves and sprays of flowers printed all along the stripes in a rich cinnamon brown. 'This would look very well if I were to cut it with capped sleeves,' the woman said. 'That way I could run the stripes in the other direction from the bodice and it would show the print to its best effect.'

Christy grumbled a little, but Isabel thought it was for the look of the thing, and secretly she was pleased to be saved from her own miserable inclinations.

Once they had all ordered their dresses – Mary chose a pretty roller-printed cotton with a contrast print hem and a blue and white stripe, and Isabel a green and white stripe and a pattern of rosebuds on white – Father said he wished to buy them all a gift from a jeweller's shop in the town to remember the journey by. In the shop, Christy went straight for a gold brooch with a great piece of red agate carved into the shape of a flower, with gold claws holding it to its pin, like leaves.

'This would suit my new brown jacket.'

Father paid for the brooch at once and the jeweller's assistant began to wrap it in paper.

Mary and Isabel looked at everything, and at last decided on single pearls fished from the Tay and hung from slender chains.

'A grey pearl for Mary,' Father said, 'to set off her red-gold hair. And a pink one for Isabel, with her dark hair and rosy cheeks.'

'We are sisters now, almost,' said Mary, as the jeweller fixed them on. Christy looked a little peeved, but her gift was much finer, and she was clearly touched by Father's generosity.

They arrived home exhausted although, in Mary's case, fizzing with ideas for the Wolf of Schiehallion – which was a cone-shaped mountain they had seen – and Lady G–. Mary had also decided on a rival for Lady G–, a character inspired by her own stepmother who, she said, would be a woman of great seductive talents and feminine wiles. This woman would be called Madame Poule, short for Ampoule, a joke as Mary's stepmother's name was Vial. She would be an accomplice of the Wolf's, when it suited her, but her background would be mysterious, deliberately so, for she had done many things she wished to hide from the world. Like Mary Jane Vial, she had been born of a Protestant family exiled from Lacunia – France, in the case of the real Mary Jane – for their faith. In this way she would speak the language of Lacunia and the language of the Old Country, and her allegiances would never be clear.

Their next story, they decided, would see Lady G– approached by the Wolf while the Accomplished Peer met Madame Poule, and both would be invited to join a plot to release a nobleman from prison in the Old Country, where he was under sentence of death for his part in another plot to return the Old King to the throne. The Accomplished Peer would think he was helping release Madame Poule's husband from wrongful imprisonment, while Lady G– would think she was helping an ally of the King. In reality, the nobleman was in cahoots with the government of the Old Country, cooling his heels in prison as a trap for the unwary. They filled page after page with scribbled plans for this story, crossing out this idea, or that. Mary clearly viewed herself as leader in the writing, and once or twice she snapped at Isabel that her ideas were too obvious, or her wording too derivative. Isabel's eyes smarted, but she bit her tongue, telling herself that Mary had more knowledge of writing and she should be grateful to learn by her side.

Again, though, the writing was interrupted, for that very week a letter arrived from Margaret. She had, it seemed, grown tired of waiting for her sisters to visit her of their own accord and had decided to summon them to Fife herself. There was no space for Christy, she wrote, but David would send the carriage the next Monday for Isabel and Mary, who should be ready to pass two weeks and more in Newburgh.

Isabel half expected Christy to be put out, but in fact she seemed quite relieved.

5

Isabel touched her knife to the beef on her plate, watching as blood leaked from it to stain the sauce in which it sat. Her gorge rose, and determinedly she cut a green bean in two and placed it in her mouth, breathing through her nose as she chewed, in and out, and in and out, until she had control of herself once more. All the while, David spoke on, lightly, calmly, telling them of an odd thing he had discovered in the garden behind the house, a stone ball about the size of an orange, with four large knobs carved in a band around it, and smaller knobs carved above and below. The garden was full of odd stonework, pools and channels that once took water to the old Abbey of Lindores, but David thought his latest find predated those by thousands of years.

'Perhaps it was used in a game?' Mary suggested, and David said perhaps, although it did not roll.

'For some sort of ceremony, then?' Mary said, and David seemed pleased, saying he thought this the most likely explanation; he believed the ancient peoples hereabout had worshipped the sun and moon and perhaps the ball was some representation of one or the other in its cycles, and linked, it might be, to fertility.

'I should like to see it,' Mary said, and David smiled and said, 'Then you shall.'

Isabel sat and listened to this flimflam, all the while wishing to scream, *Have we all gone mad? How can we sit here at the table and eat beef and talk of stupid things found in the garden when there is such horror in our midst?*

The visit had been a trial from the first evening. David had met them on their arrival, apologising that Margaret could not come down as she was indisposed. She was resting now, he said, but looked forward to joining them for the evening meal. Isabel had thought little of it then, long used to Margaret's invalid status, but when they stood changed and waiting in the hall and Margaret appeared round the turn of the stairs, Isabel's mouth had fallen open. Her comely blonde sister was quite gone, and in her place stood a living skeleton, her dress hanging off her and the bones of her face and body poking through her stretched and yellow skin.

Neither Margaret nor David had said a word, they had merely led the way to table where, it seemed, Margaret had no less of a power than Mary to bind the tongues of the company so none might speak. She gave signals to the servants to bring the tureens, clear the dishes, fill the glasses like any mistress, although it was a show only in her own case; she ate nothing and drank no more than water. Close up, Isabel could see her hair was thin and dry and faded beneath her lace cap, and she smelled strange, too – the whole house smelled faintly of her sickness, in fact, a lingering, too-sweet smell, like rotten fruit. But she smiled brightly enough, in her old, humourless way, and clicked her tongue at the servants when they did anything to displease her, which was often, as the room was small and they were forever bumping the table legs or the chairs.

Mary said nothing to Isabel that night, and Isabel could not think of a way of beginning, and so the pattern was set for their days, Margaret resting in the morning and coming down only for the mid-afternoon meal, retreating back upstairs afterwards and taking supper – if indeed she took anything – on a tray. This left Mary and Isabel idle in the mornings and evenings. They took to exploring out of doors when it was light, and to playing cards or reading by lamplight after dark. Now and then Isabel thought Mary would be grateful if she opened the subject of Margaret and her sickness, but she could not find the words, and so for many days, nothing was said.

In the topsy-turvy world of mealtimes, David seemed much as usual, paying a kind of self-important attention to Mary and to Isabel, and for her part Mary, too, carried on as though nothing were amiss. Only Isabel sat tongue-tied, playing with her food and flushing if spoken to, stumbling over her answers. Margaret ignored her, looking only at Mary, and Mary was solicitous of her hostess's comfort, offering to pass Margaret the salt, or to fetch an extra shawl, or to adjust the curtains so the low sun did not shine into her eyes. In return, Margaret seemed determined to needle at Mary, asking questions about her family that were clearly designed to upset her, about the health of the family business, how her brothers Charles and William did at school, or about her father's last play, which Margaret knew perfectly well had been a dreadful failure. David answered much of this for Mary, speaking deliberately of Godwin's generosity to others, this boy he had helped through Cambridge or that widow he had helped from a bind, and all the while praising the brilliance of his work. Margaret responded with remarks that seemed on the surface to acknowledge his points, but there was an undertow, too, of criticism of David himself.

Gradually Isabel understood that she and Mary were not really in the room at all – or at least, they were there not for themselves but to serve as proxies for some awful tussle between Margaret and David. She could not for the life of her make out what either sought to achieve. Margaret's time on earth was drawing to a close, so much was clear. Was she angry at David, or he at her? What had any of it to do with Mary and the Godwins?

Mary continued to play her part in the conversation, relating their daily adventures to Margaret gaily enough, their excursions to the ruined old Abbey and up the hill called the Black Cairn. She brought the rubbing she had made from the carved Pictish stone in the kirkyard to show, and asked Margaret what she thought the true history had been of the curious monument on the Lindores Road named for clan MacDuff.

In return, Margaret redoubled her nastiness, asking whether Mary thought perhaps to become a governess, like her mother, being so interested in matters of history. Making such a rubbing would be an excellent way to educate a child, she said pointedly.

Mary smiled and said she rather thought not. Her mother, she said, had been a teacher and not a governess. That was to say she had worked in a school, not for a family.

'But after that she worked for a family, did she not?' Margaret asked. 'In Ireland. I'm sure David told me so.'

David looked at his plate.

'Yes, but for a short time only,' Mary said, crossly. 'Then she determined she would make her living as an author. She wrote a book on the education of daughters, as well as her novel and works of philosophy. And she made many translations for publication.'

'Do you write?' Margaret asked. 'Are you an *author* too?'

Mary coloured. 'Yes,' she said. 'But I write fancies only. Flights of the imagination.'

'And what of your half-sister – it is Fanny, I think?' Margaret asked. 'Shall she find a place, do you believe? It will be hard for her, perhaps, to find a place with a decent family when she has no name of her own.'

Mary's face flamed at this last, and Isabel heard her breathe in heavily through her nose. Isabel could not understand how she could do so. They were eating pears poached in wine, and the scent was like a sweeter version of Margaret's own miasma, so the stink was entirely unbearable.

David opened his mouth to respond, but before he could speak, Mary jumped in.

'I dare say Fanny may do as she likes,' she said with a brilliant smile. 'My family moves much in society, you know.' She proceeded then to speak of her family home at Somers Town and the many illustrious personages who had visited them there, Coleridge, poor late John Opie the painter, Charles Lamb and many more. Her father, she said, dined every week with his publisher Johnson, and at his table had met Wordsworth, and William Blake, and Thomas Paine. 'The general milieu in Somers Town is cosmopolitan,' she said, 'with many French families, lately fled from the Terror, living in some style there.' She spoke of dressmakers and toymen, and fancy goods warehouses, jaunts to dinner, and circuses and to view the exotic beasts in the menageries. She boasted of salons and lectures and debates with the greatest personages of the day, and by the time she had finished speaking, it seemed London fairly glittered before them in the air.

Mary picked up her wine and sipped, seeming to consider she had won this round.

Margaret dipped her head, as if in defeat. 'Fancy,' she said, apparently without rancour. 'It sounds marvellous. Such a shame it should be so unhealthy a place. Its poor inhabitants suffer something dreadful as I understand it. Much better to be here in the fresh air I think, with clean air and water and green fields all around.'

'Indeed,' David said. 'Far nicer to be here.'

A strange look came across Margaret's face, almost like humour, but not quite. 'Why don't you take the girls to see some of the country yourself, David?' she said. 'There are places they cannot go themselves. I well remember how you introduced me to the countryside hereabouts. I shall take the memory of it to my grave.'

'The girls have plenty to do,' David protested.

'No, no, I insist,' Margaret said, and now there was poison in her tone. 'After all, Mary has had such impressive experiences in her life, but a menagerie or a circus in London can scarcely induct her into the true mysteries of the earth. Surely you wouldn't refuse her that during her time here with us.'

David took a sip of water, staring over his glass at Margaret. 'Very well,' he said at last. 'Isabel, Mary, we will make a journey the day after tomorrow. It will be an early start, so you may take your supper in your room tomorrow night. You will need clothing that will stand up to the wet. I will ask the housekeeper to make arrangements.' He stood up and left the room.

'Wonderful,' said Margaret. 'I look forward greatly to hearing your thoughts on your return, Mary. I know we are a poor place by comparison with all you have seen in London, but I trust we have some things here to impress you.'

The next day was wet and so they passed the morning in reading. The maid told them that David and Magaret both sent their apologies, but neither would be able to join them at table, and Margaret had suggested that they have a meal of cold cuts in the little library before the fire. This was a relief to both and they made of it a picnic and wondered aloud at the place David would take them on the morrow. The maid had said two men's coats had been found for them, and treated with oil so they would stand a soaking, and there was sacking to bind their legs. Mary wondered whether they might visit a great waterfall, like the one they had seen in Perthshire, but perhaps this one might have a cave behind it – she had read of such a place before.

Isabel said she did not think there were any great falls in Fife, or she would have heard of them. She wondered if they were going to sail out across the sea to an island. Not the island they could see from here, that had the awful name of Mugdrum and was no more than a couple of flat fields.

'We should have a character in our story called Mugdrum,' Mary said. 'He would be a very dull fellow indeed. For comic relief.' She scribbled that down in the little notebook she kept with her always.

'I can't think he will take us to Mugdrum,' Isabel continued, 'but I don't know of any other islands here. If there were others, we should see them from home. Perhaps we will sail further from land.'

Mary looked pale at that and Isabel remembered how sick she had been on the boat from London.

'No, I think it won't be a boat,' she said quickly. 'David will know how unwell you became. But perhaps sea stacks reached from land. Or a cave.'

After some further debate, they agreed that a cave was the most likely destination, and thought perhaps this would be useful inspiration for the further adventures of Lady G–.

The maid woke them long before dawn and she and the housekeeper, Mrs Brown, helped them wrap leather around their feet inside their boots and bind their legs with sacking and tie more leather over the top. Mrs Brown showed them how to kilt their skirts up and rejected the shawls they had selected, giving them instead coats of skin that looked to have last been worn by cavemen. 'Nonsense,' she said, when Mary said so. 'They're what farmers wear in winter.'

'Wonderful,' said Mary. She rolled her eyes at Isabel. 'They smell of farmers too.'

When they were wrapped up to Mrs Brown's satisfaction, the great waterproof coats went on over all, stiff and smelly, and then she tied kerchiefs of woollen stuff around their heads. These reeked of sheep, which Mrs Brown said meant they would keep out the wet.

'I hope there will be no gentlemen where we are going,' said Mary, and Isabel laughed. A day without having to watch Margaret disappearing had done much for her spirits.

They were hustled into the coach with a basket of oatcakes and cheese and other breakfast stuff, and David poked his head in to check all was well. He said he would sit up front with the driver to keep him right in the dark; they had a long way to travel and the girls should sleep if they could. They ate and then they did sleep, waking to discover that it was light outside but the carriage windows were covered with some sort of black stuff so they could not see where they were going. They picked some more at the food in the basket, wishing they could get out and stretch their muscles.

Some time later, the carriage drew to a stop and David opened the door, getting in with them. He had pieces of cloth in his hand and he said that these were to tie over their eyes, so they would not see where they were going and spoil the surprise. He tied Isabel's on first, and then Mary's, and then he and the coachman lifted them down and guided them across some rough ground, telling them where to place their feet so they wouldn't fall. Isabel did not much like the smell of the coachman, he stank of tobacco, but she was glad of his arm. She did not like walking thus blinded.

They seemed to enter some sort of enclosure, then, and David told them they would make their way down a ladder. He said he would go first, and the coachman would stay above, and in this way they would guide the girls down without the slightest risk of falling. Isabel didn't like this but she felt she couldn't say so, and Mary said nothing, and so they began on that horrible process, guided to step backwards into thin air while David and the coachman told them how to find the rungs below with their feet. David took hold of Isabel's ankle at one point to guide her and it felt strange and uncomfortable.

This was repeated three times, and then a fourth, and all the while the air around them seemed to get warmer and damper, and it smelled peculiar and dusty somehow. At the bottom of the third ladder they splashed down into water and Isabel was glad of the leather bound round her feet; she could feel the cold of the water as it breached the seams of her boots. It was strange and frightening, moving through the water blind, and she hoped they would reach the floor of the cave before long and take off their bindings.

One ladder more, and she had her wish. David told them they could unfasten the blindfolds and they pulled them off to see – nothing. They stood in a low, narrow passageway, somewhere deep inside the earth, and the only light was from the lanterns David and the coachman carried. The walls shone with wetness, and drips fell incessantly from the ceiling, and they stood in stagnant water up to their knees.

'What. Is. This. Place?' Mary asked, and Isabel knew she was speaking slowly and carefully so as not to scream.

'Where do you think?' David said, as though this was all a charming game and not something awful from a nightmare.

'It's a mine,' Isabel said, speaking through lips that felt numb with fear. 'A coal mine.' She had expected an opening, the sea, air and sound, and now all she could think of was the great press of earth above them. Mines collapsed, did they not? Or exploded in dreadful bursts of flame and heat. What was David thinking, bringing them here?

'A mine?' Mary repeated, whether stupid with anger or terror Isabel could not tell. 'We did not ask to see a mine! Why would you bring us to a mine?'

'Why not?' David asked. 'Are you not curious to see a place few women of your class will ever see? Do you not wish to understand how the labour of others contributes to our community? Your father believes in justice, Mary, and the rights of all to that which they need. I sought merely to open your eyes to what that means in the world we presently inhabit.'

'Why did you bring my sister here?' Isabel asked. 'My father is not a philosopher. He is a sailmaker.'

'He is,' said David, 'but his children are given to fancy themselves philosophers. I wanted Margaret to know that the freedom of those with wealth is built on the labour of those without.'

'We know this,' Isabel said, trying to keep her voice steady. 'My father has always made this clear to us. We have been among those who labour in his business often. Most worship with us every Sunday. We respect and thank them for we know what they do.'

'There is a difference between knowing with your mind and knowing with your heart,' said David. 'Before she married me, Margaret had never dirtied her hands. You have toiled in a vegetable plot, Mary, but this was done in play. You have read all your father's work and yet you admit that all you write are flights of fancy. Margaret was the same. But I am a brewer. I work with my hands, and I still find time to have a life of the mind. I seek the same for you. It is the only way men and women may ever be equal.'

Mary had said nothing all this while, and when Isabel turned to her, she saw she was white and breathing heavily.

'We must get Mary out,' she said. 'Quickly. Can you not see she is unwell?'

David stared at them for a second, and then nodded to the coachman to go first. The coachman climbed the lowest ladder, then held the lamp while Isabel pushed Mary up and then followed herself. They repeated this again and again, until at last they reached the mine building above ground, where Mary fell to her knees, seemingly struggling to breathe. There was no sign of David.

'Open the door,' Isabel instructed the coachman. She lifted Mary into a sitting position and helped her put her head between her knees. She rubbed her back and whispered reassuring things to her – they were safe, it was only sport, badly judged but not badly meant. Little by little, she heard Mary's breathing calm. David still had not come back above ground.

When Mary could stand, Isabel led her outside and over to the carriage, where they took off their sodden coats and head coverings and wrapped themselves in blankets. They loosened the leather and sacking from around their legs and then removed the leather from their feet. Mrs Brown had packed linen towels in with the food in the picnic basket and they dried their feet and hair as best they could, although they had no dry boots to put on, so they wrapped their feet in blankets instead. While they were involved in this labour, they could hear the coachman harnessing the horses and David taking his seat outside beside him, and then the carriage was moving back to Newburgh and Margaret.

Mary did not speak, in all of the long journey home, and Isabel herself had little to say, being cold and damp and tired and miserable. When at last they drew up at Barns of Woodside, Mrs Brown was waiting to usher them inside and upstairs where there was a fire blazing in the hearth of their little room.

'Mercy,' she said, 'you're both frozen solid. I have water hot for a bath next door, and the fire is lit. Come, let me get you stripped off and into dry towels while you wait.' She reached for Mary's dress to unfasten it, but Mary shook her off.

'See to Miss Isabel first,' Mary said. It was the first thing Isabel had heard her say since they had left the wretched mine. Her cheeks flushed. 'I have my blood, I will have to go second. I will sit by the fire and save wetting more things.'

Mrs Brown frowned but Mary pushed past her to sit by the fire and began to fan her hair out with her fingers so it would dry.

'Very well then, Miss,' she said, and she ushered Isabel out of the room and into the room next door where the maid was busy filling the bath with kettles from the fire. Isabel was glad of Mrs Brown's help to disrobe; her own fingers were too stiff with cold to manage her buttons. She felt she might weep with anger and shock.

'I can't think what the master was thinking,' Mrs Brown said. 'He took you down into a mine, is that right? That's a queer thing to do and no mistake.'

'How d-d-d-did you know that?' Isabel asked through chattering teeth.

'The missus told me,' Mrs Brown said. 'She said ... well, never mind what she said.'

She said it would bring Miss Mary and Miss Isabel down a peg or two, I'll bet, thought Isabel as she sank gratefully into the water. She found she didn't have the strength to think on it further, her head was muzzy and sore and it hurt to swallow. She lay there in the hot water while Mrs Brown hung bath sheets over a rail by the fire and the maid picked up the kettle and went downstairs to fetch more water.

By the time Isabel had soaped herself and washed her hair and the maid had poured water from a jug to rinse it, she felt as though she was watching the scene from somewhere outside herself. As she stepped out of the bath into a warm bath sheet held by the maid, there was a rap on the door and Mary came in.

'Me next,' she said. 'I don't need any help, thank you, Maisie. Just leave the bath sheet and the jug, I'll manage fine by myself. You go next door and warm Miss Isabel's bed with the pan.'

The maid bobbed a curtsey and went out. Isabel finished drying herself, feeling as though each movement was taking ten times longer than normal. Behind her, she heard Mary's clothes fall to the floor and Mary step into the bath. She opened the door and then, remembering, turned back to retrieve the topaz cross necklace she always wore.

Mary was still standing in the water, and she froze as Isabel turned to face her. Isabel saw, then, the strange marks on the skin of Mary's body that she had sought to hide. She said nothing, and knew she would never say anything, for despite the muzziness of her head, she knew that she needed to unsee what she had seen, or lose Mary forever. She made her eyes dull. 'My necklace,' she whispered. 'Bring my necklace when you come, Mary, would you? I feel too unwell.'

'I will,' said Mary, frowning, and Isabel turned and went out.

Maisie had heated Isabel's bed by the time she came in, and a nightgown was warming by the fire. She put it on, and slipped into bed, and then it seemed she was on fire, quite, with dreadful fevers and dark imaginings, and her throat swollen up so she could not even cry out.

She woke at one point, near dawn, to see Mary sitting at the dressing table with a candle, and ink and a pen, scrawling frantically in her notebook.

'What are you doing?' she asked, feeling her voice coarse and rough and sore in her throat.

'Writing,' Mary said.

'Are you crying?' Isabel asked.

'No,' Mary said, 'you're ill, go back to sleep. Never mind me. I have an idea for a story, that's all, and I want to write it while it's in my mind.' She turned her back and carried on scribbling, speaking under her breath to herself of things Isabel could only half hear, men and women and good faith and bad.

Isabel closed her eyes and slipped off into a world that looked like this one, only as if viewed through glass with a fault in, so all was skewed and wrong. In this dream world, there was no Margaret and David was married to Mary, and there was a child who was Mary's child, only the child was not a baby but a yearling, or even older. 'I won't tell,' dream Isabel said to dream Mary, and dream Mary stared back blankly. 'There's nothing to tell,' she said. 'No child at all. Or the child is dead. You're confused, Isabel, you've been ill.'

Isabel lay in her fever two full days, and then it broke and she woke up cool and weak, but feeling well once more. They told her they had sent for an apothecary, but he had said it was nothing to be afraid of, not the putrid sore throat or anything so dangerous, just a bad chill from the cold weather. He prescribed broths and jellies and Mrs Brown toiled up and down the narrow stairs with these and professed herself pleased with Isabel's progress, if not with Mary's, for she had great bruised circles below her eyes from sitting crouched over her desk all night.

When Mrs Brown was gone, Isabel asked to see the writings, but Mary said no.

'Could I know a little of what they're about?' Isabel said. 'Is it Lady G–?'

'No,' Mary said. 'That is, yes. It is about a man who kidnaps a woman. I mean Lady G–. He takes her prisoner and he treats her abominably. I have given him green glasses like my stepmother wears.'

No matter how Isabel wheedled, Mary would not let her see the writings, and instead she made herself everything that was charming so it seemed they were almost as close as before, although perhaps there was a distance in Mary's very jolliness, a wariness as she offered to read to Isabel, or to play cards, or to bring up her drawing things and pose for her. She only seemed easier when Isabel told her she could not remember much at all of the journey home from the mine, or what happened after. Then she cheered, making Isabel laugh with her take-offs of Margaret and David at table, her 'Margaret' brittle and vicious and her 'David' oily and obsequious. It was the first time they had spoken openly of them since they had arrived.

'Margaret is dying, isn't she?' Isabel said, relieved almost to say the awful words. 'I don't understand. She had consumption when we were children but she came through, and the doctors said there was no reason she could not live a long life, only she would always need to be careful of her health and never exert herself.'

'She has no cough,' Mary said, 'and I cannot think she has a growth or similar, there seems no pain, only she is so thin. Perhaps she will rally yet.'

'Are you angry with David, still?' Isabel asked, thinking a rally on Margaret's part unlikely.

'Only for how ill he made you,' Mary said. 'But you are nearly better, your cheeks are quite rosy again – see?' She brought over a looking glass and Isabel saw that she was indeed well again, or nearly. It really had been a passing infection.

The outing to the mine had been on the Sunday – when work paused for church – and on the Friday, Isabel was well enough to come down for dinner. Margaret met her with a thin smile.

'There is a letter for you, Isabel,' she said. 'And one for you, Mary. You may read them when we are done with the meal.'

That was an excellent ruse to ensure the dinner dragged more than usual for Isabel and Mary, but at last the plates were cleared and the maid appeared with the letters on a tray. Margaret got to her feet and David rose and hurried to her side, taking her arm and lifting her against him. Isabel and Mary had to wait, again, to open their letters until they had made their painful way from the room. Then Mary picked hers up excitedly and tore it open, perhaps recognising the seal or the hand as her father's. Isabel felt a strange pang of nerves in her stomach as she picked up her own, and she broke the seal unwillingly. She felt her lips grow numb as she read.

Mary had rushed through her own letter and now her eyes sparkled. 'I am to go home for a spell to London!' she announced. 'My father wishes me to return for the winter, to see Reynolds' new exhibition, and to attend the opening night of Coleridge's new play! Oh, Isabel, think! Such sport we will have!'

Whatever distance had existed between them since the night of the mine visit, it seemed it was gone, and Isabel felt tears prick her eyes. She said nothing, and Mary took her hand.

'Isabel? Are you not excited? You have always said you wished to see London. Oh, I know you will miss your father and your home, but the time will pass quickly and you will soon be home again, you will see!'

'I'm not coming,' Isabel said.

Mary frowned at her. 'What do you mean? Of course you must come. That was always the arrangement. I would stay here for a time, and in return, you would come to London and stay with my family.'

'Christy is to go with you in my place,' Isabel said. 'My father says he knows I will be disappointed, but he asks that I remain here to help Margaret in her illness.'

'No!' Mary said. 'This is nonsense. I care nothing for Christy, what company will she be to me? I will speak to David and he will set this right. After that ... performance with the mine, it's the least he can do.'

'It is David who has made the arrangement,' Isabel said, feeling tears prick the back of her eyes. 'And it seems all is settled already. Margaret will hear of having no one else with her but me, and my father will not gainsay her. Your father and your stepmamma have already made arrangements for Christy to travel with you and my father encloses a page from her full of her pleasure at seeing London again. The trunks are packed, and they will meet you at the boat tomorrow. You will set out from here at six. You had better get to bed.' She managed to keep the tears from falling, but there was a rushing in her ears as she stood up and left the room.

Isabel's plan had been to make for their bedchamber, but in the hallway, she changed her mind and went outside into the garden. It was drizzling and she had no cloak, but the fine mist soothed her stinging eyes. She walked out of the garden and up the hill behind the house, sitting there on a tree stump for a time until the tears came. Margaret had done this from sheer spite. Why could Father not see it? How could he leave Isabel here, alone, without Mary for company, without anyone for company but Margaret who hated Isabel, and David, and everyone? Then she fell to wondering whether Mary would ever return. She worried that she would not, worried that she had spoiled their friendship forever with the thing she had seen, one stupid turn back in a bathroom.

When at last she was spent, Isabel rose and made her way back to the house. In the bedchamber, Mary was still up, sitting by the fire in her dressing gown. She exclaimed at the state of Isabel, and began to strip the damp clothes off her, scolding her for being so careless with health so recently recovered. She threw a nightgown at her, instructing her to put it on, and then she filled the warming pan with coals and thrust it to and fro in the covers of the bed before making Isabel get in. Isabel's teeth chattered, and Mary got into bed beside her and moulded herself to her back while Isabel sobbed and shook.

'Hush,' she said. 'Hush. I'm heartsore, too, Isabel. But I won't stay in London. It's only a visit, and then I will be back. My true home is with you at The Cottage. I've never been so happy anywhere. I can't very well stay in Holborn with my stepmamma, can I? She hates me. And we have our writing to continue.'

She got out of bed and fetched a towel, and then climbed back in and began to rub Isabel's damp hair.

'Do you mean it?' Isabel asked. 'You really did want me with you? And you really will come back?'

'Of course I mean it,' Mary said. 'And I'll prove it to you. Only you must promise to help me get you warm and dry, and then we'll make a vow.'

Isabel sat up then, and Mary rubbed her hair until it was almost dry. Then she got up and went over to the dresser, opening the top drawer and bringing out a tiny red leather box.

'This was my mother's,' she said. 'It was the only thing that wasn't taken from me on the boat north when I was robbed.

I haven't shown it to you before, for it's a poor thing really, and for all that it's my greatest treasure. I didn't want you to think me silly. Look.' She opened the box and Mary saw a ring with a chip of diamond in it.

'Come with me,' Mary said, and she led Isabel over to the window. She used the diamond to scratch her initials into a pane of glass, 'MG', and then she gave it to Isabel and told her to entwine her own with them. Isabel scratched 'IB' below Mary's, very close, so the B overlapped the G, and then Mary kissed her and said she must keep the ring for now, it would be Mary's promise to her that she would return.

'I can't,' said Isabel. 'I can't keep your mother's ring.'

'It's a loan only,' said Mary. 'You will loan your trust to me, and I will leave this with you to ensure I repay it. It's called a surety. My father was always taking loans, so I know all about such things. And while I am gone, I will write to you often, and you must write to me, too, for I will miss you sorely.'

'You will be too busy to miss me,' said Isabel.

Mary grasped her hand, and her eyes were like great pools in the firelight. 'Do you know, Isabel,' she said, 'my father says my mother was so faithful to those she loved that it almost seemed she could only love one person at a time, man or woman. Her friend Frances Blood was one such. She and my mother kept a school together, with my mother's sisters, my aunts Eliza and Everina. Fanny married and left for Portugal, but there she became ill. My mother left everything behind to care for her, and so the school was lost. Even after she died, she named my sister Fanny for her, and she wrote a book in tribute to her. She loved with all her heart, you see. I think I am like her. You are my dearest friend and I love you with all my heart. I will never feel quite whole as long as I am parted from you. We will find a way to live together all our lives, and make a living from our pens. You will see.'

Isabel felt a tear fall from her eye and Mary wiped it away and kissed her cheek. Then she shook her head, and laughed, and the intensity of feeling seemed to leave her. 'How shall I come on with Christy for company, and Claire and Charles and William and Fanny moreover?' she asked. 'I shall be bored to tears. Now, let's go to bed. The sooner the day comes and I leave, the sooner I will be back again. Sleep in my bed tonight, my beloved sister, we'll keep each other warm.'

Isabel allowed herself to be led back to bed and wrapped in Mary's arms. She was worn out from crying and sleep came easily. Her last thought was to wonder whether she was the first person Mary had loved, and what might persuade her to transfer her affections to another.

Harriet

April, 1813

THE EVENING STARTED BADLY FOR Harriet when she clambered clumsily from the carriage and trailed the hem of her dress through a mound of horseshit on the street. Then there was a wait in the cold and drizzle while the Godwins' servants stirred themselves, so she knew her hair would frizz and her nose would turn red, adding to all of the other demerits of her appearance at the present time. At least she had thought to travel in her boots and bring her slippers in a silk bag.

Harriet had not wanted to come out to this dinner at all. When first she had visited the Godwin house she had been a new bride, decked out in peacock-coloured satin to complement her toffee-coloured hair and her glorious engagement ring of twined turquoises and diamonds. Mrs Percy Shelley. Back then, she had been confident of both her beauty and her talents, and had sung after dinner, an old Irish air that suited her warm, low voice. Of the children, only Fanny Imlay had been at home, Godwin's late wife's bastard daughter, and Harriet had seen how the poor plain creature blushed to look on her as she sang, enjoying the warmth of her obvious envy like a cat enjoys a fire. She had invited Fanny to stay with them in the house they had taken in Devon for the summer, but William Godwin had refused, saying he would not send the poor creature away to live among strangers.

Harriet was sorry – already she had begun to tire of always having her sister Eliza with them, and back then there had been Elizabeth Hitchener too. The pair of them constantly interrupted her time with Percy, their study and their sport. There was nothing she could say about Eliza, of course; she had earned her place with all the comings and goings with letters between Harriet and Percy when Harriet was still at school and fancying herself oppressed by her father and a prisoner of her instructors. Perhaps Harriet could have tolerated her if only she could have stopped finding fault with the Shelley sisters, but Eliza could not – Harriet thought it was jealousy, Eliza fearing that Harriet loved Helen Shelley too well.

Bessy Hitchener was another matter altogether. A madness of Percy's, that had been, taking in a schoolteacher on the basis of a six-month correspondence, only to discover that what he loved on the page, he loathed in the flesh. Harriet would dearly have loved to have shy little Fanny with her, her own creature to walk with and talk with; instead she had to bite her lip and listen to Eliza's cursing and Percy's rants on Hitchener, who had become ever more hateful in his eyes until he imagined her a veritable demon in their midst.

That peacock-clad bride who had been Harriet seemed a stranger now; after all the flights here and there she was a different creature entirely – tired, and heavy, and painfully aware of her new bulk. More than six months forward, her belly protruded below the high waist of her frock and – worse – her backside seemed determined to outdo it in the rapidity of its expansion. She had tried to plead tiredness and stay at home, but Percy had snapped that he refused to be ashamed of his wife's pregnancy, and Hogg had leered at her bosom and said she was the picture of burgeoning beauty, ripening like fruit on the branch. All this had the effect of making Harriet feel more matronly and ungainly still, and she could have wept when they were told the lady of the house had been detained by an item of business and so Miss Mary would greet them in the drawing room in her stead. The last thing she wanted was an audience with Godwin's golden child, an apparent prodigy who had charmed the likes of Coleridge since babyhood. She sat crossly on a chair in the hall to wipe the worst of the foulness from her skirt with a towel and change her shoes, thanking Heaven that at least her slippers still fitted her swollen feet.

They were shown into the drawing room then, a familiar room Harriet found gloomy, and not very fine. The furnishings were all good enough in their way, but worn-in and comfortable, nothing grand or gilded such as her own parents had bought as soon as they could afford a little ostentation. Unfortunately, Mary Godwin showed to particularly good effect against this humble backdrop. Harriet's jaundiced eye saw how artfully she had posed herself – it was the sort of trick Harriet might have used herself, once – on a low chair by a table that held a pretty crystal candelabrum. The light from the candles lent Mary's pale cheeks a glow and kindled the loops of red-gold hair she had twisted about her head in a curious style. She held a book on her knee, and remained sitting as they entered, rising at last when they were before her to welcome them with a modest, downcast gaze. Apologising that her parents had been called to attend to some business, she offered refreshments, flushing very prettily all the while, and Harriet felt uglier than ever, and dowdy, and old.

Harriet accepted a glass of ratafia and water, hating Mary even while she sat down at her invitation on a sofa with Percy beside her and Hogg opposite in a chair. Only then did her heart lift a little, for she saw that Mary was not alone, her Scottish friend Christina Baxter sat by the door. Harriet had met Christina – Christy, they all called her – several times before. She liked her very well, for she was flat-chested, with a dull complexion, and although there was nothing wrong with her features, she wore her hair in a severe fashion that rendered her quite plain. She spoke in a quiet, down-to-earth fashion and all in all made Harriet feel much better about her own attractions than she had for many months together. There had been a funny story doing the rounds about Christy and Charles Lamb. It seemed Mary had told Christy that Lamb was a dreadful flirt, and in the habit of kissing women on first acquaintance. It was all a tease – Lamb was inclined rather more to glare at women than kiss them – but poor Christy was mightily discomfited all the same.

Hogg had not met Christy, of course, and so there were introductions to make, and long explanations of Mary's sojourn in Scotland, Mr Baxter's business as a sailcloth maker and much talk of Dundee trade. Harriet could not bring herself to take much interest in whaling or the import of flax from Archangel, and she was surprised to see that Mary seemed quite engaged with these subjects. Then Hogg made the great faux pas of talking of Harriet and Percy's wedding having happened in Scotland, which was scarcely a choice and more a matter of the marriage being an elopement the Shelleys would have stopped by any means at their disposal. A woman of the smarter type might have smirked and looked sideways at Harriet, but Christy simply asked what part, and Percy rambled on about Edinburgh and the castle, and all the other sights they had seen. This confirmed for Harriet that Christy was kind, and taken together with the fact she was some years Harriet's own senior, unmarried and unashamed, was altogether a comforting person to have in attendance.

After half an hour or so of chatter, William Godwin and his wife appeared with profuse apologies for their delay in attending to their guests. When first Harriet had come here with Percy, she had liked Mary Jane Godwin, but the liking had cooled. There was something of a *too-much* in her interest in them – Percy said that Godwin was always looking for money and Mary Jane saw it as her duty to help. Even then, the woman could not hide her ire when Percy cancelled engagements or otherwise disrupted her plans and she had been quite sharp with Harriet on one occasion, as though Harriet had any say on where Percy went and when! After their return to London, though, she had come to their hotel and apologised for the sharpness of her tongue, and so here they were in her house again.

Tonight, they were an awkward number to dinner, which would not have mattered had they seated the ladies at the upper end and the gentlemen at the lower as most people did, but the Godwins liked to seat ladies and gentlemen alternately. Harriet found herself seated on Mary Jane Godwin's left while Hogg sat on the woman's right with Mary on his far side. Then came Percy, then Christy, then Godwin, and then a place was set on Harriet's right-hand side for Mary Jane's daughter Claire, who came dashing in late having been given the next day off from the school where she boarded. Hogg was very gallant to Christy, and to Mrs Godwin, Percy served Mary although he never touched wine himself, and Godwin served Claire. No one remembered Harriet at all, so she sat with no wine and had to ask Mrs Godwin if she would be so good as to fill her glass.

The talk at first remained of Scotland, where it seemed Mary and Christy were soon to return. Harriet was pleased at that, for it would mean this was the last time she would be forced to endure Mary's society. She could not bear to sit before the girl if – when – she became any larger or ungainlier. If they were invited again before she left, Harriet would have to insist that Percy allowed her to stay at home. Hogg seemed avid for descriptions of the places Mary had visited with the Baxters and her impressions of the hills and moors of the north. Mary spoke very prettily of what she called the 'palaces of nature', describing views of snowy mountains from her window, and castle ruins, and the waterfalls and ancient forests she had seen on her travels.

'It is to me almost a magical place,' Mary said, 'so that it seems... I feel as though I am... as though something is about to happen.' Then she coloured and laughed. 'That is poorly put and makes no sense, I am sorry. It is hard to express it in words. I feel I... come alive in Scotland – it sustains me and I feel it is readying me for whatever life might bring.' Then she laughed again. 'No, it is no good,' she said. 'I cannot explain it at all.'

Harriet surprised herself by saying, 'I understand. You were ill, and now you are well. You have feared what life would bring, but now you do not. That is a wonderful thing.' And it *was* a wonderful thing, she could see that, unlike her own life that lay mapped out before her with such awful certainty – more discomfort and ugliness to come, then the certainty of agony and the fear of worse, and then a child, and more children, and in this way a tie that would bind her to Percy forever. It was different for him, he believed in free love and surrounded himself with women and said that it was all perfectly fair because Harriet could make herself free in turn by giving herself to Hogg. Hogg, it seemed, would like to take her even now, or perhaps *especially* now, though the thought made her sick. They had discussed it, in front of her, Hogg saying they could both suckle at her breast like twins, and she saw the way they looked at her in that moment, Hogg like a dog looking on a bitch in heat, and Percy observing her coldly, as though she were an idea, not his wife and made of flesh and blood. She did not think she could feed her child at her breast after that. She would give anything to be back at the start, as Mary was now. She thought she might make quite different choices.

Mary acknowledged Harriet demurely, and then neatly turned the conversation to writing, telling them all that she and Christy had seen Walter Scott, although Christy demurred and said she had not seen him, only Mary, and she said to Mary it was naughty to sound so certain when she had not been at all sure at the time. Godwin and Hogg and Percy joined the conversation then in earnest, asking Godwin how he had found 'Rokeby', Scott's new poem of the Civil War.

When there was a pause in the conversation, Christy turned to Harriet. 'And what of you, Mrs Shelley?' she asked – kindly, Harriet thought. 'Are you a keen reader?'

'Harriet had a passion for reading aloud,' said Percy. 'But she has quite abandoned it since she has been as she is.'

Godwin seemed to notice her for the first time, peering over the table above the spectacles he wore. 'Why is that, my dear?' he asked. 'Seems a great shame.'

'I–' Harriet was about to say she did not know, but that was not true, she found she did know. 'Books always seemed to transport me,' she said, 'like a special music that filled me and lifted me up. It was as if I floated off my body as one might float off rocks and be carried by the words as if by water. But now ... for now, I feel tethered to my body and to the earth. I cannot escape into any other place.'

Hogg laughed at that, although Harriet could not see what was funny, and the conversation turned to the next topic quite naturally, as though she had never spoken. She speared a piece of asparagus and placed it in her mouth. As she chewed, she was surprised to feel a warm hand grasp her own and squeeze. She looked up as the hand withdrew and saw it belonged to Mrs Godwin. She did not look at Harriet, or speak, or otherwise make any gesture, and Harriet was glad, for suddenly she felt she could weep and she had no wish to, not here, not in front of these people. It was true, what she had said, but also it was true that she could not bear to read aloud while Hogg was in her house.

The rest were now discussing their friend Leigh Hunt's imprisonment for libelling the Prince Regent, and Hogg and Percy spoke a little of their own trials after the pamphlet they had published on atheism, that got them sent down from Oxford in the year '11. Mary asked then if it was true that an attempt had been made on Percy's life in the winter. Her stepmother cut her eyes at her, for which Harriet was grateful, but Mary pressed on regardless. 'We heard that you were shot,' she said.

Harriet's glass was empty again, and so she had not even the comfort of the wine as Percy prepared to give his account of that night in Tan yr Allt. While they were all absorbed by him, she took the opportunity of helping herself to a slice of mutton from a platter before her – Percy's regimen of meatless meals left her craving the taste of iron.

'We had to flee Devon last year,' Percy said. 'It was no longer safe for us.'

No, thought Harriet, *because you had the servants post your maddest writings all around the house on the trunks of trees, and seal them in bottles and set them afloat in the bay.* She had liked

Devon, longed to settle into a home at last, and instead had been forced to pack up, ending up four months gone with child and sick as a dog, in a wretched, damp place in the north of Wales. Still she had gone, for she loved Percy and he loved her. Then.

Percy then gave an account of his troubles in Tremadoc, his defence of the local workforce earning him such enmity among the gentry of the place that he had taken to sleeping with his pistols on either side of him in bed. This was an embellishment – Harriet would never have tolerated the guns in bed: they rested on a chest nearby – and of course there was never a word of how she had begged him to be still and keep clear of matters that did not concern him. Bessy Hitchener had done quite the opposite, of course, egging him on until he was quite convinced it was his duty to speak out against half the notables of the place, and damn the consequences.

It was odd, hearing the account of that night in Percy's words. Harriet remembered it clearly enough for herself. She had heard a noise below, just as she was drifting into sleep. Percy had grabbed the pistols and gone downstairs, calling out a warning as he went. There was the sound of a shot, and Harriet had hurtled out of bed, cowering behind the door in terror. There was silence for a time that seemed endless but was really only a second or two, and then all was uproar as the servants tumbled out of bed and down the stairs.

Percy told it now largely as he had then, although less frantically. On entering the drawing room, he said, he had discovered a man leaving the house by the window. This man raised his pistol and pulled the trigger, but by some miracle the gun failed to go off and instead he attempted to flee across the lawn. Percy gave chase, and the two men wrestled on the grass. (This made no sense to Harriet, because Percy was carrying two pistols and the man at least one, so how could they have wrestled one another she could not see.) Percy had shot the man, he said, in the shoulder, and the man roared out in rage that he would kill Harriet and ravish Percy's sister as revenge.

Harriet shivered at the words, even here in this brightly lit room – back then her blood had run quite cold, standing in the drawing room in her night rail while Eliza attempted to wrap a dressing gown around her shoulders. Bessy Hitchener had chided Percy, saying he should not say such things to Harriet in her condition, she should not be afeared or upset in such a manner. Percy said to Eliza to take Harriet upstairs, in fact they should all go back to their beds. Percy would sit up with Jack the gardener, he was a stout fellow and between them they would guard the house till morning. Harriet allowed herself to be led upstairs and put back to bed, shivering now as though she would never stop, and Eliza fetched a bedpan and warmed the blankets and told her to hush and think of the child, she would not wish to lose it through her distress. Then Eliza climbed into bed with her and wrapped her arms around her like they had done when they were children, so the awful shaking lessened and stopped and she dozed, only to be woken a few hours later in dread, hearing another gunshot downstairs.

'Mercy!' Eliza had screamed, and Harriet had bolted out of bed and down the stairs before anyone could stop her, almost crashing into John in the hall. Percy was in the drawing room alone, wide-eyed and raving, saying the man had returned and shot at him through the window. This time Percy's gun had failed and the rogue had run off before Percy could get a shot in in return.

'Why did you leave him?' Harriet had demanded of John, and John said the master had asked him to fetch a cleaver from the kitchen to arm himself, and he had only been gone a moment when he had heard the shot and returned.

They got Percy onto the sofa and felt all over his body, finding only a bullet hole in the side of his bedshirt. He was desperately pale and agitated, and John and the other menservants said they would keep watch so Harriet could take Percy upstairs and put him to bed. He muttered and mumbled about Leeson, a local landowner he had offended, and twitched and jumped most oddly in his sleep, while Harriet sat up the rest of the night, watching the dark sky and feeling her heart pound at the least sound below. When at last the winter sun rose, her eyes stung from the long vigil of the night, and she hurt in every muscle.

'And so, you see,' Percy told the company, 'it was unquestionably an assassination attempt. We left the next morning and ... well. Here we are.'

'How utterly terrifying,' Mary whispered, and Christy looked equally shocked. Godwin and his wife seemed less unnerved, and Harriet suspected they had heard the rumours that had dogged their party ever since – that Percy had staged the shooting to escape from the unpleasantness he himself had created in Wales, or perhaps imagined it in his state of heightened stress. He had suffered from a form of walking nightmares since he was a child, and it seemed his friends all knew it. Harriet had no idea what to think, and generally tried not to think on it at all, lest her own nerves should become as shredded as Percy's. The bullet holes had been real enough, in Percy's bedshirt and in the plaster of the drawing-room wall – she had seen them with her own eyes, and there was no question that spies had been watching them for many months together.

Talk turned then to 'Queen Mab', Percy's new poem, and Godwin said he had some advice on the manuscript. That gave

Mrs Godwin her cue to rise and invite the ladies to the drawing room, and they had enough decorum to allow Harriet her place behind Mrs Godwin as they filed out. Christy and Mary took themselves over to a card table and began to set up a game. Harriet's child was restless in the evening, and her back ached, but she accepted the tea Mrs Godwin offered and sat as elegantly as she could beside Claire Clairmont, enquiring after Fanny Imlay.

'She has gone to stay with friends,' Claire said as her mother glared at her. 'It is a relief to us, for Fanny is so gloomy these days. There is no cheering her.'

'Perhaps she missed Miss Mary when she was away,' Harriet suggested politely.

Claire hooted with laughter. 'No, not at all,' she said. 'She and Mary fight like cats half the time. She is like her late mother Wollstonecraft, that is all. Given to despondency. Fanny even talks of ending her life, as her mother once wished to do also.'

'Claire!' Mrs Godwin snapped. 'That is quite enough.'

The girl gave an unrepentant smile and asked Harriet if she would play cards. Harriet said no, thank you, she would prefer to sit still, the little beast she carried tormented her tonight, but please, the others should go ahead. Claire needed no encouragement; she was on her feet in an instant, but her mother caught her by the arm and steered her towards the piano instead. She seated herself readily enough and soon was playing, quite skilfully and very fashionably, one of Field's nocturnes.

Harriet sipped her tea and wished more than ever that Godwin had allowed Fanny to come and live with them as Harriet's foil and her friend. It seemed they had a significant item in common, for Harriet could not remember a time when she had not imagined bringing about her own end. Since childhood, thoughts of death and burial had preoccupied her, the idea of leaving her body below the ground, leaching its goodness into the dark soil, so that she could escape its confines into the wideness beyond, a vast expanse of nothingness. As a girl, she had held her breath to fainting, lain under the water of the bathtub till her eyes quite blurred, hung backwards from a high branch of an oak tree on the common, wondering whether the wood or her knees would give way first and hurl her to the ground. When she crossed the Thames with the other girls of Mrs Fenning's school to visit the great Cathedral of St Paul's, she had no interest in whispering with her classmates from one end of the high walkway below the dome, to witness the sound carried as if by God into the ear of a listener at the other. Instead, she stared at the nave below and thrilled to think of stepping out onto nothing, seeming to hang there weightless an instant, and then the glorious rush of the air as she plunged to meet the marble floor below. It had been all she could do not to drop her reticule, just to hear the smash of the glass vial of smelling salts within.

In her schooldays, she loved to read of women sacrificing themselves for love or honour, Juliet dying on Romeo's breast, Ophelia giving herself to the water, Cleopatra embracing the asp. She had admired them, thought them kin to the greatest poets and writers, seeing more and feeling more than simple mortals, and suffering more in their turn. Now she was not so sure; closeness to Percy and his circle had opened her eyes. As poets they professed to be concerned with the spirit, but since Hogg had come they seemed to her far more interested in bodies, Percy bedding her at all hours of the day and night, upside down and back to front and hanging off the curtains of the bed, and Hogg listening at the door with his hands in his breeches.

She wondered now if her old girlish enchantment with death had been a sort of daydreaming, a self-absorbed musing, divorced entirely from any real intent. She had fairly been the star player in a drama of her own devising, threatening Percy with her death if he abandoned her after all he had said and written and promised. 'Very well, then,' she had said, fifteen years old and eager to be ruined, the cherished daughter of a self-made man about to throw herself into the power of the half-brilliant, half-mad heir of a baronet. 'I shall know what to do. I shan't survive without your protection and I shan't live a prisoner, I shall open my veins first and spill my blood on the floor.'

What could he say after that? He did not question it for an instant, flattered to think her love for him so great, excited in his boyish conceit to be her rescuer.

Only later would she learn that he would not, could not sacrifice any element of his principles in order to compromise with his father and reinstate a living for himself and his bride, and he could not back down from an argument even if it threatened his life. She did not care, at first, content and cosy in their lodgings in Edinburgh, the two of them alone, lying late abed before venturing forth to explore the city, returning in the afternoon to their studies. In the evenings she sang or read, and they went early to bed. She thought they were like birds in a nest, but he called her his dormouse. No name for a woman, she saw now, but rather for a pet. She was like a pet, too, wishing to be with him always, longing with all her heart for his love. She wondered if that longing were gone, whether the bitterness that had come into her had filled its place instead, growing like the dark twin of the life she carried in her womb.

The card players had finished their hand and Mary and Christy had won. Harriet joined in the applause, thinking of

Mary's odd words at dinner. In a great flash of determination, she decided that she, too, would win, she would not sit idly by to find out what life would bring her. The coming of a child was a trying time for any couple, but they would survive it.

As the men came into the room, her eyes went straight to Percy, who said something to Godwin and then presented his 'Mab' manuscript to Mary. She felt her vision blur, but she blinked until it righted itself. He was in love with the idea of being in love, she knew that, and her task now was to remind him of the strength of that early bond when he had written that their life was Heaven on Earth. She was already rid of Hitchener, and she saw now she must also send away Eliza, and before the baby came she must find a way to dismiss Hogg, so Percy would forget that he ever thought of passing Harriet on as a trinket to his friend. She was beautiful, he was an angel, he could be frank and sweet, generous and magnanimous and she could be gay, and happy. She would survive the birth of her child, and thrive, and Percy would love the new little creature and its mother the more for the bearing of it.

'Well?' Percy said to her and she smiled.

'Well,' she said. 'Never better.'

Mary Godwin might have 'Mab' to read, but he had, after all, dedicated it to Harriet.

Part II

Fife and Dundee, 1813–14

6

My dearest Isabel, Mary wrote in her scrawling, messy hand, *you must forgive me for the very long interval since last I wrote to you. Three months! In truth, I did write sooner but the letter was spoilt before it could be sent. I filled pages and pages with the very best sketches I could make of our comings and goings in hope of entertaining you, but Claire spilt a glass of water over it where it sat on my dressing table so the ink ran and it was quite illegible. I do not think it was done in spite but one never knows with Claire. Again and again I have sat down to write another but have been called away to attend to this task or that, or to run hither and thither on my stepmamma's command – I can't tell you how much I hate the woman, she winds my nerves up to the utmost irritation. And so here is my very overdue missive, with anguish that I have neglected you so long – at least I will have much to tell you.*

There followed lengthy accounts of various dinners and outings to exhibitions and theatres, running to several pages replete with crossings-out and underlinings. Between the many pages of the letter and the fact it enclosed a pamphlet of poetry, the postage Mary had paid had been inadequate and David had been required to settle quite a steep charge before Isabel could take delivery of it. He had harrumphed at her, as well he might – the sum was a week's wages to one of the local brewery workers.

The pamphlet was a curious thing, purporting to reproduce poems found among the papers of a woman who had made an attempt on the life of the King in 1786. The frontispiece claimed it had been edited after her death by a man named John Fitzvictor who was the unfortunate woman's nephew. In fact, Mary wrote, all was composed by her father's friend Percy B. Shelley and his friend Hogg, who fervently believed the monarchy to be a means of oppressing mankind. *I admire it greatly,* she wrote, *and I trust that you will, too.* The letter ended with warm words for Isabel, whom Mary said she missed very much. *My mind naturally turns to a more countrified place, to the dear Cottage and to you, my friend <u>at home</u>. Here all is narrow and mean and I long to be in that generous house with its thick walls and wide rooms, holding us as if we were valuable, and worth cherishing.*

Isabel found she had no more energy for the letter and none for the pamphlet, and put both aside. There had been much mention of this man Shelley in Mary's letters. It seemed he was the son of a baronet and a great admirer of William Godwin's work. The Godwins hoped he would aid them in their publishing endeavours, which often saw the family in penury. To this end, he was often to dinner at Skinner Street, and Mary's letters fairly crackled with excitement when she related especially clever things he had said or done. Christy wrote of him too, and Isabel knew from her that he was married, to a very charming girl around Isabel's own age, and who was moreover many months forward with child. The family arrangements were strange, Christy said, involving the sister of the wife and at one point another woman too, and the whole lot of them moved around a great deal. Christy did not dislike

Mrs Godwin but she admitted she was often cross with Shelley, for he and his party broke arrangements as easily as they made them, and thus far no money had been forthcoming.

Isabel was glad of Christy's letters, which were less effusive than Mary's, but in their quiet way showed more concern for Isabel and the household in Fife, asking after little William and Tibby, and sister Margaret's rapidly declining health.

Little Tibby had suddenly stopped being a baby under the sole care of a nursemaid and had become quite a sturdy small girl, happy to totter along after William on her strong little legs, and chatter away about everything and anything that crossed her mind. She was a great consolation to Isabel, who would have been desperately lonely had it not been for the children's company. David was distracted, and much away attending to business. When Margaret came out of her room at all, it was to sit silently for some part of the main meal of the day, as before, and she showed no more interest in having Isabel by her at other times than ever. Every offer Isabel made to read to her, or play cards, or help see to her comforts was met with polite refusal. And so Isabel took on the role of William and Tibby's first teacher, taking them abroad any day the weather was fair. She took over a simple game the nursemaid had devised of walking to a burn nearby where there was a little footbridge. On the way, they gathered sticks and dried leaves and other bits of detritus in a basket, and then they dropped these one-by-one off one side of the bridge, rushing to the other to see the 'boat' sail away. William made a competition of whose 'boat' would go the fastest, while Tibby crowed and clapped in delight.

At home, they searched the library for books with illustrations to explore. Tibby became enamoured of a collection of maps of the north, with pictures of the great white bears of the Arctic.

She insisted on looking at it daily, tracing the outlines of the bears with her chubby fingers while Isabel read from the text. She seemed particularly drawn to one picture in which a bear seemed to be floating away from its fellows on a small sheet of ice.

'Poor bear,' Tibby would say, patting the etched lines of fur.

Isabel reassured her that white bears could leap and swim, even in the freezing waters of the Arctic, and the bear she pitied would soon be reunited with his friends. But the situation of the bear seemed to exert a sort of horrified fascination on the child, and the next day she would insist on returning to the picture and consoling the bear again. At last, Isabel painted a reunion of the bears for her in watercolour on a large sheet of paper and hung it by her bed where she could look at it when she woke, and the book was gradually forgotten.

When the children were asleep, Isabel drew, or played patience, but she felt lonely and low. She did not want to think about anyone else – not Mary, enjoying herself so in London, nor Margaret, whose condition was ever more disturbing, nor David, who she could not make out at all. In the end, she put away her paints and cards and instead she spent her free time with her nose in a book. During one of David's many absences, she poked through the shelves of the library and found the slim little volume that was William Godwin's memoir of Mary Wollstonecraft. She took it to her room hidden in her shawl, for all there was no one to see her, and immediately sat down to read. Some clippings fell out when she opened it – notes in David's hand, and a review cut from a newspaper – and she gathered them up and placed them in the drawer of her dressing table.

It was not a long book, but Isabel found it weighed on her long after she had finished it. She was not troubled by the account of Wollstonecraft's amours – if she hadn't known previously that the woman had had a married lover and borne a child out of wedlock, Margaret's needling at Mary would have been enough to ensure she was in full possession of the facts. Rather, she was perturbed by what seemed to her to be a curious association made by William Godwin between his wife's passion and intelligence, and her self-destructive tendencies. It seemed almost that her husband considered the black moods that plagued her as speaking to her virtues, so her attempts to destroy herself spoke to her character, and not against it. Isabel found that notion profoundly frightening, and determined to set it aside, but like little Tibby with her bear, she could not put it from her mind, returning to the thought to puzzle over it as she might worry at a sore place in her mouth with her tongue.

Isabel knew that Mary had not been raised by Mary Wollstonecraft, had not known her at all, really, but she wondered whether her friend could have inherited something of her mother's tendency to melancholy, or even to self-torment. She remembered the game they had played with the Bible, when they had read of the man in Gadara who was harming himself with stones. Isabel knew now, of course, that there was an alternative explanation for Mary's condition then, but she had already determined that she would put that notion aside and did not wish to think of it again, for fear that she could not be the same with Mary if she allowed her thoughts to stray too far down that particular path. The book had, on the other hand, awakened within her some disturbing new thoughts on Margaret's illness.

Margaret had always suffered from periods of sickness. After she had recovered from her childhood consumption, it seemed the infection lay dormant in her blood, and now and again it would boil up and overwhelm her. Mother had told Isabel, long ago, that Margaret knew one of her episodes was about to come upon her because she would suddenly become hot, so that beads of sweat would break out on her brow and then pour down until all seemed to shimmer and shift before her eyes. Then she would feel as chilled as if she were outside in an icy wind, and a great terror would take hold of her, for there was nothing for it but to sleep, but then she knew she would find herself in the grip of terrible, awful dreams where great black birds would hold her down with their vicious claws and pick her bones clean.

Over the last weeks, Isabel had seen and heard a number of odd things, and been unable to make sense of any of these. A doctor had come from somewhere in England, and had stayed two weeks before he left as suddenly as he had arrived. One night during his sojourn, there had been an almighty crash from Margaret's room in the night, and Isabel had peered out of her own door half asleep, to see a servant girl run down the hall weeping as she clutched her cheek, on which there was a vivid red mark. The housekeeper had come the other way, then, with a bowl and a funnel and a grim set to her face. There had been strange sounds, a cry and other noises, and Isabel had closed her door and slept fitfully, plagued by bad dreams. Margaret had not come to dinner the next day, or the next.

It seemed the servants were much engaged with Margaret, and the housekeeper asked Isabel if she could help with William and Tibby, who was uncharacteristically grumpy and unsettled with new teeth. It was raining and wet and she was hard-pressed to keep the children entertained. They played with blocks, and strung beads on thread, and they drew with chalk on a little blackboard David had gifted William. Tibby spent much time comforting her 'baby', a plump doll made of rags, and telling it that all would be well. 'Just eat a little bit, baby,' she babbled, sounding older than her years. 'Just one bite.'

Isabel fell into bed exhausted but slept badly for want of fresh air and exercise. Her mind churned over and over the odd happenings of the past days, and one morning she awoke quite sure of the facts of the matter. Margaret had stopped eating. She had decided to die.

That was the morning the doctor left, having spent some time locked up in the library in conference with David. Isabel took her breakfast alone at the table, and then she went to Margaret's room, knocked sharply, and entered without waiting for an answer. Recoiling at the smell, she made her way across to the curtains and drew them, turning back to look on Margaret's skull-face on the pillows of her bed.

'It's fair outside, Margaret,' she said, 'and I am going to take Tibby and William on a walk to the burn. When I come back I will sit with you a while. I know you have no need of me, but I have need of you. I have been dreadfully lonely since Mary and Christy went away.'

Then she left the room before Margaret could see the tears on her cheeks. She rubbed them away harshly with her sleeve, irritating her skin with the lace trimming. In the hallway downstairs, she almost fell over the doctor making his escape. David was also dressed for travel.

'Where are you going?' she demanded.

'To fetch your father,' David said, focusing on his gloves. 'He should be with Margaret.'

So there is nothing more to be done, Isabel thought. 'Yes,' she said aloud. 'That would be best.'

When he was gone, Isabel had the nursemaid dress Tibby and William in their coats and the four of them walked together to the burn. The nursemaid helped the children with their 'boats' and Isabel stared into the water, feeling her eyes smart but willing the tears not to come.

When they got home, Isabel told Tibby and William she would take them in to see their mother. She unpinned the picture of the white bears from by Tibby's bed and they took that in, too, so that Tibby might have something to distract her. Margaret was asleep when they came in, but she roused and seemed to listen as William told her he could write his name and showed her his efforts on the little chalkboard. Tibby prattled on about the bears, seated on Isabel's lap while Margaret held the picture in her poor hands that were so thin as to be like the skeletons of leaves. Then the nursemaid came in to fetch the children for their dinner. Tibby told her mother she could keep the picture of the bears to look at, and allowed herself to be led off after William. Isabel asked the nursemaid to have Mrs Brown send her own meal up. Then she lifted Margaret's hands one by one and rubbed almond oil into the skin. Margaret whispered a thank you and Isabel heard how her voice was rasping and ruined. She nodded brusquely and set about tidying the room. Then the food arrived, she ate, and when she was done she read Margaret Christy's most recent letter.

'Where is David?' Margaret asked.

'Gone to fetch Father,' Isabel said.

Margaret's eyes shone but she said nothing. Isabel asked if she could bring her anything for her comfort, but she said no.

'Will you go over to my dressing table?' Margaret whispered. 'There is a bracelet there. I want you to have it, Isabel. All my other things will be for Tibby, in time, but the bracelet belonged to Mother.'

Isabel crossed to the table and opened the case she found there, taking out the bracelet. It was a lovely thing, luminous rose-cut diamonds set in silver.

'I remember this,' she said. 'Mother would wear it when she was dressed very fine.'

'Put it on,' Margaret said, and Isabel did as she was told, holding her wrist so Margaret could see.

'I miss her, Bel,' Margaret said suddenly, surprising Isabel. No one had called her *Bel* since Mother died.

'I miss her too,' she said, and it was true, the missing of her was an enormous gaping hole inside Isabel, and she had no idea how to fill it. She knew not whether the loss of Margaret would make the hole larger; they had not been friends, but they were sisters.

'Do you think—' Margaret began, and then she began to choke. Isabel jumped up and brought a handkerchief, raising Margaret up and wiping her mouth until at last she recovered.

'What did you want to ask me?' she said. 'You said, "Do you think ..."'

'Just ... Do you believe we shall meet again?' Margaret asked. 'Mother, I mean? I long to have her hold me, just once, like I was a little lass.' Tears beaded on her lashes. 'I am so afraid, Bel. Would you ... would you come into bed with me? Like when we were wee?'

'Will I not pain you?' Isabel asked.

'I don't mind,' Margaret said, and so Isabel stripped down into her shift and climbed gently into bed beside her.

'Coorie in,' she said.

'That's what Nanny used to say,' Margaret murmured, and then it seemed she slept. Isabel lay there beside her, watching the short day darken outside the window. Margaret made a strange sound and Isabel started, thinking she had gone, but then she heard her breathing – unsteady and shallow, but still there, fragile stitches binding her to life. She lay still and listened.

'What if I can't go to Heaven?' Margaret asked all of a sudden, waking Isabel who must have drifted into a doze.

'Of course you'll go to Heaven,' Isabel said.

'Not if God knows I've ruined myself,' Margaret said. 'That would be a dreadful sin.'

'Whisht now,' said Isabel, and she stroked Margaret's cheek, feeling the strange feathery down that grew there. 'Whisht, Peg.' It had been years since she had thought of Margaret as *Peg* – it was Mother's name for her back when Isabel was *Bel*, and they were all in short dresses, even Robert. 'You haven't done anything,' she said, 'only you were sick and couldn't eat and so you became sicker.' So what if it wasn't true, she thought – what use was truth in this awful room? 'And anyway,' she said, 'Brother Robert Sandeman said "the bare death of Jesus Christ without a thought or deed on the part of man, is sufficient to present the chief of sinners spotless before God".'

Margaret was quiet again then, but her eyes were open. Isabel shifted to hold her more comfortably.

'Can I ask you some things, Peg?' she said. 'I have no one else to ask.'

She felt a motion as Margaret nodded, and she bit her lip and blurted out the question that had been on her mind for weeks.

'When a woman bears a child,' she said, 'does it leave marks on her body, after?'

'Why?' Margaret whispered. 'You haven't . . . you haven't done anything you shouldn't, Isabel?'

Isabel blushed. 'No, no,' she said. 'It's just ... something someone told me. And I didn't know if it was true. I thought you would be able to tell me. You had Mother, but I'll have no one.'

'No,' Margaret said. 'But if it soothes you any, Isabel, Mother told me very little. I learned most of what I know from the servants, when my time came. And yes. The belly and breasts mark. Red marks, like the channels you see in a bog. Once the child has come, they fade away to silver, but they never quite go away. Some women have other markings, too, patches on their face, or bands or lines of colour on their bellies.' It took her a long time to say so much, and her voice had fallen to the barest whisper as she finished.

'Were you afraid?' Isabel asked. 'When William came, and then Tibby?' She had never asked Margaret anything so personal in her life, and she did not really expect her to answer.

'Yes,' said Margaret, and Isabel felt a hot wetness on her chest as she wept. 'I hated it as I have never hated anything in my life. Growing and stretching and becoming so ugly, when I had always been so lovely, so delicate. David called me his china doll. But after the children, I could never get back to the way I was, no matter how I tried. I was always clumsy and ungainly after.'

Isabel closed her eyes so she did not have to look on the wasted thinness Margaret could not see, the great knobs of bone at her wrists and the bumps of her backbone.

'Promise me you'll see to them, Bel,' Margaret said. 'The children, I mean. None of it is their fault. They love you like a mother.'

'Of course,' Isabel said. 'But you are their mother, Margaret. And they will always love you.'

'Tell them I loved them,' Margaret said, and then she lay quiet. She seemed to sleep, and then she woke in a panic, her pulse fluttering under Isabel's hand.

'I can't see right, Bel,' she said. 'Stay by me. Hold my hand so I know you're there.'

'I will,' said Isabel.

'I feel her close,' Margaret said. 'Mother.' She seemed to calm then, and drift off into sleep.

Isabel felt her own face wet with tears. She held on to Margaret's frail body, feeling the echo in her own chest as Margaret's breath came shallower and shallower, rattled a moment, and then came not at all.

7

It was a wild and wet day when they buried Margaret, so it seemed that the very Heavens mourned, and the trees and the bushes wept with them. The purple velvet mortcloth on the coffin had darkened to black before the small procession turned out onto the road, David and Father and Robert and the other men. It looked very small, the coffin, and seemed no trouble to them to carry. Mrs Brown watched them go, dabbing at her eyes with a corner of her apron, and then she bustled off clucking about getting dry clothes hung before the fire so they would have something warm to change into after, or else they would surely follow the mistress into the grave. Isabel stood a while longer, fancying she could hear the men's steps recede down the steep road to the village, reluctant yet to turn back to the house.

Isabel had imagined for some reason that they would bring Margaret home to Dundee and lay her to rest beside Mother, but of course that was wrong; her home was here in Fife now, and she would lie in the small burying ground in Newburgh until the Last Day. It seemed a desolate thing to Isabel, to lie among strangers, and she was glad to meet the village women who came to help lay out food and refreshments for the men, for they seemed kind folk and a number spoke gently of

Margaret. Few of their Dundee connection had made the journey, the Glasites did not believe that funerals were a matter for the church, they were a matter for the folk of the place the person had lived. They would condole with the family at home, over the coming weeks and months.

A Fife woman came to Isabel where she stood in the doorway, and guided her in with a gentle arm around her shoulder.

'The menfolk'll see her right, hen,' she said. 'Come away in.'

In the late afternoon, the rain stopped and a pale sun broke through, transforming the sky with lines and washes of colour like a watercolour painting. Father and David came home and changed into dry things and then they spoke to the assembled company while Isabel sat by brother Robert with Tibby on her lap and William beside her and talked about horses and fairies in the garden and ships sailing all over the world.

Arrangements for the children had been much under discussion since Margaret's death. David had been set on keeping them here at Newburgh, arguing that they had all they needed and moreover that Barns of Woodside was their home. Father had countered that it was no home at all if it contained all they needed except family, as David was so often away that the children would instead be raised by the servants. David said that was easily enough addressed – Isabel could remain there, she and the children had grown close in the last months. To Isabel's relief, Father had dismissed that suggestion out of hand, saying that Isabel was his child as Tibby and William were David's, and he was required to think of her wellbeing, which could hardly be served by living apart from her family in a house where she was alone except for two small children.

It would also be inappropriate, Father said, for Isabel to remain in the house when David was in residence, surely David saw that? 'No,' Father said, 'and I will not have this become an apple of discord between us, David. William and Tibby will come home to The Cottage with us for now. You may stay there any time you return from your business. I will send word to Nanny Chisolm to come and set up the nursery once more. Their own nursemaid may come too and in that way, when your situation is more certain, they will travel home with their own attendant.'

It was not common for Father to stand up to David in this way, and David clearly saw that his mind was made up. He said he had plans to travel to London directly, and so would consent to release the children for now and make provisions for the longer term when he had more time to reflect.

It was a great relief to Isabel to leave Barns of Woodside behind and travel home to Dundee in the carriage with Father. Robert had gone already, travelling to Edinburgh on business, and David would be London-bound the next day. Isabel could not understand what business could be so important that he could not mourn his wife a week, but she kept the thought to herself. Her own journey home was more cheerful than it might have been under the circumstances as Tibby chattered away to her little nursemaid, and the girl blushed and stammered with nerves, and so Father was stirred from his sadness by his desire to put her at her ease by answering Tibby and speaking of this and that. Then they were on the ferry, and there was so much for William to see and point at and ask about that the crossing seemed over in an instant, and the next thing they were driving up to the front door of The Cottage where Nanny Chisolm was waiting.

They got Tibby and William settled first and left the nursemaid to unpack and bathe them, and then Nanny Chisolm took Isabel into the parlour and sat her down and called for tea. Then she sat beside her and took her hands and said, 'Now. Tell me all. A sorrow shared is a sorrow halved, and I loved her well for myself, you know. She was the first of my charges, Mrs Booth, as I know I should call her, but she will always be Miss Margaret to me.'

Isabel stared at her smooth hands in Nanny's worn ones.

'It was a strange thing indeed, Nanny,' she said. 'She was not afraid, exactly. At least, I think she was not afraid to die, until the last moments when she had a flutter of panic, but ... Nanny ... she was afraid to live.'

'I'm not very sure I know what you mean,' Nanny said. Isabel looked up and saw a frown on her kind old face.

'Do you remember—' Isabel began, and then she felt her cheeks flush red. She dropped her eyes to her hands again. 'That is to say ... Nanny, when Mary first came to stay, I think perhaps her arm didn't pain her quite as she said but rather ... she caused the pain herself. To gain her father's attention, perhaps, or to ... Och, I don't know. To make real the pain she felt inside? Like the man from Gadara in the Bible who had a demon?'

'That's a dreadful thought,' Nanny said with a shudder. 'But Miss Mary seemed to overcome her demons, if demons they were. Perhaps the arm was just bad and healed itself in the normal way.'

'I think ... I think Margaret had a demon,' Isabel said. 'But I do not know what it was.'

Nanny chewed her lip for a moment. 'She lost your mother at a hard time. Now, no –' she said, seeing Isabel about to protest '– I don't mean that it was easy for any of you. But Margaret was only just wed, and she was such a fragile creature after she survived the consumption. I had my doubts that she should marry at all, let alone bear a child ... two children. I understand the first years of a marriage are a ... trying time for any woman, although of course I never married myself.'

'Did you ever wish to marry, Nanny?' Isabel asked.

'I can't say I did,' said Nanny comfortably. 'I have known a good many fine men in my life but I've never sought to have the keeping of one. They eat a great deal, and are forever tramping mud into the house on their boots.'

'Do you think she is in Heaven, Nanny?' Isabel said. 'Margaret, I mean.'

'Aye,' said Nanny. 'Without any doubt.'

'And what ... do you think Heaven is *like*? I know the Bible says it is very beautiful but ... well. It's beautiful here too.'

'Well,' said Nanny. 'I know the Good Book says there will be streets of gold and many mansions, and I can't imagine that, precisely, but I do trust it will rain less and be warmer, for they say souls in Heaven are at peace and no one is ever at peace on a cold or a rainy day with their nose red and dripping and wet feet. And I know I will see my parents again, and I take great comfort in that, as I do from the thought that Miss Margaret is with your mother again now.'

Isabel wept for a while then, and Nanny put her arms around her and shed a few tears too, and after that Isabel felt a little better. Nanny told Isabel that she would go and see to the children, and Isabel should take herself to bed, for all it was only afternoon. Isabel did as she was bid, and slept straight through to the next morning, waking feeling more herself than she had for many days. After she had washed and dressed, a fancy took her to wear Mother's bracelet. It was too fine for everyday, of course, but still she clasped it around her arm under the cuff of her sleeve.

Downstairs, Father and Isabel sat together for a time and Father told her that Mary and Christy would be home within the week. Isabel found she was glad of it, but dreaded it also, fearing that she was changed by the last months, and worrying that Mary and Christy would now be the better friends. Father said he had some business to do before it grew too late, and Isabel said she would go and see the children, happy to escape to the nursery and let all her worries disappear under the weight of their young charges' chatter.

When the little nursemaid began to set out the midday meal, Isabel took herself to her own room. Something compelled her to sit at the desk and then she found herself sharpening a goose feather quill and opening the little crystal inkpot. It was the first time she had picked up a pen to write anything other than a letter since Mary had left.

At first, Isabel tried to write an adventure for Lady G– – she had an idea about a coded message embroidered onto the fingertips of a pair of gloves – but she found she did not have the skill of it. She could *imagine* adventures for Lady G–, but the *telling* of them was Mary's, Lady G– was her creature on the page. Instead, Isabel decided to write a story inspired by one of Nanny's tales. She remembered Nanny's horror at Mary's suggestion that these be collected and published, but she reasoned with herself that she only meant to write it down to pass the time and hone her skills with the pen, it was never meant for a reader.

The tale she chose had been a favourite when they were children and sought to terrify themselves witless. Nanny called it 'The Headless Body'. This referred, it seemed, to a creature, or perhaps a sort of ghost, that haunted a rocky mound in a place in the West Highlands called Morar. Nanny had family connections there, and she swore blind that all particulars of the tale were true. The creature was a terror and a horror, killing any that dared pass through its territory after dark, until people came to avoid the place entirely. One night, however, a man named MacDonell sent his son to fetch his neighbours to show hospitality to an esteemed friend who had visited by surprise. Failing in his mission, as the neighbours were from home, the son returned alone – or tried to. He never arrived, and the next day dawned on an awful scene. By the mound, the very ground was ripped apart, and great rocks had been thrown around with inhuman strength. There was no sign of the boy, but the entire place was crimson with his blood.

MacDonell vowed that he would not rest until the monster was slain. He waited until dark, and took himself to the haunted mound. There he heard the voice of the monster, and it told him to go home. MacDonell refused, and turned to see the monster, but before it could act, he leapt upon it and knocked it to the ground. He drew his dirk and suddenly the creature shrank away, begging not to be touched with the iron. It vowed that as long as Morar held anyone related within the twentieth degree to MacDonell, it would never be seen in those parts again. Nanny said that many in Morar claimed distant kinship with MacDonell, her own people among them, and so the creature had never reappeared.

Instead of telling the story as Nanny did, Isabel decided to tell it as if she were the creature. She dipped her pen, and began to write the creature's testimony.

I cry out to my Creator to help me understand what went amiss, so that I am denied the rest of the grave and instead became a headless creature sentenced to roam the earth a monster, in fury and despair!

I am a true creature of the darkness, now, but once I was a man, and whole, and possessed a soul. It is not easy for me to explain to you how I come to be as I am, for in looking back it seems to me that my story forks, like the forks you may see in the lines of a hand. I believe that at that fork I crossed from one state to another, and in this crossing was robbed of many of my memories, so that my perceptions and impressions of the time before are imperfect. I believe these to be true rather than knowing it, rather as an adult may rely on memories of infancy that are in truth images derived from stories told by others before his own memories were properly set down.

This means that I can tell you that I believe I was a man, and a clansman in the Highlands of Scotland, and I believe I had a family who loved me, and friends who respected me. I believe I fought in a battle for my chief – many battles, for this was the bargain the chieftain struck with his men; for a home on his land and his protection, they must take up arms whenever he had need of a war-band. In the heat and blood and fury of one such battle, I believe I lost my head. Perhaps my back had grown weak. Perhaps I had grown old. I cannot remember why we fought. I do not think I hated the man who struck me down.

In the Highland way of life, a fallen warrior is laid to rest with honour, and he does not grudge the grave-worms their feast, for he has no need of his flesh, only the bones so that he may rise on the Last Day to meet his Maker, reborn.

I do not know why this dignity was denied me.

It could have been vengeance, leaving an enemy unburied in the field for his blood to manure the soil. Or perhaps I was a greater man than I recall, and my head was taken as a trophy, hung from a warrior's belt or the saddle of his horse. Perhaps catastrophe befell all my clan, so there was no one left to bury the fallen. Then again, it might simply have been that my head was carried off by a fox or a wolf or an eagle as spoils before it could be retrieved, the jelly of my eyes a delicious treat for the young in their lair or nest, my tongue a delicate morsel for their mother.

Where was I? Ah, yes, how I came to be called a devil, and a fiend. An insect, and a plague, and an abomination. We have come, you see, to the fork in my tale. I was not lain whole in my grave, and instead I found myself roaming the earth blindly, night and day, until I came to a place my feet seemed to know. A rocky mound where there might have been a dwelling place, once, a home with children, and a wife, and friends. And so I determined that that would be my place for all eternity, and there I would grieve, and none should disturb me.

I did not begin a monster, and I can speak, you know, although it is not the speaking I remember, where the voice begins in the chest. My voice is at once silent and thunderous. My words may echo in your ears, but you may also think you were mistaken, and heard nothing but the cry of the wind. To begin with, I would bellow a warning to any who came by my place, telling them to be gone before I could extract my price in blood. This seemed to me only fair, for I had long ago discovered my physical strength to be beyond compare. I am tall, and strong, my joints like steel and my muscles like ropes of wire. No mortal man can best me.

At that, Isabel grew tired and laid her pen aside. She read over the pages, pleased with some sentences and dissatisfied with others. She sifted sand over the last page to blot the ink and then she went down to find Father.

The headless ghost occupied Isabel's afternoons for the rest of the week, documenting his gradual descent into evil until he killed the son of MacDonell in blind rage, furious to hear the boy search out friends to sit at his father's fireside in warmth and companionship while he was condemned to his lonely rock. When he recovered from the blind heat of his rage and saw what he had done, some sense of pity moved him, for he seemed to remember that he had been a father, and had had a son. And so, when MacDonell came for his revenge, he thought he would let him have it, for he knew that the holy touch of iron would dispatch his soul once and forever to Hell. At the last, he found himself too much a coward, and begged with MacDonell to stay his hand, promising instead to go from the place, the one place he had ever known, and where he knew he belonged, and tramp the earth instead for all eternity, seeking refuge in such bare and frozen places as would guarantee his peace from man.

When Isabel was done, she read the story over, crossing out words and phrases here and there and writing in better, and then she folded the pages and placed them inside the box where she kept her letters locked away. As she turned the key, she heard the sound of carriage wheels on the gravel of the drive. Mary and Christy had returned.

Isabel knew she should go down, but somehow she could not. Seeing Mary and Christy would break through the last wrappings of unreality she had gathered about herself, she knew, so all that had happened in Fife would be made fully real. Seeing them together, in all the bustle of servants and trunks and baggage, would be too much and she felt that she should not survive the shock. And so she sat there at the desk and listened to the stir below and then, at length, she heard Mary's voice call and her step on the stairs. As the door opened, she got to her feet.

'At last!' she said. 'I have so much to tell you.'

It was clearly not the greeting Mary had expected and she looked a little taken aback, but she recovered quickly.

'And I you,' she said, 'but first ...' She stood back so Isabel could see a stout, dark-haired girl standing in the doorway. 'Isabel, this is my dear friend Hannah Hopwood who has come to stay. Hannah, this is Miss Isabel Baxter, Christy's sister and my very dear friend.'

The colour rose so quickly to Isabel's cheeks that she felt a stinging there, as though she had been slapped. She did her best to bid Hannah welcome, but the proper words would not come. Hannah blushed and looked at the floor. Just then, John the footman appeared with a trunk.

'Pardon me, Miss, but where is this to go?' he asked.

'In here,' Mary said. 'That's if . . . Isabel, should I sleep in here, or would you prefer to have Christy, and Hannah and I can share?'

'You,' Isabel said, more forcefully than politely, and Mary laughed.

'Very well, then,' she said. 'We shall be as we were before.'

But they were not as they were before. With Hannah to settle, there was no question of staying upstairs and talking of all that had passed since they had seen each other last. Instead they had to traipse downstairs and pass tea things and make polite conversation with Father, who did his best in turn to draw Hannah out. This was no easy task, no matter how Father spoke of his own sister Hannah and all of their childhood adventures. This Hannah was, it transpired, the daughter of an engraver, who provided the engravings for the books published by Mary's papa and her stepmamma. Hannah liked painting and was prodigiously talented, Mary said, and Hannah murmured that yes, she was very fond of painting but not very talented, no, not at all and it was naughty of Mary to say so. Then Mary spoke of all they had done in London, and her father and stepmother's health.

Throughout all of this, Christy seemed very out of sorts and said not a word. At length Father noticed – he was quite distracted, still, after Margaret's passing – and asked her directly if she had enjoyed London.

'Yes,' said Christy, but still her eyes remained downcast. Just at that point, the maid came to clear the table, and so they all escaped. Mary said she would take Hannah outside to show her the grounds, and Christy asked if she might go upstairs and see William and Tibby. Isabel went up with her, and they spent half an hour by the fire where the children were being fed bread and broth by Nanny. Then there was an upset, and Nanny said Tibby was over-tired, it was the excitement of the carriage – she had witnessed it pull up as she returned from a walk with her nursemaid, and had been allowed to feed an apple to one of the horses. All in all, Nanny thought little Miss Tibby should have a nap, and Master William too. Christy and Isabel had best come back the next morning.

In the hallway outside, Christy stopped and shook her head. 'I can't bear to think of it,' she said. 'Here we are, all going about, full of life, and – and Margaret is dead!'

Isabel was surprised by the heat of the anger that washed over her at Christy's words. 'Speak for yourself,' she said. 'I was not going about. I was at Newburgh, her only companion. I was the only one with her when she died.'

Christy raised her hand to her face as though Isabel had struck her.

'I would have come if I could,' she said. 'But no one sent word.'

'You all chose me to be with her,' Isabel said, 'and then you chose to carry on with your own lives.'

'I did no such thing,' said Christy. 'It is cruel of you to say so. I did not ask to go to London. I would have stayed with Margaret if I had been invited but instead it was you they would have. It is always you everyone would have!' She burst into tears and fled into her own room, banging the door behind her.

Isabel stared numbly at the closed door for a moment. Then she went slowly down the stairs, readying herself to talk to Hannah for as long as she had to before she could be alone in her room with Mary.

8

CHRISTY STAYED CLEAR OF ISABEL for a while, and spent much of her time with Hannah, who did turn out to be a very talented artist with a particular gift for watercolour painting. She and Christy suited one another, they both liked to get into old clothes and aprons and never minded although they were covered in smudges of paint or charcoal, or mud from their tramps. When they were not away on drawing expeditions, they took the carriage and went off to visit Christy's friends here and there. Hannah said she enjoyed herself although Mary laughed and pointed out that she could repeat nothing of what the people they visited had said. Hannah blushed red and confessed it was difficult to understand; she had not been used to Scottish people before.

Mary and Isabel were left alone much of the time at home, and the slight strangeness brought about by their separation seemed to dissipate quickly enough. Isabel returned Mary's mother's ring, and showed Mary the bracelet Margaret had given her. She had expected that she would wish to tell Mary every particular of Margaret's awful death, and Mary was very solicitous, saying how truly shocked and sorry she was. For all she and Margaret had not been friends, she said, it was a terrible thing and Isabel should speak of it if ever she wished. Isabel found, though, that she did not want to talk of it, it was too strange and too sad and even to think of it exhausted her. Instead, she said, she would prefer to write again with Mary, and to talk of books and ideas as they had before.

Mary seemed delighted at that, taking it as an opening to tell Isabel of all they had seen, and read, and heard in London, and the people they had met. She still seemed most enamoured of the young men Hogg and Shelley who had authored the pamphlet about the madwoman Nicholson, especially the baronet's son, Shelley, who she said had the face of an angel and a fire in his breast for reform. Isabel was relieved the young man was married – she thought that Mary had changed during her time in London. Before, she had been interested in love as an idea, or a theme in a book. Now she seemed ready to fall in love herself. She carried herself a little differently, too, it seemed, a little more restrained in her movements, and her face seemed more arch, so she almost looked like Lady G–.

Isabel made a point of asking Mary about Mrs Shelley. Mary said she had formed little impression of the woman, and so Isabel was dependent for her information on Christy, who spoke of her a little at table when Father asked. Christy said she had liked her, and she was very pretty and elegantly dressed.

'There was a scandal, I think,' Christy said, 'when Shelley married her. She – Harriet Westbrook, she was then – was still at school. They eloped.' Christy blushed as she said this, perhaps remembering the German tutor.

'How about the other young man behind the pamphlet?' Father asked, swiftly. 'Hogg, I think he is called?'

Christy said she had found him difficult to understand, having a manner of speaking she had not heard before, and left it at that. Later, Mary told Isabel he was a strange young man, who seemed at least halfway in love with Shelley's wife.

'Does she encourage him?' Isabel asked, thinking the idea very odd indeed. Had they not said she was far forward with child?

'I don't know,' said Mary. 'They all believe in free love, and that marriage is a form of property and therefore unjust. They are disciples of my father and mother in that. I think it a great principle.' She gave a dramatic sigh, a new affectation she had brought back from London.

'Why, then, did they marry at all?' Isabel wanted to know.

'Ask David,' was all Mary said, which confused Isabel. What did David have to do with it?

The tale of Lady G– had been restarted, and Mary was weaving in some odd tale she had heard from the Shelleys, of a nighttime intruder bent on murder. She seemed to need Isabel's ideas less than she had, and was impatient with her suggestion that they begin to weave some elements of the supernatural into the story. Isabel had shown Mary her story of the Headless Body, and Mary said it was good, and interesting, but it had no place in the story of Lady G–.

'It is the start of something, only,' she said. 'You could make a great work out of it, Isabel. Follow the Headless Body on his wanderings throughout the Earth. He has some remembrance of human emotion; with the proper education, would he reclaim more? It would be a cunning way to examine the ideas of Rousseau. And those of my own parents.'

'Perhaps,' said Isabel, but she was not excited by the prospect of exploring the ideas of Mary's parents. She suggested, instead, that Lady G– might meet a witch.

'There were witches in Scotland, then,' she said. 'Some were burned here, in Dundee.'

But Mary would not be moved. In the end, she suggested that they begin a related thread of story. They would both continue to contribute to the Lady G– saga – Mary was enchanted by Isabel's idea of the code embroidered on the gloves, and she had seen and admired the bracelet and thought it should be included, too – but Mary only would write the pages. At the same time, Isabel would write her own adventures, with a setting in the Old Country and a cousin of Lady G– as their protagonist. In this way, Isabel could use as much magic as she liked.

Isabel was a little sorry not to work so closely with Mary as before, but she reasoned that she had always had less control over the adventures of Lady G–, and was enjoying her new writing, so she agreed. Mary helped her to decide on the particulars of her own character – blending the early life of Charlotte Corday and Anne of Denmark's Lady Jean Drummond, and named Janet for the heroine of the 'Ballad of Tam Lin', who had saved her lover from an eternity enslaved to the Queen of Elfland by holding on to him as he was turned into ever-yet more awful things, from a lion to a snake to a bear to a burning torch.

They generally wrote in the afternoon. Mornings were for breakfasting with Christy and Hannah, and then Mary read while Isabel visited the children in the nursery upstairs. Mary said she was not fond of the nursery, and Isabel was happy to have the children to herself, and time with Nanny Chisolm moreover, when she took the opportunity to ask for more stories.

All passed comfortably enough for a few weeks, and Christy and Isabel were learning to be easy with one another again, when Father suggested a journey. One of his ships was leaving for Russia, and it would call in to the port of Stromness in Orkney to take on additional crew. They could travel north as far as Orkney on board this ship, and another coming south was due to put in at exactly the right time to let off its crew, so they would also have transport back. Father was like a boy who had played a marvellous trick on his fellows – it seemed he had been plotting this since Mary had been with them before, but the sailings had not aligned until now. This would be the last chance of the year.

'What do you say, Mary?' he said. 'And Hannah? Would you like to see the furthest reaches of this country? They were the lands of the Norsemen, you know, Orkney and Shetland. Not at all a part of Scotland until the Middle Ages.'

Mary and Hannah said yes, they would like that very much, although Isabel thought that Hannah was not so sure.

'Now, it won't be comfortable sailing,' said Father. 'It's a working ship, fitted out for the cold waters of the far north. There are cabins, but not the fine cabins of a craft built for passengers. You young ladies must dress wisely for the voyage. None of your finery – warm and sturdy fabrics will be the order of the day. David and I will do well enough, I suppose, we both own clothing that will see us right, but we must round up warmer wardrobes for you all. The winds blow sharply at sea and across the islands and you will be fairly deaved by cloaks and the like, flapping around you.'

'David?' said Mary. 'Is David to come?'

'Yes,' said Father. 'He has never seen the northern isles or the north country proper. I think he has never been north of Aberdeen.'

'Have you visited Orkney, William Thomas?' Mary asked.

'Yes indeed!' Father said. 'And Shetland beyond, and then I have sailed all along the coast of Norway and all the way to Russia. I have seen whales and walruses and even a white bear, what do you think of that?'

Mary professed herself amazed at this, which was frustrating to Isabel; she could not see how Mary could think her father so innocent of the very business that put food on their table and a roof above their heads. She was also unsure how she felt about David accompanying them. He had not shown face at The Cottage since Margaret's funeral, and it was odd to think that they would take a trip together now, for no reason but their own edification. Then again, she thought, Father had made it sound more of an ordeal than a pleasure – perhaps David saw it as some form of penance.

There were just two weeks until the journey and they were all much occupied in making ready. Hannah was determined to record as much as she could in ink and paint, and she enlisted John to help her make a sort of travelling painting kit – it was a clever thing, a box with a lid hinged in two parts, so if the wind was high, she could fold back one half only and paint under the shelter of the other. There were pegs to hold her paper, and she connived an arrangement with a woodworker's clamp to hold her water, ink and colours ready at one side. She was worried at first that the water would freeze in the cold northern climate, but Father said they were not going so far north for that to be a worry, it would be nowhere near freezing in Orkney at this time of year, only the wind chill would bother them.

Father asked Nanny Chisolm if she would like to travel with them, leaving the children in the care of Cookie and the nurse-maid, but Nanny Chisolm said she had no wish to sail past her family's old home-place in the north country, her life there was put aside and she was at peace with it, but if she saw it again, she might not feel so calmly. She did offer to go with Isabel and Father into the town and help purchase their travelling outfits. She chose them thick flannel petticoats, woollen skirts, knitted jackets, shawls for the girls and woollen scarves for David and Father.

'We will look like you, Nanny!' Isabel said. 'Even Father and David!'

'Well, then, you will be plenty warm enough,' said Nanny. 'When I was a child in the Highlands, I mind the old women still wore their plaids pleated and belted about them as a dress, pinned in the front with a brooch. The thing is about good wool, it keeps you snug even when it rains. If you have wet weather on the ship or in the islands, you can pull your shawls up over your heads and be fine and cosy.'

Mary did nothing practical but seemed forever in the way at home, asking Father all sorts of questions about the islands of Orkney and his onward travels. She scribbled his answers down and said she had half an idea for a story set there, only she could not quite work the thing out.

'You haven't seen the place yet!' Father said. 'No need to write it in your mind before you go.' He patted Mary fondly on the head and she took his arm and squeezed it.

Isabel had noticed Mary spending more and more time with Father and at first she had been jealous simply of her own place – after all, Mary had her own papa in London and had no need of being the favoured child here, too. Then, after a while, a darker fear began to creep up on her – that Mary perhaps saw Father not as a surrogate parent, but as a man in his own right, and one that she might have for herself. He was not so very old, after all, only in his fifties, and Mary was used to being in the company of older people – she had been allowed, indeed encouraged, to be in company of her father's friends since infancy.

Once this disconcerting idea had occurred to her, Isabel tried to assess Father not as her father, but as a prospect for a young woman in search of a husband. He was wealthy, of course, and seemed set to become more so as his business grew and flourished. The Cottage was a fine house and although Father still had children at home, none of them were babes and there was no reason any of them shouldn't make good marriages in the fullness of time. Robert was his heir, of course, but Father was sure to be generous to any future children of another marriage. She knew him to be kind, and good-hearted, and clever. He was active in charitable causes, and many of these chimed with Mary's own interests, such as the establishment of the library at Dundee. He was faithful to the doctrines of the church, but never dour with it, and Isabel thought him – hard though it was to judge – still quite attractive. He was certainly upright and strong, his hair was thick and still dark, and he had a warm and ready smile. She remembered how other travellers had admired him when they were in Perthshire.

Isabel desperately wished she could speak to Christy about her suspicions, but the rift that had existed between them since Isabel had snapped at Christy about Margaret's death was not quite healed. She hoped that travelling together would return them to how they had been before. But the night before they were to leave, there was a tap at Isabel's door and Christy came in.

'I am come to tell you that I have asked Father if I may stay behind,' she said. 'And that he has permitted it.'

'But why?' Isabel asked. 'I thought you were looking forward to it!'

'No,' Christy said, not quite meeting her eye. 'I have been dreading it, rather. I was homesick in London, and I feel very badly that I was away when Margaret died. I do not like to think of William and Tibby left alone here while we all sail off. They have lost their mamma. What if something were to happen to us?'

'I'm sure nothing will happen,' Isabel said. 'Father has never lost a ship, and we do not undertake the truly hazardous part of the journey. Tibby and William will do very well with Nanny Chisolm and their own nursemaid. It is not for long.'

'They will miss you, especially Tibby,' Christy said. Seeing Isabel about to protest, she jumped in quickly. 'No, I do not mean that you should stay,' she said. 'You have done more than enough, being with poor Margaret for so long and caring for the children here. I know you wished to go to London with Mary and the chance was denied you. I did not bring it about, but I am sorry for my part in it. I wish now to take my turn, and for you to go and enjoy yourself.'

Isabel couldn't say much to that and so she nodded, and Christy went away. She came to wave them off, the next day, with William and Tibby and Nanny, as they were rowed out from Bottle-work Dock to the waiting ship, and they waited and waved until Isabel could no longer see them.

The sail down the wide expanse of the Tay was calm, allowing their party to find their berths and arrange their belongings before they reached the sea proper and began to be tossed and swayed about. Father had not misled them; the accommodation was rough indeed, kitted out not for ladies but for hardy sailors. The girls slept all together in one cabin, where usually the mate and the surgeon slept. They had gone below to bunk among the men for as long as their guests were aboard. Father and David were to sleep in the main cabin with the master. Isabel said that she and Hannah would share the mate's bed, and Mary could take the surgeon's, in case her old seasickness returned. The beds were curious, built-in things, so short that the girls could not stretch out at their length and the men must have had to sleep curled up like mice. The ordinary sailors slept in hammocks below.

They met the master briefly as they came aboard. He was a man called James Hope, and he was kept very busy for the first part of the journey as they made their way down the river and into the open sea. He came after that to speak with them on deck, and told them the route the ship would take, and the hazards they would navigate. He reassured them that he had made the voyage many times and never come to grief, he knew the tides and the currents and the rocks like the back of his own hand. They were sailing short-handed in this leg, he said, for their plan was to pick up crew at Orkney, and so he explained that he would have little free time as a result, but he would do his best to dine with them each evening – he expected to reach port in Stromness by evening of the third day after departure. Then he gave them some advice on the best places to sit to be safe and out of the way.

They had set sail early, and by evening they were passing the port of Stonehaven. Hannah had spent the afternoon on deck with her painting box, making sketches of the green fields and cothouses and occasional village as they passed by. Mary sat by her watching the business of the ship, how the sails were raised and lowered and the various tasks the men undertook, and scribbling notes in a little book she had. David and Father took themselves off to speak to the officers, reporting that the surgeon had been most hospitable, as he had very little to do with no sailors to dose or wounds to bandage this close to home. Isabel alternated between watching the land pass by and the sailors at their work, marvelling at the sketches Hannah conjured up and worrying that her rift with Christy, though it seemed healed on the surface, was festering below.

The meal that night at the captain's table was plain but good. The surgeon joined too, and they both went to great pains to horrify the company with tales of the dreadful and wonderful things they had eaten on their voyages, from hard biscuits like stone with beasties in and meat with maggots, to foreign delicacies like turtle soup with sherry and roasted puffin. The captain had eaten fermented shark, he said, and bread baked in the steam of a volcano, and the surgeon said he had eaten crocodile, and a soup made of birds' nests. It was a very jolly dinner, although marred slightly for Isabel by Mary clutching Father's arm in horror as each disgusting dish was described.

They slept well, lulled by the motion of the boat, and rose the next day to find themselves past Aberdeen and making their way to Peterhead and Fraserburgh, where they would turn towards the Pentland Firth – this was according to Father and David, who had been in the captain's cabin and had had a most interesting lesson in sea charts. Mary found herself a place on deck to watch and make notes, and Hannah resumed her drawing, today working on sketches of the seamen carrying out their tasks. Isabel was content to sit in a place she liked in the stern and watch the landscape fall away, far off so that people looked as small as ants going about their business. The surgeon came to sit with her a while, and pointed out different seabirds – gulls and gannets and fulmars and storm petrels.

'Have you been many years at sea?' Isabel asked.

'Yes,' said the surgeon. 'I have crossed the Atlantic seven times. I have been to the East Indies and the West Indies, and I have—' Suddenly he broke off and pointed out to sea. 'Look, Miss Isabel! A dolphin. Do you see it? No, two of them.'

Attracted by his call, the others came over to the starboard side of the ship where they stood and stared as the marvellous creatures wheeled and dived. As they watched, another two appeared, and then two more.

'Do they know we are here?' Mary asked.

'Oh, most certainly,' the surgeon replied. 'They are curious creatures, and very friendly.'

After dinner, the surgeon asked if they would care for a game of cards, and they made a four for whist, Isabel and the surgeon and Father and Mary. They learned that the surgeon was a married man, with a wife in Perth, two daughters of five and three and the hope of another child at Christmas. Isabel was a little sorry; she found him handsome and had enjoyed his attentions. Her time spent with William and Tibby had made her think that she might like a husband of her own, soon, and children.

They were now quite used to the boat, even Mary, and sorry that there was only another full day aboard. It dawned fine as they sailed round the headland called John O' Groats, which Father said was the northern tip of the Scottish mainland, and named for a man called Jan de Groot who came from the Low Countries in the time of James IV, and ferried travellers to and from the islands. They had turned west, then, to sail along the northern coast of the mainland, with the islands to the north. The surgeon pointed out South Ronaldsay and Flotta, South Walls and Hoy, where they saw the most incredible sea stack, towering quite four hundred feet out of the water. Then they were sailing north and passing a small island called Graemsay, before dropping anchor at the port of Stromness. Mary seemed out of sorts for some reason, frowning at all she saw.

It was late by the time they were at anchor, and they were to sleep aboard.

'I'd not put you ashore in that place in the darkness,' the captain said. 'It's a rough and ready sort of town. Plenty of trade, crews coming in and leaving off for the whole north part of the globe, but too little regulation.'

'The merchants seek to have it made a burgh,' said David. 'There has been much talk of it. They say it would allow them to keep order and ensure the town is maintained.'

'I will see you to your lodgings in the morning,' the surgeon said. 'I have need of some supplies.'

Mary still seemed oddly out of sorts as they were put down into a little craft and ferried ashore. Father asked if she was unwell, and she said she was not, but still she wore a frown. 'It's not how I imagined,' she said at last. 'I thought it would be desolate and deserted and ... and *rocky*. But here is a proper town, all neat stone houses and paved streets, and all around is green.'

The surgeon laughed at that and said not to worry, there were plenty of rocky places to see.

Although none of them had suffered any seasickness aboard, Hannah and Mary and Isabel found they did not have land legs when they came ashore, and they lurched and wavered most wildly. Father gave Mary his arm, David took Hannah's, and the surgeon took Isabel's, and in this way they made their stumbling progress into the town and to the house of Father's local agent, who was to be their host for the visit. The surgeon took his leave of them then, and Isabel was very sorry.

They had but three days to explore before their ship home. Father had made arrangements with his agent to hire a cart and a driver to take them all over the place to see all that there was to see. The driver was a local man and hard to understand, and he said there was too much to see in three days but he would do his best.

That first day, they saw all manner of curious things – a great circle of standing stones inside a deep, round green-grassed ditch, and another, smaller circle between that and the town, between two lochs. A little way from the smaller circle stood other stones, and one had a hole in it, right through and close to the ground. Their guide told them it was known as Odin's Stone, for the god of the Norsemen, and any bargain sealed by a handshake through the stone was known as Odin's Vow. Some local lads and lasses pledged themselves to each other by clasping hands through the hole, he said.

Isabel had a moment's terror that Father would pledge himself to Mary, but instead she was surprised to see David put his hand through and ask for her own, pledging to thank her for all of her kindnesses to William and Tibby. He stayed close to her the rest of that day, pointing out birds and cloud formations and all manner of things.

That afternoon, they saw a fine old manor house, although they did not go inside, and then they returned to the town in time to see Father's ship leave on the tide. Isabel felt a pang as she thought of the surgeon sailing away, and crossed her fingers that he might return safe and sound to his wife and children. The next day, they went to the largest town in the islands, called Kirkwall, and saw a perfect, tiny cathedral of red and yellow sandstone dedicated to the Norse saint Magnus, and the fine if ruined palaces the earls and bishops of the place had once called their own. On the last day, they went to see a sea stack. It was not the one they had seen from the boat, which was known as the Old Man of Hoy. This one was at a place called Yesnaby, and it was known as Yesnaby Castle, although this was fanciful: there was no dwelling place there and never had been. It was a wild place, with the waves crashing round the base of the stack, and the whole thing seeming ready to topple down from the two small and bandy legs of stone that bore its enormous weight.

'Happy now, Mary?' Father asked. 'Wild and desolate enough for you?' and Mary said yes, very happy, and took his arm, her eyes shining.

Isabel found herself glad they were going home, and determined to make more of an effort to spend time with Hannah and Mary together, and Christy too if she wished. She saw now that the time she had been spending with William and Tibby had given Mary far too much time alone with Father. She felt herself watched, then, and she turned to see David looking at her with a curious expression. Then he, too, looked at Father and Mary and his face grew thoughtful.

The journey back to Dundee was not so pleasant as the journey north. The weather did not hold, and so they spent more time below decks, where Mary felt miserably sick. Half of the crew had been put ashore at Orkney, and those remaining were tired from their long voyage, the officers polite enough, but with little appetite for company. In the end, Hannah and Isabel got out their playing cards and made quite a jolly party of it in their cabin, whispering over their games so as not to disturb the sleeping Mary.

* * *

Nanny Chisolm exclaimed over the state of them when they got home, and indeed they did look wild, with their hair all blown about and their faces and bodies unwashed since Orkney. Mary was still green about the gills and Nanny insisted on putting her straight to bed and getting Hannah and Isabel into the bath before they could touch anything in the house and pollute it. Isabel asked to see William and Tibby, but Nanny said it was too late. Father and David disappeared into Father's study, and it was only when she was tucked up in her own bed, with clean hair and clean linen and listening to Mary snore very inelegantly beside her, that it occurred to Isabel that there had been no sign whatsoever of Christy in the house.

9

'A GNES SENT WORD THAT HER family invited me to dinner,' said Christy haughtily, 'and Nanny Chisolm said she was happy that I should go. They are respectable people and John took me in the carriage, so I was chaperoned on the way there and back.'

'I find myself a little confused,' said Father. 'You say Agnes's family were to hold a dinner. But I understand you in fact went to an Assembly ball.'

They were all gathered in the drawing room, Christy having just arrived back from her unauthorised excursion and having been called in to explain herself to Father. Mary and Hannah were looking at their shoes, clearly wishing to be anywhere else but here.

'That came after,' Christy said. 'I did not know there was to be a ball when I accepted the invitation.'

'A likely tale,' said Father, narrowing his eyes. 'Did you not take a ball dress with you?'

Perhaps Christy could not think of a plausible explanation for that, for she tried another tack. 'I cannot understand why you are so concerned, Father. Do we not often attend the Assembly balls?'

'Yes,' said Father, 'but not without my permission. I am responsible for you, Christy. Still, I suppose there is no harm done.'

'So may we go to the ball at Cairnloch?' Christy asked, clearly sensing her chance. 'We are all invited, you and me and Isabel and Mary and Hannah. Oh, please, Father. Mr Nathaniel Gow is to lead the band. They have paid him one hundred and fifty guineas to attend!'

'Well, now, I don't know,' said Father, although Isabel thought there was more mischief than anger in his refusal. He looked at his newspaper. 'What do you think, Mary?' he asked, as he turned a page.

'I should very much like to hear Mr Gow,' Mary said. 'He was the talk of London for a time. He has played for the Prince Regent more than once.'

'Well,' said Father, 'that rather argues against than for, does it not? I wouldn't deny you any experience of Scotland, but if the fellow is such a fixture in London, there's every chance you will hear him there.'

Christy glared at Mary and Isabel saw her father smile behind the paper. 'What of you, Hannah?' he said. 'Do you have a hankering to dance a quadrille?'

'Oh no!' said Hannah, sounding so perturbed that Isabel almost laughed. 'I wouldn't know where to start. I should trip over my own feet.' Then she caught Christy's eye, and reddened. 'That is to say ... I would very much like to attend the ball and hear Mr Gow. I don't imagine I will be invited to any parties of the Prince Regent's. This will be my only chance.'

'By my count,' said Father, 'we have two points against and one point for. Christy should rightly decline the invitation, having taken up the last without my permission, and Mary may hear Mr Gow in London. Hannah dreads the quadrilles but would like to attend. Let us see if Isabel settles the matter. If she says no, then we will stay at home. If she says yes, then the decision shall be mine.'

Christy flashed a look at Isabel and Isabel looked back coolly.

'It is difficult, Father,' she said. 'But it seems unfair that Mary and Hannah and I should miss out on the chance of hearing Mr Gow. We have not broken any trust. And Mr Gow may not be so fashionable in London next year as he is now.'

'Very well,' said Father. 'Your sister reprieves you, Christy. We shall all attend. But please all have a care to the fact I am responsible for you.'

Mary clapped her hands in delight and Christy smiled, although Isabel knew she remained displeased. She and Mary proceeded immediately upstairs, and Isabel rose to follow, but Hannah sat, chewing her lip.

'Is all well, Hannah?' Isabel asked.

'Yes,' said Hannah. 'Only ... Well, I have no ball dress.'

Father peered over his paper. 'Och, don't fret,' he said. 'You may order something new on my account, or have something made over if it pleases you better. My late wife had a number of bonny gowns and no great love of gadding about out of an evening, so many of them are almost unworn and might do you with some alteration. I have already said the same to Mary. You too, Isabel. Christy may turn out in the same frock she wore to the last occasion.'

'Father!' Isabel said. 'Christy will not like that.'

'Well then,' said Father, 'she shouldn't be such a besom. Oh, don't look at me so, Isabel. I expect I will relent, but perhaps not. It will do you all no harm to remember I am the master of this house. Now be off with you.'

Hannah and Isabel went upstairs, discovering Mary and Christy coming out of Mother's room with an armful of frocks.

'Come!' Christy said. 'Let's see if any of these will suit. There is little time to have anything new made.'

'Your father says you must wear your old dress,' Hannah said.

'Father wouldn't recognise what I have and haven't worn before if a dress suddenly came alive and bit him,' said Christy. She laid her spoils out on the bed and began her evaluation.

The first dress was amber-coloured, in a soft crepe fabric, with embroidery down the middle and along the neckline of lilies and roses. At first they thought it might suit Hannah, but when she tried it on, they saw that it was too mature for her, it made her look matronly. Mary tried it next but it was awful on her, it swamped her figure and washed out her face. Then Isabel tried it, expecting to dislike it, but finding she suited it very well. The soft gold colour brought out the dark of her hair, and the roses picked up on the pink in her cheeks.

'Yes!' said Mary, with a clap of her hands. 'It needs taken in, and you need a ribbon to tie around your neck, and it's a bit short, but that means you can have shoes tied up your legs with ribbon – green, it should be – and then it will be perfect.'

Next, they all tried a draped white satin frock with a green crepe drape worn over. It suited none of them, and they agreed it should go back in the wardrobe.

Hannah's dress was found next, a long slip in pale blue silk with a fine net robe to wear over. There was also a gold scarf in a textured fabric, but they were agreed Hannah should not wear that: it did not favour her complexion. Instead, they thought, Christy could wear it over her own ball dress, a simple white gown cut with a high waistband.

'It is like the French style of the Revolution, with the gold sash,' Mary said. 'You will look like my mother. She was very lovely, everyone says. But you must not wear your hair so sternly, Christy. You pull it back too much. Let it curl around your face a little and you will be a vision.'

Lovely Mary's mother might have been, but they could not for the life of them work out what might suit Mary herself.

Her looks were very unusual, with the pale skin and the pale reddish-gold hair, and she was very slight in build. Mother's coloured dresses seemed to make her look paler, in the pale dresses she seemed quite to fade away, and almost everything swamped her so she seemed to disappear. In the end they said they would have to have something made for her when they went into Dundee to see about alterations to the other frocks.

Tibby became unwell in the week with a fever, and would not settle unless Isabel was by her side, and so she left the arranging of fittings and procurement of ribbons and fans and other gewgaws to the others. Her dress did not really need taken in, it was cut to hang loosely, and she hunted out an old pair of her slippers for Mary to compare with the new green ones she was determined to buy in town. Father had, of course, relented and said Christy could have a new frock if she wanted, but Christy said she would happily wear the old if only she could borrow a piece of Mother's jewellery to wear with it. Father seemed pleased at that, evidently thinking that she regretted her boldness in going to the ball without permission, and he agreed immediately to the loan of a jewel.

There was much else to prepare, not least the teaching of dance steps to Mary and Hannah, who were not used to Scotch balls. A dance tutor came to instruct them, and Father was roped in to partner them, with Robert who had come home for a visit but would be leaving before the night itself. David was to come to the ball, but he was spared the preparations, having gone back to Fife to attend to some matters in Newburgh.

At last the day came, and the girls gathered in Christy and Hannah's room in their shifts and dressing gowns to style their hair and apply such colour to their faces as they thought Father would overlook. Then Mary went to Mother's room to put on her frock with the maid's help, and the children's little nursemaid came to help Isabel. Christy and Hannah said they would help each other; their frocks were so simple they had no need of a maid.

Isabel had the nursemaid lace her stays and help her lift the loose dress over her head, and then she put on the slippers and ribbon Mary had picked for her. The shoes were green, as Mary had wanted, picking out the green in the floral embroidery of the dress, and they fastened up her legs with satin ribbons. The ribbon for her neck was velvet, and a darker shade of the same green, and it looked very well around her narrow white throat. She wanted to wear her diamond bracelet, but could not find it.

'You look very pretty, Miss Isabel,' the nursemaid said shyly.

'Thank you,' said Isabel, dipping her head slightly so the girl could adjust a pin in her hair, and then she went downstairs to the drawing room where they were all to gather.

Hannah came next, looking very nervous but more handsome than she was used to, and then Christy appeared, looking a little austere in her unusual ensemble, but romantic, as Mary had said, like a heroine of the Revolution. Last of all came Mary, and as she stepped into the room, Isabel felt her head spin so she worried she might pass out entirely. She blinked, and blinked again, the room came back into focus, and at last she could make sense of what she was seeing.

Mary was wearing Mother's tartan dress, her favourite morning dress that she had worn so often. It wasn't the same, of course – where previously it had had long sleeves, a gathered skirt and a high neck, Mary had had it recut as a ballgown. This must have been the chief of the errands in Dundee. Mother had worn a white chemisette underneath, buttoned under her chin, and that was gone, it was cut instead with a low neckline and a slim skirt, with ruchings across the bodice and gathers in the shortened sleeves. Along the hemline, there were small gathers decorated with ribbon, to hold the gown off the floor. The tartan was moss green and red, and blue and gold and black, and it set off Mary's red-gold hair perfectly. She had the pearl Father had bought her nestled in her throat, and she looked like a Celtic queen.

'What do you think, Isabel?' Christy asked. 'Does Mary not look fine?'

'Good God,' Father said. He had gone quite pale.

'What is it, William Thomas?' asked Mary-dressed-as-Mother, her eyes wide with alarm.

'Nothing,' Father said. 'That is – I'm sorry, Mary. That tartan gown, it was my late wife's favourite dress. She wore it very often. When I said to take her evening clothes, I did not expect you would take that one. When you walked in – well, I think I rather thought I had seen a ghost.'

Mary went very pale, and she looked ready to cry. 'I'm sorry,' she said. 'I did not know.'

'Nor I,' said Christy. Two red spots burned on her cheeks. 'At least – I knew Mother loved the dress. But I thought she would not like it to go to waste.'

Isabel's first thought had been that it was a trick, that they had taken the dress to spite her, but now she saw it was an accident and she pitied Mary – she had wished her a little less in Father's favour, yes, but this was not how she had wished her to fall from grace.

Father shook his head. 'A misunderstanding,' he said, 'that is all.' He smiled weakly.

'Should I change?' Mary asked.

'No,' said Father. 'You look very well, Mary. I am sure my late wife would have approved. You must forgive us our fright, it was very foolish.'

He turned away as John helped him into his coat. Christy held out Mary's cloak, and then Hannah's, and then Hannah held out hers. As she tied the ribbon around her neck, Isabel had her second shock of the evening. Round Christy's arm was Mother's diamond bracelet.

'Why do you have my bracelet?' she asked.

'This?' Christy said, her voice hard. 'It's not yours. It was Mother's, and now it should be mine.'

'It is mine,' Isabel said. 'Mother gave it to Margaret, and Margaret gave it to me. How do you even come by it? It was in my room.'

'I gave it to Christy,' said Mary. 'I am sorry if I did wrong. I did not know it was a secret.'

'It's not a secret,' Isabel said. 'And you didn't do wrong, Mary. But please may I have it back, Christy? I wanted to wear it tonight.'

'Father?' Christy said, holding on to the bracelet. 'Why should Isabel have it? Margaret was the eldest sister, but now it is me. Well, after Jessie and Elizabeth, but they are not here.'

'Margaret wished Isabel to have it,' said a voice behind them, and Isabel turned to see that David had come into the room. 'She spoke of it to me. It was hers to bequeath, and she bequeathed it to Isabel, to thank her for her kindness to her in her last illness.'

'There,' Father said, looking thoroughly tired of the whole evening, when it had not even properly begun. 'Let that be the end of the matter. The bracelet is Isabel's, but perhaps you will let Christy wear it tonight, Isabel? She has been most solicitous in helping everyone else, and she will be upset to have caused Mary or me our discomfort. Now, let us get into the carriage before we miss the whole affair.'

Isabel wished to say no, why should Christy be allowed to sneak about and take her things, but instead she nodded and followed Father to the carriage.

The carriage ride was less of an ordeal than expected. David seemed determined to smooth over the awkwardnesses of the evening and very gallantly asked them all for dances. Father jested that he was available if any of them found they had a gap on their cards, but imagined they would prefer to dance with more interesting and younger men.

Hannah, eager as ever to please, immediately said she would be very happy to dance with him, and Mary laughed and said William Thomas was tormenting her, he would no doubt take himself straight to the supper room with the other fathers and leave them to the dancing. She seemed to be recovering herself tolerably well. Christy was still quiet, and Isabel determined to speak to her at home the next day – this was hardly the place – to put right whatever was festering between them, once and for all.

When they arrived, a cotillion was already underway and so they had a little time to watch the dancers before they needed to worry about partners. Christy immediately spotted Agnes and her family and took Hannah to speak to them, moving slowly through the crowd – the ball seemed very well attended, perhaps thanks to the draw of the famous Mr Gow. The music was indeed very good – Mr Gow led the band on his fiddle and played very lightly, for all he was a heavy-looking man.

'You are a match to Mr Gow, Mary,' David said, and indeed Mr Gow was wearing tartan breeches in very similar colours to Mother's dress. Then David said he would fetch them some punch and left them by themselves for a few moments.

'I am so very sorry, Isabel,' Mary said. 'I did not mean to take a dress that meant so much.'

'It is nothing,' said Isabel, trying hard to mean it, although she had wanted the dress very badly for herself. 'Besides, you loaned me your mother's ring when you went back to London, and that is more precious than a frock.'

'If you are to have your mother's bracelet,' Mary said, 'perhaps your father would let Christy have another piece of jewellery. They are like talismans, these things, are they not?'

'Christy has several of Mother's things already,' Isabel said. 'I found them in her room when she was away.'

'Well, then,' Mary said. 'All is well.'

The cotillion ended and Mr Gow announced that the next dance would be a Scotch reel.

'Shall we dance as a three?' David asked, returning with the punch cups. He laid them on a table, and offered Mary one of his arms and Isabel the other.

'I did not think you a dancer,' said Mary. 'I thought you would be too strict.'

'I was young once,' said David. 'And I do not believe you fully comprehend my views. Anyway, even if I wished to comply strictly with the Glasite doctrine, I do not believe that the Bible outlaws dancing.'

Despite this assurance, Isabel did notice a few people looking at them askance. She had been so caught up in the many oddnesses of the evening that she had forgotten that David was a widower, and a new widower at that, and many would find it strange that he should be arming two young women through a dance. She put it from her mind, though – she knew David well enough to know that he would always do as he saw fit and would think nothing of others' censure.

They passed Christy and Hannah, dancing with Agnes's handsome brother Matthew and looking very well pleased with the arrangement. When the dance was over, Christy summonsed

Mary over and began to introduce her to various of her friends, while Isabel stood with David and drank her punch.

'You do not seem so close as you were,' David said. 'With Godwin's daughter.'

'Was that your intention?' Isabel asked. 'When you arranged for Christy to go to London with Mary in my place? Did you wish to separate us?'

'No,' David said, quite calmly. 'Or perhaps it would be more honest to say that Margaret wished for you to stay, and you alone. She felt that Mary dominated, when you were both with us, and she did not like her.'

'I knew that,' Isabel said. 'That Margaret disliked Mary, I mean. But not why.'

'She thought her immoral,' David said. 'Unfairly, at least in part. Margaret was too ready to see the sins of the parents in the child.'

Isabel thought that Margaret perhaps had divined that there was more behind Mary's journey north than a sore arm, but she said nothing.

'And you?' Isabel asked. 'Do you dislike her?'

'No,' David said. 'I think she has considerable intellect, but she is spoiled and wilful and wastes her talents. I had great hopes of her when her father asked to send her north, but I cannot see that her time here has improved her. Even still, if she married the right husband, she could realise her—' He cut himself short. 'I should not speak of that. Her father's idea of a good marriage is one to a man of wealth.'

Isabel's mind was racing. Had David sought to marry *Mary*? It seemed unthinkable. Then again, he had always taken her side, in Fife, until the disastrous trip to the mine.

'I was worried she had designs on my father,' she said, feeling a strange relief as she said the words out loud. 'For a time.'

David laughed. 'Perhaps,' he said. 'Godwin thinks she is ready to marry – or to make a great fool of herself. One or the other. His main concern now is finding her a wealthy partner before she disgraces herself. I don't think – in fact, I know – your father is not wealthy enough for Godwin. The publishing business's debts are great. The Godwins stand on the brink of ruin. They need a husband for Mary who would think nothing of such sums. As for Mary . . . I do not think your father romantic enough, as she understands that notion.'

'Do you think her beautiful?' Isabel asked, surprising herself.

'I care little for beauty,' David said.

'That does not answer my question,' said Isabel.

'If I must answer,' said David, 'then yes.'

Isabel was surprised to feel a sting of jealousy. She looked down for a moment and then, when she looked up, she saw that David was watching her with a curious expression.

Before they could say anything else, an acquaintance of David's approached, and led him away towards the supper room. Isabel joined Mary and Hannah and Christy with Agnes's family and their other friends. The next dance was called, and Mary and Hannah took the floor with Agnes's brother and another young man. Christy and Isabel were left together, watching.

'May we be friends again, Christy?' Isabel said impulsively. 'I'm sorry for what I said about Margaret. In truth, I was angry to be left with her. I only saw how it mattered at the very end. It was unfair of me to hold it over you.'

'Thank you,' said Christy. 'That puts my mind at ease. I didn't – that is, I knew she was ill, but she had been ill for such a long time. I didn't think she was going to die. For my part, I'm sorry for Mother's bracelet.'

'I'm sorry for telling Mother of the German tutor,' Isabel said.

'Pardon?' said Christy.

'I told Mother about your German tutor,' said Isabel. 'But I didn't know you truly cared for him – then. I thought it was just a schoolgirl liking. But then I found your letter, and I understood. You truly loved him. I'm sorry, Christy.'

Christy's eyes shone, and Isabel thought she was moved. But then she turned to look at her in full, and Isabel saw only fury in her face. 'You read my letter?' she said. 'How dare you?'

'I didn't mean to,' said Isabel, her heart pounding. 'I was sleeping in your room and I found it. I couldn't work out what it was, and then when I did, I put it back.'

'Mary said to me that you had looked through my things,' Christy said. 'A moment ago. She said that you said I had rings and brooches of Mother's. You would only know that if you had looked through my room. Why can you let me have nothing of my own?' She turned on her heel and stalked off, meeting Mary and Hannah as they came off the dancefloor. She almost collided with David as he came back to Isabel's side.

'All is well?' David asked.

Isabel nodded, looking at the floor.

'I can tell it is not,' he said. 'Come, Isabel, let us go outside into the fresh air.'

They fetched Isabel's cloak and walked out into the darkness. It was a crisp night, and clear, so the stars seemed very close.

'I have been trying to see Vesta,' said David.

'Vesta?'

'It is a celestial body – a large star, or a small planet,' he said. 'Between Mars and Jupiter. Only sometimes visible to the naked eye. Here . . .' He stood behind her and pointed out the constellation called the Plough, and how to follow its handle to what he thought might be Vesta, although he said the only way to be sure was to observe it over several nights, to see that it moved.

'Why Vesta?' Isabel asked. 'I mean, why is it named such?'

'I don't know,' said David. 'There are three others of the same sort – Ceres, Pallas and Juno. All named for Greek goddesses.'

'Vesta is the goddess of the hearth, is she not?' Isabel said.

'Yes,' said David. 'The virgin goddess of the hearth, the home and family. I seek ...' He fell silent.

'You seek?' Isabel prompted.

'I seek my own goddess,' David said. 'To watch over my own hearth and home and family. Isabel, will you marry me?'

'Me?' said Isabel, shocked into indiscretion. 'I thought you wanted to marry Mary!'

David laughed. 'Perhaps I thought of it,' he said. 'But no, Isabel. I wish to marry you.'

'I need to sit down,' said Isabel.

David frowned, but he took her arm and led her to a low wall where she could perch. He sat beside her and took her hand.

'What of Margaret?' she said at last.

'I think she would wish us joy,' said David. 'She did not wish to be ... as she was. She was denied a full life by her early illness. An idea that she was a failure as a wife and mother took root early in our marriage and it came between us. In marrying you, I would think I had put right a wrong, and I think she would agree. You are of the same stock, but well, and strong, and the children adore you. What do you say, Isabel?'

Isabel thought of her fallings out with Christy, and her life at home. When Mary first had come, it had seemed that her horizons had broadened, but now she was not so sure that had really ever been true. If ever she had entertained an idea of living in a female utopia with Mary, earning a living by their pens as

Mary's mother had hoped to do, then it seemed to her now that Mary had no serious interest in any such arrangement. Perhaps Isabel's fears that Mary would marry Father were receding, but she would marry someone, that was certain, and leave Dundee and go back to London to take up her life there. What she had done was open a door in Isabel's mind to the idea of Father remarrying, and now she was certain that it would happen, and she would not wish to be at home then. She had no interest in becoming a teacher, or a governess – so why not a wife?

'Could I have time to read, and write?' she asked. 'Children's stories, I think, I want to write.'

'Of course,' said David. 'You would be mistress of the house. If you wished to learn the business, you could do so, and I would welcome your support in my other endeavours – I am working on a dictionary, and other writings – but your time would be yours to do with as you see fit. You know I have no time for the church, although I said little of that when Margaret was alive, so as not to pain her. I believe in the life of the mind.'

'It is just as well you are not a believer,' said Isabel. 'If we married, they might cast us out from the church.'

'Yes,' said David. 'I'm almost certain they will. Could you live with that?'

'I think so,' said Isabel, thinking of the words she had spoken to Margaret as she died. Her ties to the church were ones of custom, she knew that. She had no deep or abiding faith.

'Would we live at Newburgh?' she asked. 'At Barns of Woodside?'

'Yes,' said David, 'and we could extend the house in any way you wanted, build out into the other barns. And we would travel. That is, if you wished, we could travel.'

'May I think on it?' Isabel asked. 'And have you asked Father?'

'Not yet,' said David. 'I will do so tomorrow, if you permit me. I will say you have not made up your mind.'

Isabel agreed, and they went back to the ball, although afterwards she could not have told who she danced with, what she ate, or indeed anything that happened at all.

10

'It is a horrible idea,' said Mary. 'Horrible in every particular.'

'I'm sorry you think so,' said Isabel, pulling her shawl tighter about herself.

They were in their bedroom where Mary had been seated at the desk, writing, when Isabel had told her of her engagement, settled the evening after the ball.

'He is *deformed*,' said Mary.

'Mary!' said Isabel. 'That's a vile thing to say. And it's not true. David is not tall, and he lays no claims to good looks, but there is nothing *wrong* with his countenance or his person.'

'Oh, I don't mean his looks,' said Mary, 'although you are right and he is by no means a handsome man – while you are a beauty. I mean his mind, Isabel! He is so rigid and unbending.'

'You have often said that your father thinks him a genius,' said Isabel.

'I do not doubt the power of his mind,' said Mary. 'But he is self-formed, self-taught and that has limited his powers of perception in the extreme. He cannot function as a husband must. You cannot have failed to see that in his dealings with Margaret – your own sister?'

'I am not Margaret,' said Isabel. 'And I wonder if some of your prejudices against David derive from his humble origins, Mary. We may differ in that, you know. You tell often of the great and good, coming to visit your father in his London house. We mixed with all sorts of people here.'

'You sound like David, now,' said Mary. 'When he took us to that awful mine and lectured us on the failings in our characters. That is what he will do, Isabel. You will become his creature, unable to think for yourself.'

'I do not think so,' Isabel said. 'Or at least, no more than any wife. We none of us may speak for ourselves, in the end.'

'My mother did,' Mary said.

'I do not understand your mother to have been entirely happy,' said Isabel. 'And society did not welcome her ways of living.'

'But you will be doubly oppressed,' Mary wailed. 'Not only as a woman, but as the wife of a man who has himself experienced oppression, and resents society for it. He will insist on finding you below him. Besides,' she said poisonously, 'he only wants you to fulfil *his* desires. He has no thought of yours.'

'I really think you are too unfair,' Isabel said. 'Is it not a revolutionary act to care for another? And I truly believe David cares for me.'

'And what of your children?' Mary said. 'They would be ... Would they be both William and Tibby's siblings, and their cousins? This is wrong, Isabel. Surely you see that?'

'I did not expect you to make so much of it,' said Isabel. 'After all, you grew up in a house where none of your siblings shared both parents, did you not?'

'Yes,' said Mary, 'and perhaps it might behove you to think of why, then, I would spare another child the pain of such a life.'

'William and Tibby love me,' said Isabel, holding to that thought as a shield against Mary's words. 'And I love them. I will treat them as my own son and daughter, you know I will. No child of my own body could be dearer.'

'Oh, I know you love them,' said Mary, and suddenly it seemed her anger was spent and instead she was close to tears. 'That is what is so diabolical about it. I wonder if this was something they planned together, when they sent me away with Christy to London. Was this Margaret's doing? Setting up a new wife for her husband after he killed her?'

'Mary!' Isabel shouted. 'I really think you are being cruel.'

'What does your father say?' Mary asked. 'Oh, don't bother answering, I know what he will have said – he is as much in thrall to David as anyone else.'

'David consulted *your* father on the matter,' said Isabel. 'When he went to London.'

Mary's mouth fell open. 'Good Lord,' she said. 'He carries all before him. I can see it matters not what I have to say on the matter. When is the happy day to be?'

'February,' said Isabel. 'And I hope that you and Hannah will stay for the wedding.'

Mary took a deep breath. 'Of course,' she said with a bitter smile. 'Why would we not? It would be a pleasure.' She picked up her shawl, and left the room.

When she was gone, Isabel realised how her heart was thudding in her chest. She had thought her defences equal to Mary's reaction, but now she saw she had been wrong. For a moment she thought about sinking onto her bed and weeping, but then a spark kindled somewhere in her and she took up a pen instead. Mary was wrong – she would not lose her own mind, or her own voice, and she would start now as she meant to go on. Without plan or premeditation, she began to write. She had no idea where the words came from, they seemed to bubble up from some source within her and flow out in ink.

Once upon a time, she wrote. She paused and then began again.

Once upon a time, there lived a widow with her two daughters in a small cot. With no man to look to them, they had no choice but to shift for themselves, tilling the land and harvesting its bounty, rootling and combing for what they could glean from the forests and the slopes.

They had a cow for milk and a spring for water, and a hive for honey-bees, and in spring they harnessed their pony and ploughed their rigs, and then they planted the sturdy, old seeds that belonged to the place, bere and rye and oats. Then they prayed for sun, and rain, and when the reaping time came, they cut and stooked and dried and ground and stored the grain away to make their daily bread and porridge and brose. There was just one place they would never till, and that place was the fairy hill, where the little people lived in the dark quiet of the earth. It would be a sin to dig into their home with iron or wake them with chatter, and unwise moreover, for the fairies were known to extract their revenge on any mortal foolish enough to disturb their peace.

In this way the mother and her daughters passed their lives, and though they had no money, the golden honey of their bees and the company of each other were riches enough, and any strife they had was of their own making only. For the mother was kind, and knowledgeable, and patient, and the daughters therefore wont to judge her dull, and they were bonny and joyful, and at times she was wont to judge them silly. Like ponies in harness, they sometimes chafed, and that was how the daughters found themselves one day with their knives and their baskets, on the side of the fairy hill. It was spring, and their loads were heavy, for already they had found a bounty of chickweed and dandelion, goose grass and gorse, maythorn and nettle and garlic.

'Look!' said the younger sister. 'There are rubies on the hill.'

They looked, and it was true, the hill gleamed with red – wild strawberries, tiny and bittersweet, shining like jewels in the sun.

'Those belong to the fairies,' her sister said. She was older by a year and wiser by a mile.

'Come,' the younger sister said. 'We can take a few and never bother the fairies, for there are plenty to share.'

'We mustn't,' said her sister, but by then the younger was halfway up the hill, cramming the small jewels into her mouth, and her sister had no choice but to follow.

Just then a cloud passed over the sun, and the hill seemed to split asunder. A great door opened and the sisters tumbled into the dark. They had no chance to do as they knew they must and thrust a knife into the wood of the door, for iron offers safe passage to a visitor to fairyland. Instead they clutched and tumbled, rolled and bumped, until they came to rest on a floor of flagstones far, far below.

'Well, well, well,' said a voice, and they looked up to see a fairy in fine robes, a handsome man with a flowing beard, and eyes the colour of ice. He peered at them and then he said, 'Steal my riches, would you, wretches?'

'Oh no,' the younger sister said, but her sister took her arm and squeezed.

'We are sorry,' she said. 'It was thoughtless of us, and very wrong, and we offer you our apologies. Please tell us what we can do to make amends.'

The robed man smiled at that, and his smile was cold, and he waved an arm to dismiss them. Another man came and took them to a place that seemed to be a kitchen, where great fires blazed and a fairy in an apron sharpened a knife.

She was the cook, it seemed, and she set the sisters to work kneading great lumps of dough for bread, and shaping them, and putting them to rise. The heat was awful, it was like the fires of Hell itself, and they sweated and they struggled, but on they worked. If they slackened their pace, even for a second, there came great growls from behind, for the fairy cook had set two dogs upon them to guard them. At least, the fairies called these beasts dogs, but they were like no dog truly seen, more like lions, and one was green and the other red.

They slaved in this way for day after day, and the eldest sister gritted her teeth and bore it, but the youngest snivelled and cried and wept for her mother until the fairy cook said she could take no more, the bread was inedible with all the salt and stodgy with the water. She came with a cleaver and a knife and with one stroke she had the girl's head clean off, and then she made short work of the butchery, cutting all that was left into joints she hung on hooks to dry. The meat of the shoulder and thigh she cut into chunks for stewing, and threw them into a meal trough under the table, and then she told the elder sister to jump to, or she would be tomorrow night's meal.

The elder sister could barely see for tears, but she bent her head and kneaded all of her fear and grief and fury into the bread so that it rose higher and was finer than any bread made in that place before. Then she bent to the trough, filled her apron pocket with meat, and walked from the kitchen. She did not know where she was going, but she closed her eyes and thought of her mother's love, and in that way she found herself coming to a passageway that seemed lighter than the others, a door was there and cracks of light showed around. She put her *hand on the door and she said a prayer, and the door swung open. She stepped through, and as the light hit her, she heard the awful barking of the dogs, and she put her hands in the pocket of her apron and pulled out great fistfuls of meat and threw them back, over and over until all the meat that had been her sister was gone. And the dogs seemed satisfied, and the girl ran home, her apron foul with her sister's blood, and she fell into her mother's arms and sobbed and sobbed.*

For all its embellishments, the skeleton of this tale was one of Nanny Chisolm's stories as she had told it one Hallowe'en – Mother had had cross words for her when none of them could sleep for a week afterwards – but Isabel planned to continue it, to make it her own. She picked up her pen again and she wrote:

The years passed, and the mother died, and the girl was left quite alone. She knew herself handsome still, with hair the colour of chestnuts, and breasts like apples. She had long worn her hair tied back, and the plainest of clothes, but now she loosed her locks and dressed herself in a flowing frock of linen, dyed rosy with madder. She went to tell the bees what she had planned, and she sprinkled cinnamon around their hive so they would know it was time to move on. She unfettered the pony and the cow, and kissed them, and then she walked about the house, touching the good, plain things they had used and loved, wood worn smooth by the touch of their fingers and iron they had oiled and cleaned. She left the door open and she walked out of her life and back to the fairy hill.

There was no door, of course, in the way there is a door on a house, always in the same place, but the girl knew that a door would appear for her, and appear it did. She raised her fist and thumped, and the door swung inwards. She thrust her knife in the wood and stepped inside. She trusted to her heart, and it told her where to turn, so that eventually she came to the great room where the fairy king sat on his throne. The years had not touched him as they had touched her, for he was immortal. She bowed her head to him.

'You have come again,' the King said.

'I have,' she said, and she looked in his cold eyes and saw a spark of fire that echoed in her own. 'I have come for you.'

'For revenge?' he asked. 'You cannot be revenged on me, you know. Not here. This is my kingdom.'

'Not revenge,' she said. 'I have never lain with a man and now I wish to lie with you.'

He quirked a brow at her, and she held his gaze until she saw the spark in his eyes kindle to flame.

'Very well,' he said, and he rose and took her hand. They went together to another room, where there was a fine bed dressed with furs and velvet, and there he bedded her, or she bedded him, it was not quite possible to say.

'Will you go now?' the king asked, and she thought he looked a little sad. 'You left your knife in the door, you are free to leave at any time.'

'No,' she said. 'I will stay a while longer. But I may go, some day. We will have to see.'

And in this way the girl had her revenge, after all, for the king of the fairies came to love her, you see, and to taste what it was to be mortal, for mortals live with the fear of loss, and he could never be certain of keeping her. And the girl loved him, in her way, and she was content.

And for all I know, she is there still, in the fairy hill, where lions slumber on velvet cushions after the hunting is done, and every night is feasting and song and the golden music of the harp.

As she finished, there was a knock at the door.

'Come,' she said.

Mary put her head round the door.

'I'm sorry,' she said. 'I said far more than I ought. Can you ever forgive me?'

'Yes,' said Isabel, calm now that the poison was poured into the paper, the fairy sister dead and gone.

Mary came and sat beside her. 'You have been writing?' she asked. 'May I read?'

'Yes,' said Isabel, and she sat in silence, clutching her worn-down quill while Mary read all she had written.

'It is beautiful,' said Mary, at length. 'And awful. Am I the sister?'

'Yes,' said Isabel. 'No. It is an old story. I thought of you for a while as I wrote, but it is not you.'

'And is David the king of the fairy hill?' asked Mary.

'Yes,' said Isabel. 'And no.'

'So you love him?' said Mary. 'Or at least, you want him?'

'Yes,' said Isabel. 'Or ... I believe so.'

'Well then,' said Mary. 'I will endeavour to be happy for you, my dearest friend. And please do not have Cookie put me in a pie for your wedding.'

'You will stay, then?' said Isabel. 'Until I am married?'

'Oh course,' said Mary. She put the pages of the story in Isabel's hand, and squeezed her fingers briefly. Then she rose and busied herself about the room.

Telling Christy and Hannah her news was easier, but still Isabel was stung by the way they goggled at first. Later, Christy seemed to come round to it all very well, realising perhaps that she would become queen bee in The Cottage once her final remaining sister was gone, and Mary suggested, moreover, that she was a little jealous of Isabel and would enjoy no longer being compared unfavourably to her for looks.

Strangely, once the news was broken, things went back almost to how they had been. David was home only for a brief visit at New Year and otherwise was much away on business – so much so, in fact, that he wrote to Isabel that he thought perhaps they should consider taking a London house, in time. Father was much engaged with the church elders, who maintained, as expected, that a marriage between a man and his late wife's sister was against canon law. Isabel was not much worried about that for herself, but she was concerned about the effects on Father. He said she should not worry herself, he rather enjoyed making arguments.

Perhaps, he said, he would start authoring pamphlets again as he had in his radical youth, and give Mary's father a run for his money.

Mary and Isabel still spent the greater part of each day together, or with Hannah and Christy, reading and writing and exploring as best they could in the winter cold. Hannah painted a portrait of Mary and Christy and Isabel together, against a backdrop of the snowy Tay, and Father was delighted with it and had it framed.

The short days of winter passed in scudding clouds and sleet storms and the occasional crystal day, and soon January was past and only a few days to wait until Isabel would be Mrs David Booth. Robert came home from Edinburgh to stay a week before the wedding and a week after, with Mary's brother Charles Clairmont who worked with him at the printers in Edinburgh. They took Mary here and there while Isabel sewed her initials on the linens Father had bought for her trousseau, and packed her new things and her old things into trunks ready to go to Newburgh after the wedding.

The night before the wedding, Mary was to bunk in with Hannah and Christy. First, though, she came and helped Isabel put her hair in papers, cream her face and trim her nails and complete all the other little tasks that would make her ready for the morrow. Isabel protested, saying that the wedding would be a quiet affair, just their family and Nanny and a few friends, but Mary was determined.

'Are you afraid?' she asked, as she rolled up the last of Isabel's curls.

'No,' said Isabel. 'A little ... nervous.'

'You know what happens, don't you?' Mary said. 'The man puts his prick inside you, between your legs. It hurts the first time but they say not after. Unless you get with child, in which case, if all goes as it should, there's hell to pay nine months later.'

Isabel laughed, although her stomach turned queasily. 'I was thinking of the wedding itself. Everyone looking at me.'

'I know,' said Mary. 'But we neither of us have a mother, and so I thought I should take on the mother's role as best I can.'

'Thank you,' said Isabel, mock-seriously. 'It is very good of you to keep me informed.'

'Many ladies in novels seem to like it fine,' said Mary. 'And we always thought Lady G— liked it. And some ladies become tousy-mousy for other ladies. I think I could.'

'You?' said Isabel. 'I had rather begun to suspect you had grown fond of my brother Robert.'

Mary flushed, but she did not deny it. 'He is a charming boy,' she said, 'but my papa needs me to marry a fortune.'

'David said that once,' Isabel said. 'But I am surprised to hear you say it.'

'It is true,' Mary said, 'although I don't know how to go about it.' She cut her eyes at Isabel and grinned. 'We can't all be swept off our feet by a brewer, my dear.'

'It is funny to think we will not be like this again,' said Isabel. 'I will miss sharing a room with you.'

'And I you,' said Mary. 'Here, let me cut a lock of your hair, and I will give you a lock of mine.' She fetched a pair of scissors and freed a lock of Isabel's hair from its papers, cutting a curl from its length before wrapping it up again. Then she snipped one from her own head and tied both neatly with a length of thread. Isabel placed hers in her shagreen box in her trunk.

'What will happen to Lady G–?' Isabel asked. 'Will you write more of her?'

'Perhaps,' said Mary. 'I dare say she will find another woman to love. And live on her wits. She is fully a creature of paper, after all. Not half paper, like my family. We still need to eat, and pay for coal, and candles and the like; our genius on the page will not feed us.'

'Will you take the pages?' Isabel asked.

'Yes,' said Mary. 'And I will ensure no one ever sees them, for I imagine they would do great damage to any literary dreams I might still hold. Will you take Madame Pretender?' She stood and crossed the room to look the fine old doll in the eye.

'No,' Isabel said. 'I think she should stay here. For now, anyway.'

'I agree,' Mary said. 'This is a grand old house, and Barns of Woodside is plainer. Fine in its own way, of course, but not the dower house of a lady. Now . . .' She stood up and held the sheets so Isabel could climb into bed. 'Do you want me to leave the candle, or blow it out?'

'Blow it out,' said Isabel. 'Although I don't think I will sleep a wink.'

'Have Elspeth in the bed with you,' Mary said. 'She will keep you company.' She tucked the little doll under the covers, kissed Isabel, blew out the candle, and crept from the room.

Mary Jane

29 July, 1814

MARY JANE SHIFTED UNCOMFORTABLY IN the cramped coach seat, trying to find a means of arranging her skirts that might provide a modicum of respite from the broken spring that had been poking her in the behind since Gracechurch Street. The coach was a disgrace, the velvet on the seats worn bald and the stuffing collapsed under the weight of too many years, too many arses, and too little care from a greedy operator who thought of his profit first and his customers' comfort second. As a businesswoman herself, Mary Jane had quite different values, but she had been in no position to wait for a better option. She was already behind by a day, chasing off in pursuit of her stepdaughter Mary, run away to France with Percy Shelley, taking Mary Jane's own foolish daughter Claire Clairmont along for good measure.

No matter how she wriggled, it was no good; her dress was cut in the new fashion with a high waist and a slim skirt and it had no spare fabric in it. Cheaper than the old frocks, of course, having yards less fabric, and handy in the shop, where you weren't always knocking things off shelves and tables, but no match for the sharp end of a spring or a collapsed cushion.

Perhaps it was apt that Mary Jane should suffer so, she thought – she had always found Mary Godwin to be a pain in the proverbial. Just so long as she could still stand when she arrived, that was all. What she had to say would be said drawn up to her full five feet – indeed, she felt she might lift off the ground with fury once she got into her flow.

The other passengers seemed to doze as the coach jolted on, the driver apparently determined to hit every wheel rut and pothole between London and France. Mary Jane stared out of the window, feeling her eyes smart with lack of sleep. It had been midday when they realised the girls were gone. A stifling, stinking day, and no coach seat to be had until the next morning. Godwin had been struck quite dumb by his daughter's transgression, sitting in a chair in the bookshop with his mouth opening and closing, one hand clutched to his chest. Curse Mary – if she caused her father to take a stroke and die, Mary Jane would kill her with her own hands.

It was all over the neighbourhood by the time she set off, Mary Godwin run away with Percy Shelley at just sixteen, his child bride deserted and Mary's stepsister Claire Clairmont gone along for good measure. They were headed for Paris, it seemed, although what they planned to do there was anyone's guess. They said the idea was Claire's, which any fool could see was nonsense. The girl was daft enough, that was true, and she and Mary had been like cats on heat for that spoiled little lordling Shelley in the last weeks, but Claire was bone idle and would have been hard pressed to transport herself to the other end of Holborn, let alone France. No, Mary Jane could read clearly enough the hand that had written this particular farce, and it belonged to Mary.

Damn the girl! she thought again, always so sly and conniving, proud to think she knew better than anyone and carrying on accordingly. Mary Jane couldn't tell her anything, of course, what wisdom could a *stepmother* possibly have? Just a woman who had navigated her own hard times, two children born out of wedlock and only her wits to rely on to bring them all to safe harbour. Not so dissimilar to Mary's mother Wollstonecraft, when all was said and done – she had conceived Gilbert Imlay's bastard in a tollbooth outside Paris, trailed all over the world behind the man, and then repeated the error by marrying Godwin with her skirts just about under her chin. Mary had arrived just weeks after her parents' marriage, and now the girl seemed quite desperate to follow the ruinous pattern set by her mother.

Mary Wollstonecraft had achieved legendary status, of course, by the simple expedient of dying. With one stroke, the tale was written – the dead mother was sainted, the living recast as poor shadows of her beauty, her bravery, and her brilliance. Mary Jane's own role was written then, too – the wicked stepmother casting a cold shadow across the cradle, one greedy hand on the poor father's back while with the other she holds out an apple with a poisoned cheek.

It was funny, really, that Mary Jane should be so cast, when she herself had translated Perrault's fairy tales from the French, and many more writings of a similar nature besides. Had her hand paused as she wrote of the stepmother condemned to dance herself to death, the iron shoes heating on the fire, and the other one, cast in her bindings into the agony of the flame? If it had not, she had had cause to think of them many times since, her eyes meeting the gaze of Mary Wollstonecraft each morning, in the portrait hanging above the fire in the drawing room in the Polygon. That wretched painting still hung in William's study, even after Mary Jane's efforts to prise him out of his first marital home succeeded and they settled into the new rooms above the shop, where they could at last make a place and a living of their own.

But of course the portrait came too, a daily irritant like a grain of sand or grit, chafing at Mary Jane no matter how she sought to smooth it over with smiles and patience. She wondered if she would have liked Mary Wollstonecraft – the woman, that was, not the painting or the sainted memory. Would they have been friends? They said her friendships were fervent, she loved the artist Frances Blood with such a passion that she named her bastard with Imlay for the woman ten years after her death. The Blood woman had been an artist, able to conjure a plant from pen and colour that seemed so real you might think you could pick it from the page and smell its perfume. All that talent went to waste in the end. She died in birthing a child, poor Fanny Blood, just like Mary Wollstonecraft did in her turn.

Hard as it had been to follow in her footsteps, the circumstances of Mary Wollstonecraft's death made it hard for Mary Jane to hate her. It had been an awful business, by all accounts, Mary born healthy but with the afterbirth stuck, so they had to call a doctor to come in haste and haul it out of her mother's body piecemeal. After all the awful agony of that, he had still missed some, so that the poor creature rotted from the inside out. Some said she had brought it upon herself, refusing a doctor in favour of a midwife only, but Mary Jane couldn't see that that had anything to do with it. The midwife hadn't caused the afterbirth to stick, had she? It just happened, sometimes. There but for the grace of God goes any woman who has birthed a child.

Lost in her miserable musings, Mary Jane must have dropped off, for she woke with a start to find an elderly woman shaking her arm and telling her they were in Rochester and would make a stop to eat, Mary Jane had slept right through the first change of horses. The coachman was loosening the beasts as the passengers alighted from the coach, groaning as cramped muscles stretched and full bladders complained. Mary Jane gathered her things and followed her fellow travellers into the inn where they were to refresh themselves. They took their turns behind a screen with the pot, ate some soup and cold meat and rough bread, and then they were back in the carriage and jolting onwards. The next real stop would be Canterbury, for the evening meal, although Mary Jane would have preferred to continue on to Dover with no stops at all, if she could.

Most of the passengers dozed off, their bellies full, and Mary Jane and the old woman eyed each other for a time. Then they found they could no longer sit in silence and exchanged some pleasantries in low voices. The old woman asked Mary Jane where she was bound, and Mary Jane said that she travelled to see her daughter in France. The old woman said she travelled only as far as Dover; she had a son there.

'He has caused me much pain,' she said, surprising Mary Jane, although why she was surprised she did not know; now she thought about it, it seemed that children were as like to cause pain as not.

'My daughter likewise,' she said. Then she asked if the woman's son met her off the coach. The woman said no, she would have to seek accommodation for the night and see her son in the morning. And so, in this way, they agreed that they should share a room in an inn Mary Jane knew and be pleased to do so, for they both found comfort in the presence of the other.

They were untroubled by brigands on the road and arrived in Dover that evening, some twelve hours after leaving London, or nearly, and they went straight to the inn, where Mary Jane bought ale and they both took turns with the pot and lay down in their clothes in the dark. There they whispered the truth of their situations to one another, and found they had much in common indeed, for both were on the trail of a prodigal. Claire had been stolen away by Mary and that whoreson Shelley and gone to France, and the old woman's son languished in debtors' prison here in Dover.

'I worked hard all my life,' the old wife said, 'and stewarded what little I had with care. I am sure it was likewise for you. I cannot comprehend how I can have raised a child so ready to throw it away on a whim.' Then she wept a little, while Mary Jane patted her hand, and said nothing of her own time in debtors' prison, an experience she had done her best to forget. She decided to offer the woman some money in the morning. She had rarely had a woman-friend in her life, and she had found it had soothed her.

The bulk of Mary Jane's money was hidden in a pocket concealed inside the fall-front of the plain dress she wore, but she had some small coin in a purse and this she tied round her wrist before she slept. It was a trick she had learned when she had fled from France; to dress respectably but plainly, like a woman of the middling sort, and to keep enough about you to satisfy a thief that it was all you had. If you lost that purse, it was no great hardship, and any search of your person was generally avoided. Mary Jane was, in fact, carrying a significant amount of money in her ample bodice, the shop safe emptied along with a stash she kept under the floorboards of her son William's room, hidden even from her husband. Shelley was always in need of ready money, this they knew, and Godwin thought he might be persuaded to travel onwards without the girls if they could offer enough inducement. Mary Jane had agreed, although as far as she was concerned, Mary could go to hell with Percy Shelley, so long as she could retrieve her Claire.

Mary Jane did not expect to sleep, but she did, waking untroubled by cutpurses if not by fleas. She and the old woman rose and used the pot, drank and ate a cold breakfast downstairs, and said their farewells. By eight o'clock, Mary Jane was at the quay buying her passage to Calais. She had two pounds less in her purse, having given this to the old woman, and refusing to take anything from her for the room. If she was required to give up Mary to retrieve Claire, she told herself, that small act of charity would ease her conscience a little.

The packet wouldn't sail, it transpired, until late afternoon and so Mary Jane occupied herself in admiring the goods in the merchants' shops on Main Street and taking coffee in Dame Lydia Tebbet's tavern, where all discussion seemed to be of a new cotton-manufacturing enterprise in the town. It was still hard to believe the war was over but the mood in the streets certainly seemed to confirm it; there were soldiers about, and sailors, for sure, but they seemed relaxed enough, and there were plenty of imported goods to be had.

The packet was called the *Prince Leopold*, and the passengers were reassured by the master as they embarked that conditions were fine; they would leave Dover on the tide and land on that same tide in Calais. Mary Jane was pleased to hear it, she knew the palaver of landing on a small boat and dreaded it; she had no love for the water and hated to be passed down like a parcel into the waiting craft as it bobbed on the waves. She found herself a place above decks where she was out of the way and watched as Dover Castle and the great chalk cliffs retreated. She had been afraid she might feel ill, but she didn't, or at least, it lasted a few moments only and then she was well again.

In the great rush of packing and leaving, Mary Jane had thought only as far as Paris, and not beyond, and so now she had her first chance to formulate a plan for how the miscreants might be discovered. Paris was half the size of London, perhaps, but that still was a great throng of streets to search and she had no real idea where to start. She thought she should try to find her father's people when she arrived. She had neglected the bonds for many years now, since first she took the name Mrs Clairmont in order to marry Godwin. Her own folk could not be trusted not to betray the deception – they all knew she was no more a widow than she could fly in the air, she was still plain old de Vial as she had been born. Then the war had intervened, and letters to France were hardly possible, with Bonaparte rampaging all over Europe, but she was sure she still had ties there. Thank God she spoke the Parisian tongue fluently.

The sailing was calm, although the master passed her by and said she was lucky, the night before had seen a strange summer storm in the Channel and the folk aboard the packet had been in fear for their lives. They had sailed late then too, he said, to catch the tide, and halfway across a thunder squall had struck them and the crew had had to bail the waves from the boat. They got the sails reefed, at last, and all was well, but one young woman had been most unwell and he had thought they might lose her. A pretty piece, she had been, he said, if a little too thin, with fine reddish-gold hair, and her face had been as green as the glass in a bottle.

'Poor creature. Was she travelling alone?' Mary Jane asked, feeling her heart race in her chest, but doing her best to sound no more than idly curious.

'No, with a young man and another young woman,' the master said. 'Though not a lot of use they were to her, the lass seemed almost beside herself with fear and the man had to hold her up while the other lay by him and seemed like to part from her own insides.'

'French?' Mary Jane said.

'Heavens, no,' the master said. 'As English as I am myself, all three of them.' He shivered, and spat over the side. 'A bad crossing that. Twelve hours it took, and I had my doubts that we'd see the other side. Still, we made it across, and the lad got the two lasses off and into an hotel. Reckon they'll still be there, the sick one didn't look fit to go on anywhere.' He smiled. 'And here we are today as though none of it ever happened, over and back again like a sealed bottle, neat as you like.'

He said he'd better get on, then, and Mary Jane smiled and nodded, thanking whatever power had seen fit to send him her way. She knew Mary's seasickness of old, even a calm voyage could discommode her. Of course they would be holed up somewhere in Calais, and a sight easier to discover there than Paris. If their crossing had been so long, and she made haste, she would reach them before they had spent so much as a night under the same roof.

The master was as good as his word and they were borne into the harbour at Calais on the very tide on which they had sailed from Dover. As soon as they had disembarked, Mary Jane found a porter on the quay and asked after the hotel the English party of yesterday with the poorly lass had gone to. The porter hadn't seen them, but he asked among his fellows and soon enough, Mary Jane had the name of the place. She thought better of going there at once, though, and asked to be taken to a different inn. There she took a room, stowed her things and hurriedly changed into a fresh dress and a hooded cloak. Ten minutes later, she was outside the hotel.

She did not have long to wait. Barely half an hour had passed before Claire came out of the hotel with Percy Shelley and turned into the town. Shelley seemed as confident as ever but Claire appeared shifty, looking around herself as she followed him into the throng. There was no sign of Mary.

When they were out of sight, Mary Jane walked into the hotel and asked for a room. Once that business was done – her luggage, she said, would come on the next packet – she asked whether there was a young woman here with red-gold hair. 'She was very ill on this morning's boat,' she said. 'I was worried for her, and I would like to pay my respects.'

The clerk said yes, the young woman was here, and he told her the room. Mary Jane thanked him, took her own key, and made her way straight to Mary's room. She rapped on the door.

'Yes?'

'*Eau douce, madame,*' called Mary Jane. '*Et des serviettes. Ouvrez la porte, s'il vous plaît.*'

There was a pause and then the door was unlocked and she saw Mary's pale face peek out. She seemed to take a second to recognise her stepmother, by which time Mary Jane had pushed the door open and swept past her into the room. Mary stood by the door, apparently dumbfounded.

The room was cluttered and dirty, as was Mary's wont, and Mary Jane sighed and began to clear the detritus away, stacking dirty plates and shaking out the gowns and wraps that were strewn over the settle.

'Come in, Mary,' she said, 'and sit. See – I have made a space here for you.'

Still Mary stood by the door, and so Mary Jane took her by the arm and led her to the sofa, closing the door behind them. Mary perched on the edge, stiffly upright.

'How could you, Mary?' Mary Jane said. 'How could you do this to your father? After everything that happened last year?'

'Where is my father?' Mary asked, looking round as though she thought Mary Jane might have packed him in her reticule.

'In London,' Mary Jane said. 'Where else would he be? The care of children is a mother's lot.'

'You're not my mother.'

Mary Jane closed her eyes. 'No. But I have tried to be a mother to you. I have done my best.'

'Your best?' Mary sneered. 'Sending Claire to piano lessons and away to school while I stayed at home?'

'You had your time "at school", Mary,' Mary Jane said. 'I arranged for all of that, or have you forgotten?'

Mary's face flamed. 'Of course I haven't forgotten.'

'Well, who do you think came up with the mysterious malady of the arm?' Mary Jane demanded. 'Who made the arrangements for you to go to Ramsgate, and went with you moreover? Who hushed all up, if not me?'

'You told my father,' Mary said, and Mary Jane heard the pain in it, the child who had valued her father's approval above all.

'No,' she said. 'I did not tell him. Or at least, I alerted him, but I did not mean to do so. I ... I did not see. You were so young. A child, only. Until he took you to Doctor Cline, I did not understand.'

'How could you not have understood?' Mary fairly shouted this, then seemed to realise where she was. She continued in a hiss. 'You are always so quick to remind us that you are a woman of the world. How can you not have seen?'

'I ...' Mary Jane did not have a ready answer to this. 'I never sought to send you away in the summer. This was a choice of your father's. He thought the city unhealthy. And I ... I did not think that the Hopwood house would ... Well, that you would be in any danger there. You were much among adults from your youngest years.'

'I trusted them,' Mary said. 'Too much, it seems. And I see that was not your doing. But, Stepmamma ... If you told no one of my ... travail, then how does Claire know?'

'Claire?' Mary Jane echoed, stupidly. 'She doesn't.'

'She most certainly does,' Mary said. 'You must have told her.'

'No. Never.'

'How can it be, then, that she told me she knew all and unless I brought her with me, she would expose me?'

Suddenly weary, Mary Jane sat down beside Mary on the sofa. 'Claire said . . . that? I don't understand. I thought we had managed it so no one knew. Just you, and me, and your father. And Dr Cline, but he was sworn to secrecy.'

'Of course,' Mary said. 'You are always such an efficient manager. Such a shame it all came to nothing, after all. Nothing for you to manage. In the end.'

'Not so very far from the end,' Mary Jane said. 'There was plenty to manage, Mary.' Suddenly, she thought of the child she herself had lost, her first son with Godwin. It had been years since she thought of him, the poor mite. William, they had called him, though she could see it had pained Godwin to give his name to a child who never drew breath. Another William had come along a little over a year later, and sometimes it seemed that the first had never existed.

'Perhaps we shouldn't think of it,' she said. 'What's done is done. I would not have wished such a thing on anyone. But as it happened, you were able really to attend the school. No one thought anything amiss.'

'A few months in school,' Mary said, 'while Claire—'

'Enough, Mary,' Mary Jane snapped. 'You throw my mothering in my face and suggest I cannot perceive my own biases. But credit me with a little sense. You have plenty of advantages. Claire has few. Tell me again what she said to you, for I promise you she does not know of the thing from me.'

Mary glared at her for a few moments and then she slumped. 'She said she knew of the "dreadful evil" that had befallen me,' she said.

'Those were her words? "The dreadful evil"?'

'Yes.'

Mary Jane shook her head, cursing Godwin for a fool, and herself for worse. All of them, fools and dolts.

'Those are not Claire's words,' she said. 'They are my words. In a letter to your father. I told him we had no longer need fear the dreadful evil we apprehended. In this way I sought to tell him how matters had ended, but written in such a way that another reader might understand I was referring to your arm and the many conditions that we might have dreaded. The lepers' disease, or consumption.'

'My father showed Claire the letter?'

'I doubt it,' Mary Jane said. 'But you know his study. He is not a tidy man. His papers ... He destroys so little and all is always strewn about. It's where you inherit your untidiness. But that letter, alone, is not enough to alert Claire. She is not so very wise.'

'She saw my own letters to my father too.'

Mary Jane raised her hands to her head, which was beginning to pound. 'I see. And those letters were perhaps less ... carefully edited than mine? You spoke of your ... loss?'

Mary had begun to cry. 'The letters are very incriminating,' she said. 'I have them now, Father gave them back to me. And I kept all his to me, although they were unkind. I locked them in a box but Claire has the key. All my writings are in there too. She could ruin me. And I am ... ruined again already.'

'You mean you are with child?' Mary Jane asked. 'Oh dear God, Mary, do you learn nothing?'

'How should I have learned?' Mary demanded, crying in earnest now. 'Hopw— The old man put his *thing* in me without my permission. I had no idea what was happening. And this ... well, I did not seek it, but how could I have stopped it?'

'How indeed?' said Mary Jane, and in that moment she wished she had stayed here in France, had never returned to England, never met Charles Gaulis and borne him Charles or borne Claire to John Lethbridge, never needed to meet or marry Godwin to legitimise her family. God! What a mess she had made of it. Perhaps Mary Wollstonecraft had had it right. Perhaps Mary Jane should have made her living with her pen. She had been ten years older than Mary was now when she met Gaulis, and many times more worldly, and still she had been caught in the same bind.

'Shelley has money,' Mary said, recovering a little, 'or will have. And he will have a title, when his father dies. It is not the same as what happened before.'

'He has a wife, Mary,' Mary Jane said. 'And a title is neither here nor there. Claire's father, too, has a title, and little good it did me when I bore him a bastard.'

Mary stared at her and she realised she had never spoken openly of her situation before, to anyone. Even Godwin. Oh, he knew well enough – of course he knew, had married her once under her assumed name, as a widow, and once under her own, to make it legal, a spinster with two bastard offspring – but she had only ever glanced at it, never said the words out loud.

'What am I to do?' Mary asked, tears flowing again, and fleetingly Mary Jane thought of saying, *Oh, I am mother enough to you to manage the situation again now, am I?* But she had not the energy. Her only concern was limiting the damage to Godwin; he had been ruined before and she would not see him so again. Their business depended on his creditors and she had worked too hard to lose it all now. All those hours with the account books, all the night hours bent over translations, all the times she had had to hide when printers and paper merchants came calling, looking for payment.

'There are ways to avoid getting with child,' she said. 'If you had asked me, I would have told you.'

'Oh,' said Mary, her face pinched. 'I did not know. It seems they did not work for you, though? Or my mother.'

Mary Jane laughed. 'No, they do not always work. And I ... well, I hoped that a child would ... focus the mind of my paramour. Three times. I was wrong. Twice.'

She saw Mary puzzle that out.

'There are also ways to ... slip a child,' Mary Jane said. 'But they are dangerous in their own right.'

'No,' Mary said clearly. 'I am here with him, and he is pleased.'

'He has a wife,' Mary Jane repeated. 'And a child. In England. And is she not with child again?'

Mary coloured. 'He says she can live with us, as a sister.' Even as she said it, she looked unconvinced.

Mary Jane snorted. 'I'm sure she will be delighted to accept this kind offer. And I'm sure society will have nothing to say of it. But it seems to me you do not need another sister, Mary, there is already a sister here with you.' She took a deep breath and aimed for a steady tone. 'Will you let me take Claire home with me? I will consult your father there, and we will see what we can do. Perhaps there is a story to be told of the first wife, some wrongdoing or other. Perhaps her coming child is not Shelley's at all?'

Mary narrowed her eyes. 'Could you do that?' she asked.

'Of course,' Mary Jane said. Of course she could do it. Harriet Shelley had done no wrong but to be wronged – but she was a woman, wronged by a man, and that man was a baronet's son and a poet. How likely was it the world would find *him* in the wrong when it could find *her* so?

Mary seemed to rally a little at that and, for the first time, she looked Mary Jane full in the eye. 'I would be very grateful if you were able to help me in this way,' she said. 'As you have helped me before. I appreciate that I have not always been grateful, and I am sorry for it. I would be pleased to assist you in my turn. If you wish to take Claire home, I will not do anything to interfere. But she has my key. I am in her power, and not the other way.'

And so there is it, Mary Jane thought. *Self-interest will always out.* 'Let me speak to her,' she said. 'When they return, send her to my room.'

They made their arrangements, then – Mary was to say to Claire that she had begged some rosewater from a neighbouring woman, having lost her own, and please would Claire return it? Then Mary Jane took herself to her room and sat in the dark feeling every beat of her heart echo in a ring of pain around her head.

In an hour, or a little more, Claire knocked on the door. She started at the sight of her mother, but Mary Jane took a firm grasp on her arm and drew her into her room. Claire stared at her coolly as she lit the lamps.

'Captain Davies told Shelley a fat woman had asked for him,' she said.

Mary Jane considered rebuking this rudeness, but found her head was too sore.

'Shall I order some dinner?' she said. 'And a bottle of wine? I hope you might spend the night here with me, Jane.' It was a deliberate choice, using the name they had used throughout her daughter's babyhood and childhood. She hoped it might awaken such fondness as remained between them.

It did not.

'Claire,' her daughter said. 'I prefer to be called Claire.'

'Of course,' Mary Jane said. 'Claire. Although I still find it hard to remember, when we called you Jane for so long at home.'

'But yet my given name was always Clara,' the girl said. 'I think Claire becomes me better. Is there meat? I am hungry, Shelley will give us no meat.'

'I will order meat,' Mary Jane said, 'if you will wait here while I go down?'

Claire nodded at that, and Mary Jane went below and arranged for a meal to be brought, and for a boy to bring her bags and settle her balance in the other inn. It was good to speak French again, she found it allowed her to imagine a different life for a moment or two. By the time she mounted the stairs again, she had begun to formulate a plan.

As they ate, she told Jane – Claire – a little of her own beginnings, in Exeter. The inn her merchant father owned with her mother, her beloved mother's death and her flight to France to live among her father's people. She spoke at length of her happiness there until the Terror, when she and her sister fled to Cadiz and then on to England. She was deliberately selective in her narrative, choosing, for example, to maintain the fiction of her marriage to Charles Gaulis but she did not spare Claire the details of her own birth, holding back only the name of her father. Since her conversation with Mary, Mary Jane had reassessed her daughter's cunning, if not her intelligence, and would not trust her not to presume upon her father if given half a chance, and that would surely risk the payments Mary Jane received for her upkeep.

Mary Jane wove her fiction skilfully, as befitted a writer, to show herself as sympathetic to Claire's frustrations, like her daughter a bold and brave survivor of a world designed for men. By the time she had finished, Claire had agreed to spend the night with her mother and went to tell Mary and Percy so. The boy had come with the luggage by this time, and Mary Jane stripped to her shift and got into bed. She was almost sure Claire would agree to come home the next day before any real harm was done – to herself if not Mary, for spending the night with one's own mother in a hotel room was scarcely a scandal – but she came back in an ill humour, having been teased by Shelley. She sought then to engage Mary Jane in argument, rehearsing all her petty frustrations and jealousies, the ways in which she felt Mary had benefited more from Mary Jane and Godwin's love than she had. And then it was out. She knew the truth of all her stepsister Mary's woes and was ready to barter with them for her own freedom. She turned Mary Jane's elegant narrative back on her then, saying a mother had no right to enjoy her own freedoms, only to tie her daughter to her apron strings.

Mary Jane was almost fainting by then for lack of sleep, and in the end she knew that all she cared about was Godwin. Between Claire and Mary, they would be the death of him, and then where would Mary Jane be? And so she agreed to her daughter's demands. In exchange for the key to Mary's box, Claire could do as she pleased, travel onwards with Mary and Shelley and ruin herself if she liked. She spoke fluent French, unlike Mary – of all their gripes and jealousies, it was true that this was one skill Mary Jane had imparted to Claire and Claire alone. Mary Jane gave Claire the names of her grandfather's sisters in France, telling her she could turn to them if she really found herself in need. Then Claire threw herself into bed and began to snore, while Mary Jane turned the key in the box and fed Mary and Godwin's letters – stupid letters, ill-advised letters – to the fire. She returned the box to Mary in the morning and told her to say she lost it on her travels. They both knew well what an ill-judged memoir or the publication of thoughtless letters could do to a woman's reputation.

'I will deny it always,' she promised Mary, 'and now there is no evidence at all to gainsay me.'

Mary took the box, seeming less pleased than she might have been to have gained Claire in exchange, and Mary Jane took her leave. She found passage on a packet and began the weary journey home. She could not bear the thought of telling Godwin that Mary was again with child.

Funny, she thought, that she should so often play the midwife. Perhaps, though, that was the lot she had chosen in life. What else was a publisher, after all, and had she not seen many great works brought to term? She knew William's friends looked down on her – a second-class wife, an indifferent intellect – but she had seen William right many times when the thinkers of the first class had failed him. Moreover, she had seen their own works into print, *Tales from Shakespeare* and *Swiss Family Robinson*. Were these not as much her legacy as their own? She had brought them into the world and they would not die, but survive and thrive. All those supposed radicals, looking down their noses at a woman whose great passion was the education of the young.

Part III

Fife, London, Dundee, 1814–1823

11

Isabel did not hear of Mary's elopement until the guilty parties were already on their way back to England from the Continent. It was Christy who let it slip – perhaps David had never intended to tell her at all.

Christy had come to Newburgh to help with William and Tibby while Isabel recovered after the loss of an almost six-month child. It had been a dangerous time, and they had been concerned for her life. She was slow to regain her strength, weak from loss of blood and a fever that followed, and prone to long fits of melancholy. The doctor David brought said she would recover, and there was no reason she should not conceive again, but for now she found she would much prefer to stay abed with the laudanum bottle and the tincture spoon. David tolerated this for two weeks and then he sent for Christy.

'I would prefer Nanny Chisolm,' said Isabel.

'No,' said David. 'Then you'll never get out of bed. Christy will be better for you. You'll have to get up, even if it's only to avoid listening to her lecture you on your failings.'

David knew Isabel well, she thought, for her grief at the loss of the infant – it had been a boy – receded a little in the heat of her resentment of the intrusion of her sister into the world they had created here for themselves. It would be in her interests to be better so that Christy might leave them again and all could be as it was before.

Looking back, Isabel saw that she had expected her marriage to David would be a tame and comfortable thing, more akin to friendship than her ideas of romantic love. She would look after William and Tibby, and the house, and help David with his dictionary and his other writing, not quite a housekeeper nor yet a secretary. A helpmeet. He had promised she would have time to read on her own account, and write if she wished.

In all this, she had been more or less correct. She instructed the housekeeper and assisted David, and when neither David nor the children needed or wanted her, she read and she painted, and sometimes she wrote.

David was more generous than she had expected with his money, telling her to do as she would with the strange old house – it seemed to have grown up rather as a ramshackle old village might, unplanned and responding to need, a room added in this odd location and a staircase in that to make the row of ancient barns into a dwelling place for a family. One day, he said, they would choose a house of their own, but for now they should make the Barns their own. She had not known the place was leased, had thought David owned it, but he reassured her that the lease was long, and she had great pleasure in the ordering of hangings and furnishings and in placing them about the place to bring it to life.

They had discussed brothers and sisters for the children, and she knew that meant doing all that led to infants. She wanted it, half wished she had waited to marry a man who might be a lover as well as a protector and a friend. She'd expected that bedding David would also be a passionless thing, a necessary matter performed in the darkness to the purpose of getting with child. In this, she had been completely wrong. It was a little as though she had bought a lion pup, thinking it would grow into a domestic cat.

They had travelled to Newburgh alone, the night of the wedding, as Father had insisted on keeping William and Tibby at The Cottage for a fortnight more while Isabel settled herself into her new home. It had been full dark when they arrived, so early in the year, and the little white houses were closed and shuttered for the night as they passed through the village and up the hill. But Barns of Woodside was far from shut up – there was a candle in every window and Isabel was near blinded by the lights of the fires and the lamps as David hoisted her over the threshold. There was no sign of anyone else but a great spread of cold cuts and chutneys lay ready by the fire in the drawing room, with rich red wine to toast one another.

It seemed they were quite alone, the servants out or hiding in their rooms, and they left the meal uncleared when they were done. David took Isabel's hand and led her upstairs to their room – it was his old room, not Margaret's, and she was grateful for that – where another fire blazed and the covers of the bed were turned down. He helped her undress, right down to her shift and then he sat her on the bed and lifted that off her, too, so she sat shyly feeling a red blush creep up over her skin and wanting to gather up the sheets to cover her nakedness. He unpinned her hair, and then he began to stroke her, gently, all over, touching her in all the soft and secret places, so she felt a sweet soreness rise up in her and her breath come fast. He asked her then if she wanted him, and she said yes, but shyly, eyes downcast, and he lifted her chin and looked straight at her and asked again and she said yes, yes she did, and it was true. There was no more Margaret, no more Father or Christy or Mary, just this place and the two of them, and she felt it was all she wanted until the end of her days.

He did not say he loved her then or in the weeks that followed, but he said he wanted her, and he called her his goddess, and he could not keep his hands from her. The servants had, it seemed, been sent home on holiday and only one maid came up each day to bring food and lay the fires. David did no work in this time, or if he did, his work was educating Isabel in the myriad ways, places and times they might take pleasure in each other, adding to the lesson she had already learned – that men of fifty were not so close to their dotage as she had once imagined.

This honeymoon lasted two weeks, and at the end of that time, William and Tibby and their nursemaid were brought over from The Cottage by Father's man John, and the rest of the servants came back from their family farms and villages and got on with putting the place to rights before settling into the normal rhythms of running any house. William brought endless tales of the journey across the Tay and the nursemaid brought letters from Father and Mary and Christy. Father's was all good wishes for the newlyweds, Mary's full of missing Isabel and a suspicious lack of mention of Robert, and Christy's full of a great many unwise things that Robert and Mary had done and said, so unwise, in fact, that it seemed Mary's father had called Mary home immediately for fear she might accidentally make a most unprofitable marriage.

Isabel read the letters quickly and laid them aside, not wanting the outside world to intrude yet on her new life. Already she found it a challenge to go back to rising in the morning and dressing in the usual way to face the day. It seemed then almost that there were two Davids, and two Isabels – the pair that went about their business, quiet and sober and industrious, listening to children's chatter and eating at table, and the pair that came together half-violently in the breathing darkness of their nighttime room. There were times Isabel thought she might laugh out loud for the strangeness of it. Perhaps David felt it too, for then he took to asking her to join him in his study to read aloud the pages he was writing for an educational charity. While she read, he dropped his breeches, lifted her frock, and tested her ability to keep her place most sorely.

Isabel missed her courses the first month, but waited until the second month had passed without any show before she told David what she suspected. She was happy to be with child, thinking it best that any children of hers and David's should be as close in age to William and Tibby as possible, so that none should feel themselves an outsider. She thought David was a little sorry it had happened so soon; he said he would be jealous to share her. Still she had no idea if he loved her, but she thought he hungered for her no less than before, or perhaps more still. He was a caring attendant when she sickened and grew faint, but that aside, his manner towards her did not change even as she grew heavier and rounder.

In her fifth month, Isabel wrote to Mary at her parents' house, to tell her of the coming child. She enclosed a sketch of the children, and another of the strange stones outside the village that had fascinated them, but there was no word back from London.

When all came to grief, it was entirely without warning. Isabel rose feeling well, and breakfasted with David before going upstairs to prepare the children for a walk out to the burn. As she reached the nursery, a nagging ache in her back became severe, reaching all of a sudden right around her belly so she thought she would retch from the pressure of its grip. Then there was a gush of fluid and she called out for Mrs Brown, but David came instead, alerted by something in her voice.

'Take the children away,' said Isabel through numb lips, and she saw how he had turned grey in the face, so he looked again old and stern like Margaret's husband of yesteryear. Then her eyes rolled back and the floor seemed to rise up before her.

Christy said they had had to burn the carpet at the top of the stairs, she had bled on it so much, and her dress was ruined too, but they had managed to get her shawl cleaned. Isabel had no proper memory of being carried to her bedroom or of the hours of her travail, she had been unconscious for some of it and the rest had passed in a blur of pain and terror. David had ridden like hell for a doctor and Christy said that was all that had saved her; the man had managed to deliver the poor wee mite so the bleeding might at last be stemmed. He hadn't been able to stop the milk coming in, nothing could do that, and Isabel had had a fever from it that made her mad for a night and a day. She thought Margaret was in the room, and Mother, and the only thing that would stop her from throwing herself from the window was David lying beside her and holding her down, no matter the pain from her poor swollen breasts as she struggled. Christy didn't know about that, thank goodness, and so couldn't torment her with it in her attempts to be kind.

'I'm sorry,' Isabel had sobbed when the fever broke and she awoke, weak but aware for the first time in days. 'I'm sorry.'

'Nothing to be sorry for,' said David. 'And much to be glad of, Isabel. We thought you lost.' He looked tired, and old. 'Rest now,' he said, 'I'll bring the children in later,' and he kissed her forehead and went from the room.

She did sleep, although her dreams were full of mothers searching for their children.

When she woke, Christy was there, the mess by her bed was tidied, the laudanum bottle and spoon gone and a fresh glass of water sat ready on the table. Christy sat on a low chair frowning over some mending by the light of a lamp. When she saw Isabel's eyes open, she poked her needle into the fabric and picked up the water glass, holding it for Isabel to sip.

'I can manage,' Isabel said.

'You gave us an awful shock,' said Christy, ceding the glass to Isabel. 'Father was beside himself until we heard you would live. He wanted to come, but David thought that might upset you more. We are all very sorry, Isabel.'

'It is good of you to come,' said Isabel. 'I know we have not been the best of friends for a long time now.'

'That is all forgot,' said Christy. 'When we thought you might die, Isabel! I wished many things said, and many unsaid. And David says you are not improving as you should. I am no nursemaid, as you know, but I will do anything to help you.'

'There is nothing to do,' said Isabel. 'Only ...' She began to cry and Christy came to her and rubbed her arm. 'Only I must see to the milk. It still comes in.'

Christy's cheeks flamed red at that, but she asked very gamely what she should do. Isabel asked her to bring the dish and the cold compresses. She expected Christy to turn away but she didn't, she sat and handed all to Isabel.

'When will it end?' Christy asked, when Isabel was done and the milk tipped into a bucket.

'Soon, they say,' Isabel said. 'There is almost nothing now. And it does not hurt as it did.'

'I'll ask Mrs Brown to make me up a bed in the room,' Christy said. 'So I will be nearby if you need anything in the night.'

Isabel opened her mouth to say no, but then she thought it might be reassuring to have Christy near her for a time. And so the bed was made up, and Christy helped Isabel see to her other needs, and then they heard David's knock at the door and suddenly William was leaping on the bed and Tibby looking set to follow as David sought to catch her and pull her back.

'Careful, William,' Christy said, 'we mustn't break Isabel. She has been very sick.'

'I won't break,' said Isabel, hugging William to her. She looked David in the eyes, over the little boy's head. 'I won't break.'

William and Tibby chattered away, then, until Isabel grew tired. 'You go downstairs with Papa,' she said. 'I need to sleep now. Tomorrow, perhaps, I can get up and we could play in the garden a while.' She accepted their kisses, and David's, but she did not remember them leaving the room, knowing nothing until Christy roused her to take a glass of water in the dark.

Getting up the next day was hard work, for Isabel was as unsteady on her legs as a newborn foal. Once or twice she doubted she would manage, but at last she was upright and dressed – after a fashion – in her dressing gown and shawl. Her hair was in an awful state but she tucked it into her cap as best she could, thanking her stars that they hadn't cut it as she lay in fever. She and Christy ate breakfast in her room and then Christy called for Mrs Brown and each took one of Isabel's arms until she was safely down the stairs. She made her own way out to the garden where she was met by David and the children and a very charming scene. They had laid out a cloth on the grass with cushions for themselves, and a comfortable chair had been carried out for Isabel and another for Christy.

'Look, Isabel!' Tibby roared, overcome with excitement. 'It's a picnic!' David did his best to shush her, but Isabel laughed.

'It is a picnic, my darling,' she said. 'How clever of you to keep such a lovely secret.'

'We are going to eat a pie and strawberries!' William announced.

'Delicious,' said Isabel, although she wasn't in the slightest hungry.

They sat outside for the rest of the morning and Isabel watched as William and David made a tower from Tibby's blocks and toppled it, over and over. Christy joined them and they made a new game of hiding the blocks in the garden for each other to find, calling out 'hot' and 'cold' as the seeker came closer or strayed further. Isabel dozed for a few moments and woke to find that David had been right, her sadness had receded a little now she was up and outside in the air and warm. David seemed lighter, too, and while it was clear that Christy was not yet used to the new configuration of the family, William and Tibby gabbled on and spared them any awkward silences.

When they had eaten, Christy went inside to wash and David said he would take Tibby upstairs for a nap and William could come and draw in his study. Tibby kicked up a great fuss and in the end he picked her up and put her over his shoulder. He paused to kiss Isabel's forehead as he passed and she smiled up at him while Tibby pounded his back and howled.

When she returned, Christy brought a bonnet with a wide brim for Isabel. 'Your nose is turning pink,' she said. Then she sat on the blanket at Isabel's feet and raised her own face to the sun.

'I wish I didn't burn so easily,' said Isabel. 'The sun is such a blessing. You are lucky to be able to enjoy it.'

'You must not grudge me that,' Christy said. 'After all, you were always the prettiest.'

'No,' Isabel said. 'Or if I was, it was only till Mary came. I was not the prettiest then.'

'Nonsense,' said Christy. She shook her head. 'And little good her prettiness has done her, in the end.'

'What do you mean?' Isabel said. 'Have you news of her?'

Christy turned to face her. 'Do you mean you don't know?'

'Know what?'

Christy's eyes were wide. 'I suppose it was when you ... became unwell. Isabel – Mary has eloped.'

Isabel felt her heart leap in her chest and raised her hand to still it. 'Not with Robert?' she said.

'No, no,' said Christy. 'Not with Robert. With the poet we met in London. Percy Bysshe Shelley.'

Isabel frowned; she could make no sense of it. 'But he is a married man.'

'Yes,' said Christy. 'But, Isabel, you have gone so pale. I'm sorry, I shouldn't have told you like this. You're still so weak. Let's go inside and get you into bed. I want you to sleep for a bit and then I promise I will tell you all I know.' Seeing Isabel make ready to protest, she stood and took her arm. 'No,' she said, 'come. I am only just becoming used to this friendly David you have coaxed out of his shell. I don't want him to fall out with me and become terrifying again.'

Making their way upstairs was a trial, and Isabel was shaky and shivering, so Christy had to bustle off to fetch a warming pan and hot tea to drink. There was the business with Isabel's milk to deal with, then, and clean rags to fetch for her private parts, and by then there was no fight left in her.

'Sleep now,' Christy said. 'And we will speak when you waken.'

Isabel did as she was told, surprised and a little discomfited to find that it was evening when she woke. David sat by her, reading by the light of a lamp.

'Did you know?' she said, meaning Mary's elopement.

'Know what, my love?' he asked, with a smile that did not quite mask the concern in his eyes.

'Nothing,' she said, thinking that he had never spoken to her of love before. 'I was dreaming.'

'Yes,' said David, placing the back of his hand against her forehead to check for fever. His frown lessened when he found her quite cool. 'We kept you outside too long, I think. Tibby wants another picnic tomorrow, of course, but I think the weather will not hold.'

There was a knock at the door and Christy came in with a tray.

'Mrs Brown has made you a broth,' she said. 'And jelly with port and spices.'

Isabel was surprised to find that she was hungry. David helped her sit up and Christy placed the tray on a table by the bed. 'Have you eaten?' she asked.

'Christy has but I have not,' said David. 'I have been here with you. And now I will leave you to your meal, and go down to my own.' He closed his book, nodded to them, and made his escape.

'Tell me,' Isabel said, the instant the door was closed. 'Tell me all.'

'It is as I told you,' Christy said. 'She has run off to France with Percy Shelley. I wrote to you of him and I'm sure Mary spoke of him.'

'She did,' said Isabel. 'And I thought she had some partiality to him. She was forever poring over those poems he wrote about the mad woman who tried to stab the King. She said he had the face of an angel.'

'He was striking,' Christy said. 'But I found him unsettling, Isabel. There was an intensity to him that felt to me most uncomfortable.' She laughed. 'He seemed to me a little as you do, since your illness. You are very thin, you know, and your eyes seem large in your face. He had that look, and his way of speaking was as if he were acting in fever. He told us the strangest story, when we were in London, of an attempt on his life. I could not for the life of me decide if it was true or a ... fever dream of sorts.'

'And Mary has caught his madness,' Isabel said. 'But still I do not understand. How can they elope? He is already married.'

'Quite,' said Christy, 'and there is more. His wife is with child.'

'Still?' said Isabel, stupidly. 'But it is an age since you were in London and you said she was some months forward then.'

'No, no,' Christy said. 'I mean, she is with child *again*. Their daughter was born last year. Ianthe, they called her. Now his wife is some months forward again.' Only then did she redden, realising that Isabel might not relish talk of childbearing.

'Don't worry yourself, Christy,' Isabel said. 'I hope I may be with child again myself some day and it cheers me to hear of other women's success. Although I pity this Shelley woman. It would be dreadful to be so abandoned. But did they not try to recover her? Mary, I mean.'

'Of course,' Christy said. 'Her stepmother went after them. They'd taken her stepsister Claire along too.'

'Did she find them?'

'Yes, and she attempted to bring Mary and Claire home, but they would have none of it. It seems poor Mr Godwin collapsed, when he saw her come home without Mary, and for quite some time they were worried he would not recover from the shock.'

'Does David know?' Isabel asked.

'Everyone knows,' Christy said, with a hopeless shrug. 'Mary is quite, quite ruined, and the Clairmont girl with her. And poor Harriet Shelley is ... well, I don't know what she is. Disgraced, I suppose, although I cannot see that the fault is hers. I liked her, you know. She was very beautiful, and she seemed good-humoured.'

'Should I write to her?' Isabel asked. 'Mary, I mean. Perhaps I could reason with her.'

'I don't see how you can,' said Christy. 'Write to her, that is. She is somewhere in France. Whether you could reason with her ... I don't know.'

'There is a lot of port in this jelly,' Isabel said. 'My head is spinning.'

'I don't think,' said Christy, 'that it's the port.'

Over the days that followed, Isabel gradually recovered her strength, and within two weeks was going about her life almost as before, although David would allow her to do no work more arduous than agreeing a sauce for the meat with Mrs Brown. Christy took her leave of them and returned to Dundee, and Isabel was surprised to find her eyes fill as they made their farewells. She blinked the tears away, though, and determined that she should be bright and happy for David and William and Tibby.

12

Isabel thought many times of speaking to David of Mary's situation, but somehow could not find an opening. She skirted near it, once, by asking whether he had heard from William Godwin, but David said no, it had been some time since they had corresponded, and then he began to speak instead of a letter he had received from Isabel's father, so she had no chance to ask more. For David's part, it seemed as though Mary had never existed and Isabel wondered if he felt now as he had when they were newly married – jealous of intrusions into the little world they had created for themselves.

Isabel expected that Mary would write to her, eventually, but no letter ever came, and as Christy had said, Isabel could not very well write to her without any idea of her whereabouts. She had little to write about on her own account in any case, for all that occupied her was domestic – David's dictionary work was now in full flow and she was busy with her own project of getting with child again. The doctor said there was no reason she should not and the only obstacle was David, whose fears for her health at first kept him at a distance. After a week or two of frustration, he went from home on business for a night and Isabel instructed Mrs Brown to move his things back into their room. There, as she had predicted, he did not long withstand temptation.

She said nothing when it happened, telling herself at first that all might go amiss, and then, when the first months had passed safely, that David would be nervous and curtail her activities unnecessarily. She could not bear to sit in idleness, knowing that the dark undertow of fear she carried with her would overwhelm her if she had too much time to think. Aside from some episodes of sickness early on, she felt quite herself, and so she worked on quietly, holding her secret to her even as the year turned and the first small stirrings within her gave way to definite pokes and proddings that made her shift and turn in her chair.

She knew this could not last forever, of course, and one morning in late February, when she woke to the odd silence of snow outside, and David already up and dressing, she turned her head and said, 'I have something to tell you.'

'Have you now?' said David comfortably, sitting down on the bed beside her. 'I wondered when you would think to take me into your confidence.'

'You knew!' said Isabel.

'I did,' said David. 'Though there were times I thought the babe would be here already before you said a word.'

'I thought you would not be pleased,' said Isabel.

'Of course I'm pleased,' said David. 'But a bit afeared also.'

'I think that all will be well,' said Isabel, feeling oddly certain it was true. 'How long have you known?'

'A while,' said David. 'Some months ago I suspected, and lately I have been sure. But you have been very coy with me, wife. I was sure you would tell me on your birthday, but that was more than two weeks ago, and you said not a word.'

'Months?' Isabel was surprised. 'I thought myself quite inscrutable then, and there was certainly nothing to be seen, I was thinner even than before. How on earth did you know?'

'Something in your eyes,' he said. 'You seemed to look inward, as though you were listening to something only you could hear. Sometimes you looked right at me and did not see me.' Then he laughed and pinched her cheek. 'And the nipples of your breasts are darker, I have been studiously avoiding noticing. When shall it be, do you think, if all goes well?'

'June,' said Isabel. 'Or thereabouts. But I cannot sit idle until then, David.'

'I would not ask it of you,' David said, and his face grew solemn again as he rested his hand over the gentle swell of her belly. 'Only please have a care, Isabel. I would not lose either of you.'

So like that David knew, and then the servants knew, and Isabel found that now she was permitted to do as she pleased, she no longer wished to do very much at all. The winter dragged on into March in snow and hailstorms, and no visitors could come or go, or even letters make it through the drifts, so it seemed that the whole world had drawn in around her and her little family and the new life she carried.

When, at last, it thawed, a great pile of letters was delivered to the house. There were three from Father, and David read them to Isabel that evening as she sat by the fire. Just then, there came a knock at the door and Mrs Brown came in to say there was a man come to take delivery of a parcel and David cast Father's letter down and went to see to the matter. Idly, Isabel took the letter up and read on, a great much of it dull and then a part she could not make out at all. She read it over again, and then she found she could not sit, and took to pacing before the fire, pulling her shawl tighter about her.

'What does this mean?' she demanded, as David walked back into the room. 'Father says Mary is much upset at a letter from you. I do not understand.'

David seemed at a loss for a moment, and then he saw the letter on the chair.

'I will explain,' he said. 'Only sit down, Isabel. You are very pale.'

'No,' said Isabel. 'What have you done?'

David took her by the shoulders and tried to make her sit, but she slapped him away.

He held his hands out to her, palms first, and stepped back, as one might retreat from a nervous horse. 'Very well,' he said, his mouth a firm line. 'If you will not sit, I will not speak more of this tonight.'

Isabel held his gaze for a moment and then, defeated, she sat. After a brief pause, David sat in the chair beside her.

'It seems they returned to England in September,' he said. 'They planned to stay in Europe, but they ran out of money and turned back. Mary wrote to you at the end of October. I kept the letter for some weeks, trying to decide what to do. By the end of that time, I knew – that is, I was sure you were … as you are. And so I did not give you the letter. I thought the risk to your peace of mind too great. And so I wrote to her to say that your connection must end.'

'That was not your judgement to make,' said Isabel. 'It was my letter. You had no right not to tell me.'

'It is my child you carry,' said David, 'and yet you chose to say nothing of it to me. I do not think that was your judgement to make, but you made it, and I have never rebuked you for it.'

'That's different,' said Isabel, although she felt herself well caught.

'I don't think so,' said David. 'You did not tell me, I think, because you feared that all would come to grief again, and you would not worry me. You chose to bear the burden alone. And I chose not to tell you because I shared your fears. I too feared you might lose the child, and I would have done anything not to have you upset. So I kept the burden of knowledge to myself. I have buried two wives, Isabel. I dread the loss of you, and it had almost come to pass not three months before.'

'I am well,' said Isabel. 'You could have waited until you saw I was well.'

'I will not count you well again,' said David, 'until the child is born, and you are recovered. Only then will I sleep easily in my bed once more.'

'The two cases are different, though,' Isabel insisted. 'There is no choice in one, it will go on as it goes. There is a choice in the other. I might have wished to write.'

'Isabel!' said David. He had never spoken sharply to her before and her eyes filled at the shock of it. He saw, and rubbed an impatient hand over his face. 'I'm sorry,' he said. 'I did not mean to bark at you. But you must know you cannot continue to correspond with Mary Godwin. She is living with this man out of wedlock.'

'She is my friend,' said Isabel.

'And you are my wife,' said David. 'And have we not suffered enough for it already? None of your father's church will so much as look at us.'

'I do not care about that,' said Isabel.

'No?' said David. 'The effects on your father distress me, and I worry that you are pained by the fact your old friends do not write, or visit.'

'No,' said Isabel. 'It is enough for me to be here with you.' It was true, she thought. Or perhaps some of her pride in their isolation was a means of showing she did not care.

David stood and held out his hand to her. 'Come,' he said. 'We will have no more cross words tonight. We will say goodnight to the children, and then we will take ourselves to bed.'

Isabel thought of asking if he still had Mary's letter, but she was too tired to prolong the quarrel. She took his hand and let him help her to her feet.

* * *

A few weeks later, they woke to the oddest sky Isabel had ever seen. It was full day, and overcast, but there was a yellow pall over all, not the mellow golden warmth of the sun but a peculiar mustard tint to the clouds. She stood by the window wondering while David washed at the jug.

'Is all well?' he asked.

'The sky is strange,' said Isabel. 'And I feel odd.'

He was at her side in an instant and caught her as she swayed. He put her back to bed and sent a serving man for the doctor. While they waited, he told her there had been a great volcanic eruption in the South Seas and strange skies had been reported all across the country.

'Like a portent,' said Isabel. 'But I feel well again now. It was a moment's faintness, is all.'

'I don't believe in portents,' David said sternly. 'And nor should you.'

'We saw the star called Vesta,' said Isabel. 'Was that not a portent of our marriage?'

David's lips twitched. 'No,' he said. 'It was an excuse to stand close to you. I am a rational being, Isabel. You will not convince me to look for signs in the heavens.'

'You called me a goddess,' said Isabel. 'That night we saw Vesta.'

David smiled down at her. 'Did I? Well, that only goes to show how unreliable such notions are. Vesta is a virgin goddess. Quite an unfitting soubriquet for a wanton like you.'

'I was virginal then,' said Isabel.

'Still,' said David. 'I think then you were more a sprite. Or a pixie.'

The doctor arrived soon after, and looked at Isabel's hands and feet and then poked and pressed at her, and asked about sensations in her body, how often she urinated, and whether she was sure of her last courses, and then he frowned and poked some more. David stood with his back to them while this was going on, staring out of the window at the yellow sky.

When the doctor was done he said he saw no particular reason for worry, the child was positioned well as far as he could tell and moving exactly as it should. He thought there might be a slight disturbance in Isabel's humours, but there was nothing to do about that, just to keep to a good diet and gentle exercise, only he recommended she not walk too far from the house and always have her husband's arm, or someone else's, to protect against falling if there was any faintness. He spoke a little more to David outside the room, and when David returned, Isabel wanted to know what he had said. David said only that the child might be more advanced than they thought.

'But that cannot be so,' said Isabel. 'You know that as well as I. You kept yourself from me very studiously.'

'Of course,' said David, 'but to be on the safe side he recommends having a midwife on hand a little before you reckon your time will be, and he says to fetch him as soon as things begin.'

They found a woman locally who was well regarded and she came up to see Isabel a time or two over the last weeks. By this point, Isabel was so uncomfortable that she wished they were all right and she had mistaken her dates, but Mrs Duncan the midwife agreed with her and said that the child was perfectly comfortable where it was, and she thought simply that it was large. Isabel panicked a bit at that, but the woman said not to fuss, she had seen many women smaller than Isabel delivered perfectly safely of babies bigger than she thought this one would be.

Unbeknown to Isabel, David had written something of their worries to Father, and Father wrote that he would come at the beginning of June and stay until Isabel was well again. He would travel with John, who could take William and Tibby home to Christy on the return journey and in that way they would not have to worry about their care.

Isabel was horrified, but David said perhaps it was a good thing. After all, Isabel's mother had done the thing seven times perfectly safely. He teased her about her interest in portents and said that Father might prove a lucky charm.

Father arrived as promised with John, who was to spend the night before leaving with William and Tibby in the morning. Father embraced Isabel as best he could past the great globe of her belly, and said he had feared he would find her ill, but she looked stronger than he did himself.

'Always the bonniest of my daughters,' he said. 'And what do you think you have in there, Bel? Another Isabella, or a Thomas for me?'

Isabel laughed and said two Isabellas were quite enough for any house – Isabella was also Tibby's proper name. If it were not a Thomas, then they would need another name.

They sat in the parlour and took tea, which Tibby insisted on serving them, naming each recipient as she carried the cup unsteadily across. 'Papa,' she said. 'Grandfather.' 'Mama.'

Isabel found her eyes were wet.

'I thought she called you Isabel,' Father said.

'Her real name is Isabel*la*,' Tibby told him. 'And Papa's real name is David. I don't know your real name.'

'William Thomas,' said Father, solemnly.

'That is two names,' said Tibby.

'Yes,' said Father. 'Some people have two names. My father was William too, you see, and so I needed another name so everyone would know who was being talked of.'

'My name is Isabella too,' Tibby said. 'But it doesn't matter because her other name is Mama.'

'I see,' said Father. He finished his tea and placed the cup on the table. 'Do you think you could pass me the parcel by the door, Tibby? I think there is a gift in it for you, and one for William, and one for Mama.'

Tibby bolted over and returned with the parcel, climbing on Father's knee as he cut the string with his pocketknife. Inside was a cloth doll for Tibby, a set of toy soldiers for William, and two paper-wrapped packages for Isabella. The first of these was from Christy, and contained a journal, a book of verse and a baby's crochet jacket in pale buttery yellow. The second was from Father, a soft tartan shawl and a brooch of clear crystal.

'It reminded me of that dress of your mother's,' Father said. 'And the old women say crystal is good for healing.'

David rolled his eyes and Father laughed. 'Whether or no there is any reason to it, it is a bonny thing in its own right.'

Tears came easily to Isabel in these days, and she was moved by her gifts, but thankfully Tibby saved her dissolving again by taking the little jacket for her 'baby'.

'It's not for you,' David said, rescuing it from her grasp. 'It's Mama's.'

Tibby snorted. 'It will never fit her,' she said. 'She is far too fat.'

David got up and marched the children out, leaving Isabel and Father to their laughter.

The morning, by contrast, was wretched, Tibby crying and clinging to Isabel's legs as David did his best to untangle her and get her into the carriage. William was braver but his lip still trembled. Father told them Aunt Christy was waiting at the ferry, excited to take them home to The Cottage and make a whole trunk of clothes for Tibby's new 'baby' and take William out on the pony, but Tibby would not be consoled, howling and thumping David's back as he carried her up the steps. Her little tear-stained face stared back at them as the carriage drove off, and Isabel had to blink yet more tears from her own eyes.

'Now, now,' Father said, taking her hand and tucking it under his arm. 'They'll have a marvellous time with Christy. And they'll be back before you know it, although they'll be wildly jealous, Isabel. David, when Robert was born, I brought Isabella upstairs to meet her new brother and can you guess what she did? She pulled back her hand and slapped him, right across his little face.'

'She has not much improved with keeping,' David said. 'But perhaps you would take her a turn about the garden for me? I have some letters to write.'

It was pleasant, rambling slowly in the garden with Father talking of this and that, and Isabel found she had a sudden burst of energy and said they should walk part way up the hill behind the house. In the end, they walked all the way, and stopped for a short while at the top so Isabel could sit and catch her breath. Father stood beside her, looking up into the yellow sky.

'May I ask you to do some things for me, Father, if there should be need of it?' Isabel asked. 'David will not let me speak of my wishes should ... well, should I not survive the coming ordeal.'

'It is natural, I think,' said Father, 'to wish not to tempt fate.'

Isabel laughed. 'He insists he has no beliefs in portents or bad luck, so he would not like to hear you say it, but I think you are right. For me ... It would ease my mind to say a few things, and then I may forget them.'

'Very well,' said Father, 'although I can make no undertakings for David. What would you have me know?'

'If I should die,' Isabel said, 'I would wish to lie beside Mother, in Dundee. I would wish Christy to have Mother's diamond bracelet, the one she always wanted, and Mary Godwin to have the pearl necklace you gave me that is the match of hers. All else is for Tibby. And I would have you all know that I have loved you all very well.'

'Och, Bel,' said Father. 'We know that. So, is that all? Are you lighter now for the telling of it?'

'Perhaps,' said Isabel. 'But still very heavy indeed. I think I will need your help to rise from the ground.' He bent to raise her, but suddenly she found herself unable to breathe, the core of her overcome with pain and pressure. 'Wait,' she said, 'not yet. A moment. Just a moment.'

Father sat down beside her and put a hand to her back. 'You might have said something sooner, lass,' he said. 'We wouldn't have walked so far from the house. I don't fancy my chances of carrying you home.'

13

Isabel woke to bright daylight from a drugged sleep. For a few seconds she felt calm, and in no pain, and she lay as still as she could to prolong the sensation. David was slumped in a chair by the bed asleep, and beyond him was the empty cradle.

Perhaps her waking changed the quality of the silence, for just then David stirred and opened his eyes. He started when he saw her watching him.

'You're awake,' he said.

She tried to ask how long she had been asleep, but her voice would not come. She put a heavy hand to her throat, feeling it swollen and sore.

'Here,' David said. He rose and poured a glass of water, helping her sit up to drink it. As her weight fell on her poor hurt parts, she whimpered in pain.

'Brave lass,' he said. 'Can you manage a minute while I call for Mrs Duncan?'

Isabel nodded, and he lay her back against the pillows and left the room. While he was gone, she ran her hands down her body, finding her belly loose and empty and her breasts full and warm and sore.

'What time is it?' she asked in a whisper when he returned.

'It's midday,' he said. 'I heard the clock in the parlour chime the hour. Midday on Thursday.'

'Thursday?' Her pains had begun on Tuesday.

'You had a long and difficult time,' David said. 'Do you remember it?'

Isabel shook her head. 'No. At least, it's all a muddle. I remember the first part. But then the doctor gave me laudanum, I think.'

Just then Mrs Duncan came into the room with a swaddled bundle in her arms.

'You must not be upset,' David said. 'Her face is marked from your travail, but do not let that fear you.'

Isabel began to try to scramble up and away as the midwife advanced on her with her bundle.

'No,' she said, 'I don't want to see it. I don't want to see it. Please don't make me. David, keep her away!'

David looked at the midwife in horror. 'What's wrong with her? Has she lost her mind?'

'Lord, she thinks the bairnie dead!' said the midwife. 'Whisht, lass, whisht! All's well – see for yourself!' And she thrust Isabel's baby into her arms, though she almost dropped it, all her muscles seemed turned to water and David had to leap up to catch the baby and hold them both steady. He had turned grey in the face, poor David, and then he had to put up with the midwife redding him up for not telling Isabel at once that all was well.

All the while Isabel was gazing at the poor bruised face of her daughter and weeping, though whether in relief or sorrow or something else entirely, she could not have said. At last the midwife had finished her scolding of David and the baby set up a wailing so Isabel's tears came faster still.

'Is she hurt?' she asked. 'Does she cry for pain?'

The midwife laughed. 'Lord, no,' she said. 'She's hungry. Come, lass, we'll put her to suck and your man can take himself off and drink a glass of brandy for his nerves, they're fairly shot through.'

David did as he was told, grumbling that Isabel had seen the baby before she slept, they all said so, so how was he to know she had forgotten? The midwife shook her head, but she said it was true, Isabel had seen the mite once they got her free, and breathing, but she had been in and out of consciousness between the pain and the laudanum and the tiredness.

They got the baby on the breast then, and it stung, and then it was fine and soothing, almost, and Isabel lay and stared at the child while the midwife told her the doctor had saved them both, he had guided the child out with his instruments, which was why Isabel was so sore.

'Is she big?' Isabel asked. 'I can't tell.'

'Big enough,' said the midwife, 'and awkwardly positioned. You screamed like you were being torn limb from limb, lass, and I suppose it felt like it too. Your man and your father took themselves outside but they said they could still hear you screaming.'

'Poor Father,' Isabel said. 'Poor David.'

'Poor them nothing!' the midwife said. 'Your father has been a fine help,' she went on. 'We despaired of you for a time, and while we were busy upstairs, he sat at the kitchen fire with your wee lass on his knee, feeding her boiled water from a spoon. He's got a fine touch with wee ones, and a fine voice for the lullabies.'

'Can you sew cushions?' Isabel asked. 'And can ye sew sheets? And can ye sing ballooloo when the bairn greets? He always sang that to us.'

'Aye,' said the midwife, 'he sang that one. Now let's get the wee soul winded and you can sleep some more. Nothing like it for the healing.'

'My father gave me a crystal,' Isabel said. 'To keep me safe. I know it's silly, but I would like it close.'

'It is close, lass,' the midwife said. 'It's in the bairnie's wrappings. Now, sleep.'

Father stayed above ten days more, maintaining he wished to help, but really, Isabel knew, wishing to see the danger of childbed fever past. There were times she was almost sorry she had lived, being so very sore that the normal workings of her body pained her so that she cried out. Mrs Duncan stayed too, to help her with such matters, so they were fairly overrun.

They called the baby Catherine, and in time, the dreadful bruising of her face subsided and she proved to favour Isabel in her looks, with the same dark hair and brows and rosy mouth.

Isabel, too, healed from her ordeal, although she chafed at the time it took and worried incessantly that she was damaged beyond repair. Between her own discomfort and Catherine's needs, it seemed that night had turned to day, and even when Catherine settled between her periods of endless wakefulness or hunger – Mrs Duncan said these were normal, all babies had them – she found she could not sleep and instead lay awake while every form of catastrophe that might befall them spooled out in her mind. This left her so tired in the day that she could not muster the energy to do anything; it seemed that any plan she tried to fix on slipped from her mind like smoke. In the end, she stopped getting up at all and instead she stayed in bed where the pillow was always wet with the tears that seemed to fall from her eyes unceasingly.

As autumn wore on, Mrs Duncan was needed elsewhere and David said he would send for Christy – he had business matters to attend to and could not countenance leaving Isabel alone while she was in such a way. Christy came at Christmas and her face when she beheld Isabel was a picture, but she cooed over Catherine and said immediately that she would stay with her while Isabel had a bath, that would make her feel better, and then Christy would go down and order a nourishing meal, they would both benefit from that.

Dully, Isabel did as she was told, sitting in the water thinking of nothing. At last she realised the water was cold and she got out, to find the baby asleep. Christy sat Isabel in front of the fire in a clean nightgown and took a comb to the tangles of her hair. They ate together by the fire, and then Isabel fed Catherine and Christy changed her, and then Christy changed into her nightgown and took the warming pan to the bed while Isabel settled Catherine. Christy slept in with Isabel, and before she blew out her candle, she rubbed milk of roses into her own and Isabel's hands and feet. In the night, she brought Catherine to Isabel for feeding, and put her back in the cradle after.

The next day, Christy insisted Isabel rise and dress after breakfast and come downstairs. Isabel protested that she was too tired but Christy would not be moved. The baby was put out of doors in a wicker basket, well wrapped up, and Christy sat Isabel in an easy chair in the drawing room while she unpacked a great trunk she had brought with her. This, it transpired, contained a project she called her 'filagree'. This seemed to consist of thousands of little pieces of paper, glue and brushes, wicked little knives, and a vast sheaf of paper covered in sketches and lists. There were various trays and plates, a little spirit boiler for the glue, varnish, and sheets and sheets of gold hammered as fine as tissue. All of this Christy arranged on the table in the drawing room.

Over the next weeks, they settled into a routine. If David was at home, he worked in his study, but for many weeks he was away. Christy rose in the morning, helped ready the baby for the day, and then took herself to the drawing room where she stationed herself at the table and worked on the filagree, rolling and folding hundreds of little paper pieces to different tightnesses and shapes, over and over again, following the directions on her papers. Once each was glued into its final form, she sliced it into fine slivers so the trays were gradually covered with dozens and dozens of little shapes formed of paper cut as thin as wire.

At first Isabel watched, and then she found the little curls of paper fascinated her, so she wanted to make some herself. Christy showed her what to do, and she found it oddly satisfying, trying to make sure the folds and quills of each piece were all exactly of a size so that Christy could cut identical slices to fill her tray. The repetition was soothing, and at the end of every morning or afternoon, she could see that she had achieved something, although the pattern danced before her eyes. It was easier, too, to speak to Christy while their hands were busy and their eyes bent to their work.

'The doctor said there should be no more children,' she said one day as she glued a paper into the shape of a peacock feather. 'I always imagined I would have a large family. Like our own at home.'

Christy carefully laid a sliver of paper onto her tray. 'I am sorry to hear that,' she said. 'But you have William, and Tibby, and Catherine. That is a wonderful family to care for.'

'Yes,' said Isabel. 'Just not the family I imagined. And David will be often away, so I will be alone. No one calls, not since my marriage.'

'It is the same at The Cottage,' said Christy, and Isabel felt her cheeks redden. She had not really thought before of the effect of her excommunication on her sister.

'Do you see Agnes still?' Isabel asked.

'No,' said Christy, running her fingers over a row of paper curls. 'None of our old friends from the Meeting House.'

'I'm sorry,' said Isabel.

'I have made my peace with it,' said Christy. 'I have my work, and I write to those friends I do have, and we are making new acquaintances all the time. And really, I think this is what you must do too, Isabel. You must make your peace with what has happened. So, there will be no more children. Well, you must appreciate those you do have, and find ways of fulfilling yourself. You were always reading at home. And you and Mary wrote. And you painted and drew.'

'Yes,' said Isabel, feeling wretched. 'I wish I could be still like you, Christy.'

'Well,' said Christy. 'I learned some years ago that my life would not be exactly as I wished. I was angry for a spell, but now I have had time to make my peace with it.'

'Angry with me?' Isabel said.

'Yes,' said Christy. 'As we said once before. But that is long past now.'

'Do you write to London?' Isabel asked.

'Yes,' said Christy. 'In fact, you may see what Hannah has sent me.' She wiped her hands on a cloth and picked up a cardboard folder, from which she took a little parcel of tissue paper.

Isabel took the parcel and unfolded it, revealing a little oval portrait of a young woman with dark auburn hair and a sweet, solemn face.

'It's lovely,' she said, 'but I don't recognise her. Who is it?'

'Fanny Imlay,' Christy said. 'Mary's half-sister. I am making this all for her. It is to be a jewellery casket, and the little watercolour will be inset in the lid. When all of my paper pieces are glued into place, and stained, it will look very fine.'

'What is she like?' Isabel asked, wondering that all Christy's work should be for this unknown person. 'Mary said she was dull and morose.'

Christy laughed. 'Mary is not kind,' she said. 'I did not find Fanny dull. She is shy, I think.' A smile played around her lips. 'I think she and I have much in common. We have both suffered from having a very vivacious and pretty sister. Two, in Fanny's case. Perhaps we seem morose by comparison.'

'We have just talked of our fallings out in the past, and I will not rise to your bait now,' Isabel said, surprised to find she was amused. Then she bit her lip. 'Have you heard anything of Mary?'

'Only that she has borne Shelley two children,' Christy said. 'A girl last February came early, and did not live. And this January, she has had a boy. William. Did you not hear?'

'No,' said Isabel, feeling chilled. 'I imagine David knows but he would not have told me of it. We do not speak of Mary. He thinks it would upset me.'

'It upsets me,' said Christy, 'to think of any woman throwing herself on the mercy of such a man. And poor Harriet Shelley, quite abandoned.'

'You said she was with child when ... when her husband left her,' said Isabel. 'Harriet, I mean. Does her child live?'

'Yes,' said Christy. 'She has a son of more than a year, and her daughter must be two, rising three now. She lives with her parents, I think. But I cannot think how she is to go on. She cannot go out in any kind of society while her husband openly lives with another woman, who bears him more children still.'

Isabel rested her head on the back of the chair and closed her eyes. 'I do not know how to feel about Mary,' she said.

'No,' said Christy. 'I think she is lost to us, Isabel. Unless something changes, but I cannot see how it can. How is any of this to be made right?'

'Do you think,' said Isabel, with a sudden impulse, 'that we might bring William and Tibby home now? They will be quite the strangers. They have been gone above six months.'

'Yes,' said Christy. 'And Father wrote to me last week to say that the frame for my box for Fanny has been delivered. That can come in the carriage with them.'

To their surprise Father, too, came in the carriage with the children, and spent a pleasant two days with them. William seemed to be half a head taller and just as cheerful as ever. They had expected Tibby to be strange with them, but she proved as adaptable as always, no less talkative than before. She had brought home her cloth doll and an incredible wardrobe she and Christy had begun and Cookie had helped her continue at The Cottage. Isabel was required to admire all of the tiny garments while Father bounced Catherine on his knee and told Isabel she was too thin and must eat more. He had brought the box for Fanny Imlay, and once he had left again, Christy began the painstaking work of glueing her paper curls onto the sides. William and Tibby wanted to help, but Isabel said no, and instead they began to make their own glued pictures of butterflies decorated with lentils and caraway seeds and dried peas and peppercorns and juniper berries. Isabel managed the glue in its boiler, and the children stuck their treasures into it, and in this way they were all busy and became comfortable with each other again.

At last the butterfly pictures were finished, and Christy had completed her own glueing, and then she said she would gild her work. This involved spreading glue on the patterns and allowing it to seize up, before floating a sheet of hammered gold onto the glue and brushing it, so that it only stuck to the pattern of the paper. For a week, great flakes floated in the air like golden snowflakes and William and Tibby laughed and tried to catch them as they clustered on their eyelashes and in their hair. Tibby wanted to gild her butterfly, too, but Christy said no, it was handsome enough as it was, and so instead Tibby and William and Isabel gathered the last of the dry winter leaves from the garden and gilded those and hung them by the fireplace where they would shimmer and shine in the light of the flames. Isabel was reminded of poor Margaret's hands in her last days, and then, possessed of a strange notion, she dabbed cooling glue on the children's cheeks and stuck gold to them and said they should go outside and wave to their mama in Heaven; she could look down through the stars and see her children shining below.

As Isabel fed Catherine that night, she saw that the baby's cheeks were dusted with gold, and indeed gold glinted here and there on her own breast. She laughed at the thought she might gild herself on purpose, below her clothes, to surprise David, and was surprised to feel a rush of longing course through her. She had not thought she would be excited by bedding ever again.

They went on quite comfortably in this way, William and Tibby settling back in as though they had never been away. William was almost of an age to begin his schooling properly, and they spent a deal of time with a battledore David had gifted him, practising his letters.

When David returned, he said he was pleased to see Isabel looking so well, and so comely, and suggested that they take a trip together late in the summer, to London. Isabel's tummy fluttered with excitement but she fretted about leaving Catherine. David said she could come too, and Christy said it was a fine plan, and moreover that Isabel could do Christy a great favour by delivering her jewellery box to Fanny Imlay in person. The box was finished now, with its exquisite gilding all complete and the little watercolour portrait inset on the lid, and very fine it looked too. Christy said she had not wanted to entrust it to the mail, and so it would be very convenient if David and Isabel were to take it.

And so, in this way, it seemed all was arranged and she and David were to travel south. *To Mary*, she could not help but think, although she knew that Christy was right and Mary was lost to them, no matter that her hair was in Isabel's travelling case and her letters in David's study and her slim form and laughing voice still haunted Isabel's dreams.

14

They left in August, a most beautiful season for travelling. The weather was fine, the heather bloomed on the high slopes and the parks and rigs were lush with growth, promising a plentiful harvest to come.

Isabel set out on the journey almost like a new bride, with new trunks, and a new wardrobe, and not one but two women to help her – William and Tibby's little nursemaid, who had the care of Catherine, and a girl they had engaged to serve as a lady's maid for the duration of the trip. The nursemaid travelled with them in the coach, where she whispered to Catherine but otherwise sat in shy silence, and the lady's maid rode on the high seat with the coachman, proud to show off the new carriage costumes they had purchased for her.

Christy had laughed at Isabel, taking two such inexperienced maids with her to London, but Isabel hadn't risen to the bait; she knew she needed to build her confidence again after so long in exile in Fife.

'It's as well you have me to mind you,' said Christy. 'I'll wager you have not thought of calling cards, have you?'

Isabel had blushed and said she hadn't.

'Here,' said Christy, handing her a parcel wrapped in tissue. 'I ordered them some weeks ago. I didn't think you would have any, and I'm sure you will see the Godwins and others in London. Their circle is not so very smart, but all the women have such things.'

Isabel opened the tissue to discover a box of visiting cards in the name of Mrs David Booth. They were beautifully calligraphed, and the paper was embossed with lines radiating out from the name to the edges, like the rays of the sun.

'Thank you,' Isabel said, her eyes misting. 'It is really very kind of you.'

Christy looked pleased. 'Do you have a case for them?' she asked.

'No,' said Isabel. 'I never had cards before. I was so young when I lived at home, and I haven't called on anyone since my marriage.'

'I will give you mine,' said Christy, and Isabel saw how pleased she was to feel more experienced in worldly matters. Silently, she reached out and took Christy's hand, squeezing it hard.

'You will have a marvellous time,' Christy said. 'But if ... If you do see Mary, Isabel ... well. Have a care.'

In truth, Mary was rarely from Isabel's mind on the journey south. They stayed some nights in Edinburgh, where David met with printers and publishers in the day, and in the evenings they went to the Assembly Rooms and to hear a speaker in a coffee house near Parliament Square, and to a concert held by the Musical Society in a beautiful oval room painted in a pale blue-green like a duck egg. Isabel had never lived in such a large place or moved in such varied society, and she began to see how Mary's and her own experiences had differed.

Their next stop was in the Border country, where David had agreed to attend to some business for Father in the wool mills. While he discharged his commission, Isabel travelled about viewing the ruins of the great Abbey churches and the peel towers and fortified houses that seemed dotted everywhere among the hills and waters, built by long-ago landowners in hope of saving their cattle and their gold from the attentions of the reivers. She thought of Lady G– and realised she had written nothing since Catherine's birth – no, not since before she had lost the first child, more than two years ago now.

They travelled south past stretches of water that seemed vast to Isabel, but paled by comparison with the great sights of the Lake country which they reached a few days later. They had almost three weeks in the Lakes, marvelling at the rugged mountains and fells, and the still and sulky waters that transformed in the occasional blink of sun into calm mirrors of the glories all around. Again Mary seemed everywhere, never more so than on their pilgrimage to see Dove Cottage, where Wordsworth and his sister had lived plain and thought high, and Wordsworth had written his poem of the daffodils. They saw Rydal Mount, where the great man now lived, and David said that Godwin's friendship would be enough of a recommendation to visit, but Isabel trembled so to think of disturbing him, that David laughed at her and agreed they should drive on by.

After the Lakes, they saw Derbyshire, spending another whole week visiting the great house at Chatsworth, the Old and New Halls at Hardwick, and Haddon Hall, a most picturesque place with rooms in the style of England's old Queen Elizabeth, and glorious gardens and terraces. Isabel thought once more of Lady G–, who might have visited such a place in its heyday, and plotted and schemed in its dark-panelled rooms and long corridors of rough local stone. They discovered that a curious mineral was mined in the region, banded with purple and yellow and called Blue John by the locals, and David bought Isabel a glorious, lidded urn made of the stuff, with gilded mounts. The innkeeper offered to arrange for them to visit the mine if they wished, but David took one look at Isabel's face and declined the invitation.

After Derbyshire, they stopped only through necessity and were in London in four days more. David had taken lodgings in a part of the city called Bloomsbury, which was a green and elegant place of garden squares and wide avenues, where fashionable people took the air or visited the coffee houses and the great museum of antiquities and natural history of which the city was deeply proud.

For her part, Isabel was glad at first to be done with inns and sleeping in a house she could call her own, if only for a few weeks. Soon, though, she found herself discomfited. She had not kept company for a long time, and the thought of beginning again feared her a little. She had an excuse to stay at home, because Catherine, who had been a ray of sunshine on the journey south, was starting teeth that pained her and suddenly she became hot and restless and cross. Between tending to Catherine, resting herself and organising laundry and other domestic matters, Isabel was able to avoid setting a foot across the door for more than ten days after they arrived. But she knew she could not put it off forever, she had Fanny's box to deliver if nothing else, and so she had the maid hang and steam her gowns, and tried to calm her nerves.

David, by contrast, was out and about every day. He had much business to discharge in the first instance, but eventually he had sufficient leisure to go to the Godwins to arrange for Isabel to call on Fanny. He returned very disappointed, saying they had seemed all at sixes and sevens. Godwin had been from home and Mrs Godwin had been very out of sorts, saying that Fanny had left and gone to her aunts on her late mother's side. She had not even invited him into the house, instead calling down to him from her perch halfway up a ladder in the shop.

'The aunts are in Dublin, are they not?' Isabel said, half disappointed and half relieved. 'If Fanny is gone to Dublin, there is no way I may call on her. Poor Christy will be sorry.'

'Do not distress yourself,' David said. 'I saw Charles Lamb this morning, and he said his sister has seen Mrs Bishop. She is staying, it seems, in Newington Green.'

'Mrs Bishop?' Isabel asked.

'Eliza Wollstonecraft,' David said. 'Fanny and Mary's mother's younger sister. She was married, you know. It was a scandal at the time. She had a child, and she was much distressed thereafter. Mary Wollstonecraft believed the cause of her distress to be cruelty on the part of her husband, and so she removed Eliza from his house. She left behind her child. It was a scandal at the time.'

Isabel shuddered, thinking how distressed she, too, had been after the birth of Catherine. Would she have abandoned all had Christy come to remove her from David's house? She could not say for sure she would not.

'So she is Mrs Bishop,' David continued. 'And she is staying in the house of her friends the Birches. They were great friends of the Wollstonecrafts. I could not understand what Mrs Godwin meant when she said Fanny had gone to her aunts. How could she have travelled to Dublin alone? But this makes sense of it. She must have gone to Mrs Bishop in Newington Green.'

'Well, then,' said Isabel. 'I should go there. I won't try to carry the box with me, but I can call, and speak with Fanny, and we can arrange to have the box delivered later.'

Isabel found the cards Christy had given her, and the next day she dressed herself in one of her new morning dresses with Father's rock crystal brooch, a short jacket and her tartan wrap, and took herself off to Newington Green. It was further outside the city than she had expected, and she worried that the hour for calling would pass, but at last they arrived, about two hours after noon.

The house was in a terrace, built of brick and very higgledy-piggledy. Isabel knocked on the door and inquired for the lady of the house, and for Mrs Bishop and Miss Imlay, saying she was a friend of the Godwin family. The maid said her mistress was from home, and she did not know Miss Imlay, but she thought Mrs Bishop might be at home, and she asked if Isabel would be pleased to send up her name. Isabel handed over her card and the maid showed her to the drawing room, bobbed a nervous curtsey, and scurried upstairs.

In a few moments, the maid returned and said that Mrs Bishop would be down directly. While she waited, Isabel amused herself by looking around the room, which was pleasantly if not very fashionably furnished, with many engravings of literary and political personages in pressed brass frames.

Ten minutes or so passed, and then the door opened and a woman of middle height and no great elegance of dress entered and said she was Mrs Bishop. She wore spectacles perched on her nose, fingerless mittens and a great shawl, although the day was mild and Isabel was warm in her jacket and scarf.

'How do you do, Mrs Booth?' she said. 'I do not believe we have met before.'

'No,' said Isabel. 'And I think, if you have heard of me at all, that it will be under my own name, before I married. I was Isabel Baxter, then. Your niece Mary Godwin stayed with my family in Dundee in the year '12, and then again for almost a year from June of the year '13. We were good friends.'

'Ah,' said Mrs Bishop, although Isabel thought there was some reticence in her manner. It would be natural, perhaps, that Mrs Bishop should wish to avoid discussion of Mary, given the difficulty of Mary's present situation, and so Isabel decided to turn the conversation to Fanny instead.

'I come at my sister Christina's request,' she said. 'Christina is my elder sister, and she has travelled to London twice, meeting your niece Fanny on both occasions. She wished me to visit Fanny to arrange delivery of a gift Christina has made for her in remembrance of their friendship.'

'How lovely,' said Mrs Bishop. 'Françoise – Fanny – lives with her stepfather Godwin and his wife in Holborn. I can give you the address if you do not have it.'

'Oh,' said Isabel. 'My husband called there yesterday. Mrs Godwin said that Fanny had left for Ireland, to join your sister at her school.'

Mrs Bishop raised her hand to her throat. 'To join Everina at Dublin?' she said. 'She ... I have not heard of it.'

The woman seemed perturbed, and Isabel reddened.

'I am sorry if we have misunderstood,' she said. 'Mrs Godwin said Fanny had gone to her aunts, and then we heard that you were here, and so we thought she must plan to travel back with you. It was wrong of us to assume, and I am very sorry to intrude on your privacy under a misapprehension.'

'No, no, please do not make yourself uneasy,' said Mrs Bishop, her own cheeks colouring. 'It is only ... It is very strange. Fanny did wish to join us, last year, but we do not have room. We wrote to say so, and she wrote back that she understood. And now ... well, I have not long arrived here, and I have had a letter from Everina already. She says nothing of Fanny. And I cannot think Fanny would try to travel to Dublin by herself. It is at least a week's travel, and the crossing is not easy.'

By the time she had finished speaking, the woman seemed quite distressed, and Isabel rushed to reassure her. 'I am sure we have misunderstood,' she said. 'I had the message second-hand, by my husband. Mrs Godwin must have been talking of some future hope of Fanny's.'

Mrs Bishop still frowned, but then she remembered herself and made a clear effort to play hostess. 'You said you are visiting from Scotland?' she said. 'Have you been to London before?'

'No,' said Isabel, 'although my father, and my sister, and my husband have been here often. You were born and bred here, I think? How long do you stay on this visit?'

'Eight weeks or so,' said Mrs Bishop. 'My hostess is an old friend of my family's. She helped my sisters set up their first school, here in Newington Green. That was many years ago now.'

'It was very impressive,' said Isabel. 'To make such provision for daughters, when no one else thought to.'

'My sister Mary wrote on the education of women,' Mrs Bishop said. 'Have you read any of her works?'

'Oh yes,' said Isabel. 'I believe I have read everything she ever wrote. I admire her greatly.'

Mrs Bishop looked gratified. 'Before you travel back to town,' she said, 'you should drive past the chapel on the north side of the Green. It is where my sister worshipped. She found Dr Price's ideas most inspiring. The building itself is very stark, but I suppose it is merely a vessel to serve a purpose. It need not be beautiful for that.'

'Indeed,' said Isabel, thinking that the description fitted Eliza Bishop too. She had a look of Mary Wollstonecraft, but faded, somehow, as though one of the engravings Isabel had seen of the dead sister had been hung in direct sunlight for many years. But when she spoke with passion, a light shone within her so it did not matter. Isabel wanted to touch her hand, as if to ask for her blessing, but she was too shy. Instead, she stood and smiled.

'I have kept you too long,' she said. The twenty minutes etiquette permitted for a call were almost past.

'I have not offered you any refreshment,' Mrs Bishop fretted.

'I have no need for refreshment,' Isabel said. 'It has been such a pleasure to meet you.'

The little maid was summonsed, and Isabel began to curtsey, but Mrs Bishop stopped her, taking her hand firmly and shaking it.

'If you . . .' she began, but then she stopped and began again. 'My niece Mary had a difficult start in life, losing her mother and then feeling that she had lost her father too, on his remarriage. She does not find it . . . easy to make friends. I am glad she had you. I . . . I hope she may find her way back to . . . She is not an easy girl and . . . Well.' She shook her head. 'I must stop rambling. Don't forget to visit the chapel. And if ever you visit Dublin, please do not hesitate to call on us at the school.'

'I will be sure to do so,' said Isabel, and pressed Mrs Bishop's hand. The maid showed her to the door and Mrs Bishop stood behind her watching until Isabel was seated in the carriage. She raised a hand in farewell.

The driver took Isabel to the chapel – it was closed so she could not have gone in even if she had wished – and then back into town, where she found David at home before her.

'How was Eliza?' he asked.

'Very kind,' Isabel said. 'But Fanny is not there. There must have been some misunderstanding.'

'Really?' David said. 'But I saw Mrs Godwin again today. I asked whether Fanny was with her aunt in London, and she said she was. She said they are to travel back to Dublin without delay.'

'Mrs Bishop plans to spend some weeks in London,' said Isabel. 'Eight weeks, I think she said. She has only just arrived, and she has had a letter from her sister in Dublin. Fanny is not there.'

David frowned. 'It is all most odd.'

'Christy said once that Mrs Godwin told a strange untruth to Father,' Isabel said. 'Did he tell you of it? They called and asked to see Mr Godwin – I think there was some arrangement whereby they were to visit. Mrs Godwin would not let them in, and she told them a dreadful tale about Mr Godwin burning his legs and being so badly hurt that he could receive no one. But the next day, who did they see but Mr Godwin himself, walking down the street, showing no sign of any injury. Christy said that Father thought perhaps they had quarrelled and so Mrs Godwin had sought to keep Father and Christy out of the house.'

'How strange,' said David. 'I wonder where Godwin has gone now. Mrs Godwin says he is not at home, and the servants say likewise.'

'Hopefully he will return soon,' Isabel said. 'As I say, perhaps it is all a misunderstanding, and Fanny has gone somewhere with him.'

'Perhaps,' said David, but he didn't sound convinced.

As it happened, David did not see Godwin again on that journey. He called again more than once, but it seemed Godwin was still from home, and at no point was David admitted to the house. By the second half of October, they knew they could no longer delay their journey north without risking bad weather on the road. Isabel knew it pained David to go without seeing his friend, and she was saddened to have failed in her own commission for Christy. The beautiful box was loaded into the carriage in its packing case with the other trunks and chests, and they returned north a rather more subdued and uneasy party than had departed from Dundee three months before.

15

Isabel had a sudden vision of Eliza Bishop as she stood at the grand, black-painted door waiting for her knock to be answered. She had never seen the woman again after that day when she had called at Newington Green, and she realised now with a flush of shame that she had not thought of her in the seven years since. Had she returned to Dublin and taken up her teaching once more? When had she known that Fanny Imlay had died by her own hand, in an inn at Swansea – indeed was already dead when David was knocking on the Godwins' door in search of her?

Isabel had not heard of the terrible thing for many months, it seemed the Godwins had done their very best to hush it up, but at long last David had had word of it and had told her. Isabel had felt quite faint when she heard, and now she wondered how the Wollstonecraft sisters had taken the news, poor Fanny's own aunts, who had refused her a place with them when she had asked. What had kind, resourceful Mrs Bishop been going to say to Isabel of Mary, before she stopped herself?

Her mind was still full of these unseasonable musings, when the door swung open and she saw Mary herself standing before her, waiting behind a maid who bobbed a curtsey and stepped aside so Isabel might walk ahead of her into the house.

Thankfully Isabel's feet seemed to work by themselves, as she felt quite incapable of instructing them, and she glided forward, staring at Mary, who stared back, standing ramrod straight and unnaturally still. She was dressed all in black, relieved only by a clutch of blue and yellow silk pansies pinned at her breast. She did not smile, but at last it seemed the spell that held them broke, and she reached out and took Isabel's hands in her own cold ones.

'Come into the parlour,' she said. 'And we will call for tea.'

Her hair was darker than it had been, and her face was thinner.

'You are still in mourning,' Isabel said.

Mary stroked the sheeny silk of her skirt. 'I had planned to lay it aside before now,' she said. 'But I have been editing my late husband's work, and I found a poem he wrote not long before he drowned. It says, "The silk-worm in the dark green mulberry leaves; His winding sheet and cradle ever weaves; No net of words in garish colours wrought; To catch the idle buzzers of the day— But a soft cell, where when that fades away; Memory may clothe in wings my living name." When I read that, I thought I might wear my widow's weeds a little longer.'

She has not changed, Isabel thought. *It has been nine years, and she has been halfway across the world, and she has not really changed.* Out loud, she was horrified to hear herself say, 'There is a story that you have kept your husband's heart.'

'Yes,' said Mary, although she did not elaborate as to whether she meant *yes*, such a story existed or *yes*, it was true. 'We would have liked that, in our youth, would we not?' she said. 'It would be quite at home in the sort of story we wrote, or one of Nanny Chisolm's. Is she still alive?'

'No,' said Isabel. 'She died last year. She was almost ninety.'

'And you live in London now?' Mary said.

'Yes,' said Isabel. 'With my father, in Hackney. Although I travel soon to The Cottage. It is sold, you know, and soon it will be cleared. This will be my last visit. It will be strange to bid it farewell.'

'We were sorry for your father's money troubles,' Mary said.

'It seemed he could never quite get out of the bit,' Isabel said. 'The sailcloth trade suffered greatly when the war ended, of course. He weathered the difficult conditions as best he could for years, but then his bank collapsed.'

'My father has been glad to have him here in London,' said Mary. 'He has been an excellent friend, and championed my father against many attacks. Do you think you will all stay here forever?'

'I don't know,' Isabel said. 'It is very convenient for business, and Father and David come alive in the salons and lectures. But we miss Scotland.' A sudden memory came to her, and she smiled. 'Remember poor Margaret, Mary? Barely clinging to life as she told you that London might be wonderful, but the air was not healthy?'

'Yes,' said Mary, and she laughed, looking like her younger self for a moment. *'Why don't you take the girls to see some of the country yourself, David?'* she parroted, in a voice uncannily like Margaret's.

Isabel laughed too, and then she shuddered. 'The mine,' she said. 'That awful mine.'

Mary shook her head. '"Poor" Margaret certainly had us stitched up that day,' she said. 'Did she haunt you? You used to believe in the second sight.'

'No,' Isabel said. 'Or ... once or twice I thought I saw her, making her way out of a room in that awful way she had, holding on to the furniture, like an infant who has not yet become steady on its feet. But it was my imagination only. I no longer believe the dead walk.'

'Perhaps not,' Mary said, 'but I think there are different kinds of ghosts. I wonder if the new inhabitants of Barns of Woodside see our initials on that window, and wonder who we were. Do you know who lives there now?'

'No,' said Isabel. 'The house was leased, and the lease was sold. We were gone before they took possession. I do not miss it. How is your boy?'

Mary smiled, a real smile it seemed to Isabel, so she saw the others for what they were, a polite fiction of pleasure only. 'He is well,' she said, 'and strong. I fancy he resembles my father in the face, but Shelley's sister says he is like her brother as a child.'

'Are you on good terms with the Shelleys?' Isabel asked. 'I understood your husband and his father did not always see eye to eye.'

'Sir Timothy supports me with an allowance,' Mary said. 'Not for me, you understand, but for little Percy Florence. It is a very mean sum indeed, but even then he holds it over me, tells me it will stop should I publish any reminiscences of Shelley. Still, I have the poems to put in order, and that is no small task. I would have no time for a biography at the moment in any case, and one day Sir Timothy will be with us no longer and then we shall see. And you? You have a girl, I think?'

'Yes,' said Isabel. 'Catherine. And of course we have William and Tibby, Margaret's son and daughter. They are quite big children now. You have stepchildren, too, I believe. Do you see them?'

Mary glared. 'No,' she snapped. 'How could I? They live in the country with their aunt and Shelley was not allowed to see them. The family of his first wife went to court to keep them from him. Such pain they caused him.'

'I suppose their pain was also great,' said Isabel. 'Such a sorry business all round.'

'I don't know what you mean,' said Mary.

'She drowned herself, did she not, your husband's first wife?' said Isabel. 'Oh, I know she was buried under some other name, but various of your father's friends told David the true particulars. The thought of that, a woman with child so desperate as to take her own life, it has haunted me rather. Many nights I could not sleep for thinking of her.'

'I am surprised to hear it,' Mary said. Isabel had forgotten how her nostrils took on a white cast when she was cross but wished not to show it. 'After all, you did not know her.'

'Christy knew her a little,' said Isabel. 'They met when you brought Christy to London. She was very upset to hear of her death.'

'Her death was no business of mine or Shelley's,' said Mary. 'Shelley understood she had fallen into prostitution and in that way met a lover. Some say he was an officer, and others a groom – whatever he was, he abandoned her. Her parents opened the doors of their home to her, but she was with child by the lover and she did not think they would tolerate it. She left their house before her belly showed and took rooms in a lodging house in town. Quite a good part of town. The name she was buried under was the one she went by there.'

'And she died in the Serpentine?'

'Yes,' said Mary. 'The balance of her mind was clearly disturbed. It was the fault of the man who had fathered her infant and abandoned her, and her own want of honour.'

Isabel stared. 'Want of honour? Were you not living with her husband at the time? And surely she was abandoned by her husband first?'

'No,' said Mary. 'The marriage was troubled long before he met me.'

'Ah,' said Isabel. 'I must have misunderstood. I thought you knew them before their daughter was born. There was a son after that, was there not? David seemed to think the unborn child also fathered by her – your – husband.'

'I do not think so,' Mary said. 'He had no wish to get another child on her. She would not feed her own children from her body. One of many wounds that drained the love from the marriage.'

'Whether she fed her children from her breast or not,' Isabel said, appalled, 'she was their mother. And a daughter. Her parents must have felt the loss most keenly. And her sister.'

'Do not speak to me of those people,' Mary said. 'I cannot think of their behaviour to Shelley without abhorrence. Harriet herself sought to harm him, even in death. She left a letter, you know, on the table with her rent money, full of recriminations. She went into the river wearing his ring so all would know she died his wife, and blame him. He said it had long been a trick of hers, to threaten self-destruction. He called it a theme with her. He never wished to marry her, you know, knew himself not in love, but she threatened to open her veins and die before him on the floor. He said there were times it seemed as if his living body had been yoked to a dead one.'

'It seems—' Isabel began, but Mary cut her off.

'My own mother suffered from an excess of passion and considered harming herself,' she said. 'But her passions were sincere. Harriet Westbrook was a silly girl. She came to my father's house, did you know that? Shouting and carrying on and demanding they should refuse us entry. Shelley did not abandon her, she had an allowance from his family's funds, and her own father paid her twice as much again. She had far more money than we did, she wrung us dry, and still she sent her creditors to our door any time we set foot in England. I walked out in shoes with holes in the soles and struggled to buy medicine for my poor sick child, and all the while the receipts poured in for bonnets and ribbons and new frocks for Harriet. And Shelley did write and ask her to join us in Switzerland. She could have given birth to her child there, with us. Charles, I mean. Her second child. Shelley's heir.'

'I don't understand,' Isabel said. 'Do you mean that he asked her to live with him while he lived with you?'

'Yes,' said Mary. 'You would not believe the letter her sister sent in response. Oh, do not look at me so, Isabel. Harriet Westbrook married Shelley knowing his mind. She was not a clever woman. Pretty, and pleasant enough in her way, but her intellect was limited. He believed in many types of love, and he did not support monogamy. She thought him a genius but she never really understood him.'

'I wonder ...' Isabel said. 'Are *words* rather different than *deeds*? I think your father was opposed to marriage as an institution, but I understand he was displeased when you eloped with a married man, and there is nothing wrong with his intellect.' She had a sudden desire to laugh, but she thought it best to refrain.

Mary exhaled sharply. 'My father and I are long reconciled, as you well know. He and my stepmother stood witness at my marriage.'

'You asked me to join you, too, on your travels,' said Isabel. 'Did you mean for me to be a lover for your husband?'

'Of course not,' Mary snapped. 'I thought of nothing but my love for you. Did we not kindle one another's minds, Isabel? Were you not the spark that set my imagination aflame? I thought we would grow together as writers, as thinkers.

I thought you would make great work with us. But you preferred to embrace the very form of marriage that Shelley hated. A bind that kept you at home, and silent. Your husband making choices for you.' Her voice dropped, and she spoke to her hands. 'Could you not have written to me yourself, Isabel? Did I have to hear it from your husband?'

'I did write,' said Isabel.

'Oh, yes,' said Mary. 'Cold letters one might write to a stranger. And then you sent your husband to tell me you would not come to Italy.'

Isabel closed her eyes, remembering the day Mary's invitation had arrived, enclosed within a letter from Father, who was with them at Marlow and seemingly enchanted by Percy Shelley and his circle.

'You have opened my letters!' Isabel had stormed at David, caught yet again in the familiar grooves of their disagreements over Mary, going round and round and round until she felt heartily sick of the whole business. 'Why may I not open my own letters? What can you fear from it?'

'I fear that Mary might work her charms on you,' he had said. 'You were her creature before; I would not have you so again. She is conniving and manipulative. She has already got your father as tightly wound round her little finger as ever he was in Dundee.'

As if she could hear Isabel's thoughts, Mary said, 'I spoke with your father, you know, when he visited me at Marlow, back in the year '17. The poor man arrived on the very day my little Clara was born. My second Clara, that was, Clara Everina. He came back again, later, and we spoke much of you. He said David kept you from writing to me. And that you half regretted your marriage. Was that true?'

'David did not stop me writing to you,' Isabel said. 'I knew for myself that I could not write to you as long as you were unwed. And then . . . I could not see how to write to you when all you did was ask me to go away with you. As for my marriage . . . well. That has been a thing that has given me both pleasure and pain. We were very young, Mary, when we made the choices that shaped our lives.'

'It hurt me that you sent him to tell me you would not come,' Mary said, and Isabel saw that it was true, the wound was clear in her eyes, still unhealed after all of the long years between.

'David asked me to accompany him,' Isabel said, 'when he visited you in London and told you I would not come to Italy. And I refused. He was angry with me. He saw how he would be cast as the villain of the piece.'

'Were you afraid you would agree to come, had you seen me?' Mary said. 'Was that why you refused?'

'No,' Isabel said. 'I refused because I was angry with David. He thought you would enchant me, and I would run away with you. By demanding I come, I thought he was testing me, and I saw no reason why I should have to prove myself to him. To anyone.'

'And did you really never wish you had come?' Mary asked. 'Afterwards, I mean?'

'No,' said Isabel. 'I was married, with a child.'

'I told you to bring her!' Mary said.

'You told me to bring Catherine,' Isabel said, 'but you forgot about William and Tibby. David said this was a flaw in your family. He said you saw such children as a hindrance. As your father and stepmother saw Fanny.'

'My father took Fanny in as his own,' said Mary. 'And she loved him as her father.'

Isabel knew that David held quite a different view on the matter. He remained on friendly terms with Godwin, but he had never trusted the man again after he realised how he had been lied to in London, how the Godwins had dissembled with their stories of aunts and Dublin. Something in him had hardened, upon discovering his hero was flawed. 'He was prodigiously *proud* of his kindness to Fanny as an infant,' he had ranted. 'But then he discovered Mary to be such a prodigy – his own child, who could have predicted it? – and *someone* had to make up the parcels and serve behind the counter of the shop. Little wonder poor Fanny felt there was no place for her in the world.'

'Can you really tell me that none of it plays on your mind, Mary?' she asked now. 'Not just Fanny – also your stepsister Clairmont?'

'Claire is well enough,' said Mary. 'When Shelley died, I paid for her to go to her brother in Vienna and now she plans to travel onwards to Russia and find employment as a governess.'

'Did your husband love her?' Isabel asked. 'They say he did.'

'Your husband accused him of it,' Mary said. 'I was hard pressed not to laugh. If ever there was a pot calling a kettle black, it was your husband accusing Shelley of loving two sisters.' She smiled a smile that was not in any way kind.

'She must have been gravely saddened by the loss of her little girl,' Isabel said, refusing to let Mary rattle her.

'Yes,' said Mary, raising her hands so the palms were upwards, 'as I was gravely saddened by the loss of my two Claras, and my first son William. And my husband's foster daughter Elena. Children die, Isabel, I wish it were not so but so it is. Sometimes others are born in their place, sometimes not. I almost died with a miscarriage myself in Italy, I would have, had Shelley not put me in a bath of ice to stop the blood. And as for

Fanny ... I do not know why she did what she did. My father would not let us go to the place after, or attend her funeral. For a long time I did not know how she had done it. I do not feel I really knew her at all, now. Three years between is a big difference when one is fourteen and one's sister seventeen.' She looked at her hands as though she did not recognise them, and folded them again in her lap.

'We did sow sorrow, Mary,' Isabel said. 'For ourselves and others.'

Mary's eyes flashed. 'I understand the sorrows you think I have sown,' she said. 'What were yours?'

'I too lost a child,' Isabel said. 'My first. As you say, though, children die. But before that, I was unkind to Margaret, and she died. Oh, I might not have been able to save her, but I cannot pretend I even tried. All I have is the cold comfort of knowing that I was with her at the last. And I was unkind to Christy, whose behaviour to me was always faultless, aside from her great crime of accompanying you to London, which was no crime at all and not of her doing in any case. And I was angry with you, because I loved you, and I thought you had rejected me.'

'Rejected you? I never rejected you,' said Mary. 'We have just been talking of how I wanted you to be with me.'

'Not then,' Isabel said. 'It seemed to me that you rejected me when you returned to Dundee after your visit home to London. First I thought you had replaced me with Hannah, and then I thought you had designs on my father. It was only later that I understood your husband had come into your life in London. Perhaps you did not love him, then, but you had started to think of marriage, not friendship. You told me once, you know, that you were like your mother, and she could only have one great love at a time.'

'I remember,' said Mary, pale again, and calm. 'Perhaps I am like that still. But I don't think I will ever love a man again. My son is enough for me now.'

'I am glad,' said Isabel. 'I have not known the love of men to give the joy I once thought it would. My own marriage has placed three great burdens on me.' She counted on her fingers. 'First there was shame. We were cast out from our church, pointed at and spoken about for breaking the rules we lived by. Then there was loneliness. I went from all the bustle of home and Dundee to be alone in Fife with David and the children, and no one came near us, or wrote, because we had been excommunicated. The third burden has been resentment. My husband resented me because I let you all paint him an ogre, a dreadful bully who wished to deny me the chance to see Italy, and your friendship, and I resented him for it, and you for helping sow the seeds of the whole mess as I saw it. There are times these burdens weigh upon me until my whole life seems a succession of weary hours and silence and solitude, and my husband not my friend. Perhaps that is why I think now of Harriet Shelley, and your poor sister Fanny. I can see how it must have been for them, and I pity them.'

'Harriet did haunt Shelley,' Mary confessed. 'At first he said he bore no guilt but later, whenever he was melancholy, he would say he was thinking of her. I hated her for it. I do not think I could say this to anyone but you.' She picked up her teacup and drank.

'I hated you, for a time,' said Isabel. 'I remembered only your sins. Taking my mother's dress, and telling Christy I had read her letter, and then speaking of my marriage with my father when he visited you at Marlow.' She smiled at the look on Mary's face. 'Of course I knew you had spoken to Father of me. It was very obvious. I knew you could not accept that I had chosen not to write to you. There had to be an explanation beyond the obvious. And of course I understand that he agreed with you that David was an ogre and my marriage made in error. Surely you remember that Father always wishes to please. It makes him most agreeable, and not a little malleable, and he was always vulnerable to your charms.'

Mary laughed then. 'True,' she said. 'For my part, I was always jealous of that easy bond you had as a family. And also for my part, I hated you. When you would not write to me, or see me.'

'I did read your book,' said Isabel. '*Frankenstein*, I mean. I read it when it was first published. I know it did not bear your name, but your father sent it to mine.'

'Did he read it also?' Mary asked. 'Your father?'

Isabel smiled. 'He did. He takes great credit for it. He believes that much of it arises from the time you spent with us. Our journeys in Scotland and his ships' journeys to Archangel. It is a great source of pride with him.'

'You made up perhaps a third of my early readers, then,' said Mary. 'Almost no one read it until Mr Peake staged his play at the Opera House. I went with my papa. We were both very surprised to discover I was famous.'

'Did you like the play?'

'Yes. I think Peake understood the book. The Creature had no name – in the programme, he was indicated by two dashes only. I thought that very clever. Did you like it? The book, I mean.'

'Yes,' Isabel said. 'I have read it many times. I think it a wonder.'

'Thank you,' said Mary. 'It is like my son; it is what I have taken from the time of my marriage. I could not have written it without the losses I endured. My boy William, and my baby girls.'

Mary excused herself, then, to use the privy, and Isabel looked at her bag on the floor by her feet. In it she had an envelope with a lock of Mary's hair, and another with three sheets of paper, written all over in Mary's hand. She had found these under the lining paper of the desk drawer in the room she and Mary had shared, the night before they left the house at Newburgh forever. It had seemed that she was guided directly to the place by some unseen hand. She had sat there in the cold room, on the bare mattress of the bed, and read. It was a story of Lady G– as a young woman, suffering an assault by an older man. Isabel knew at once that these were the pages Mary had written on the night of the mine visit. She read on, finding that Mary had given Lady G– a child, born from the assault, that had come too early and had died.

Isabel had sat for a long time when she was finished reading, and then she had folded the sheets and placed them under the velvet cushion in the base of her jewellery casket, where they had remained ever since. She understood their potential to harm Mary, and part of her reason for coming today was to see them safely back in her keeping. Mary could choose to destroy them if she wished.

Mary came back in and settled herself in her chair with a wan smile.

'Did you have a baby before?' Isabel asked. 'When you were with us in Dundee, I thought …'

Mary's face froze. 'I don't know what you are talking about,' she said. 'I have welcomed one man into my bed, and one man only. And that man was my husband.'

It does not follow that one must welcome a man into one's bed to have a baby, Isabel thought, *and your husband was not your husband when you welcomed him to your bed, either*. But she said nothing of that. 'I brought something to give you,' she said instead, lifting her bag onto her knee. Before she could open it, though, Mary covered her hand with her own.

'It has been good to see you, Isabel,' she said. 'But I am afraid I suffer from megrims, and I feel one coming on. Keep your treasures for another day, when we can meet again and imagine ourselves back in the garden of The Cottage.' She stood, looking very pale, and reached out as though to place her hand on Isabel's cheek, stopping short and placing the hand to her own breast.

'I am sorry,' she said, and she was gone.

Isabel waited while the little serving girl fetched her wrap, and then she walked out into the street. For a while she wandered aimlessly, coming quite by accident to Hyde Park. She was tempted to walk to the Serpentine to pay her respects to poor Harriet Shelley, but then she thought it too morbid. Instead, she turned and walked to St Paul's, finding a toyman's stall in the yard there and buying gifts for the children, a little library of miniature books for Catherine and a card game for William, and an elegant doll for Tibby to dress; she was cunning with her needle. She wondered if Harriet Shelley had missed her children, at the last. They must have been with her parents, or in the country with the relatives Mary had mentioned. She hoped Mary's son would survive, and thrive – he was still only four, and she knew the boy William had died at three, so it was not a given. She said a brief prayer for him, and turned back east.

Isabel journeyed north the next week, and by the time she arrived at The Cottage, Mary had written to her friend Leigh Hunt to tell – selectively of course – of the meeting with Isabel. Then it was everywhere, so brother Robert heard it and brought the tale when he came to help with the last of the packing.

'She told Leigh Hunt that she found you disturbed in your reason,' he said, pacing up and down on the dark patch on the floor where the hearthrug had been. 'She is saying it upset her greatly. She claims she would not have met you had it not been for your childhood affection.'

'She always was a storyteller,' said Isabel. 'And the heroine of her own story moreover. Sit, Robert, you will wear out the floor!'

'It's a damned cheek,' said Robert, but he sat. 'What was really said, Bel?'

But Isabel would not tell him. Instead, she teased him about his love for Mary.

'I think I had a lucky escape,' said Robert.

'Perhaps Mary would have done better married to you,' said Isabel. 'I do not think she is very happy now.'

'She is a celebrated author, though,' said Robert. 'I do not think she would have been so, had she married me.'

They turned to talking of happier things then, and Robert left reassured that Isabel was not distressed by the slander. She waved him off in his carriage and returned to the drawing room where the children were at play. They had set upon the treasures from their mama's bag with great joy, and while William read to Catherine from her books, Tibby began to pull out scraps of silk and lace from the rag bag to design a dress for her doll. Watching her, Isabel was taken by a curious fancy. Begging the loan of scissors and needle, she took the Lady G– pages from her travelling bag and climbed the stairs. There, she took Madame Pretender from the packing case where she lay, and carefully removed the underdress from below her gown. Measuring the petticoat panels against the pages, she carefully trimmed them to size and tacked them along the hems. Once she was done, she re-dressed the doll and stroked a finger down her nose where she always thought she could feel a roughness in the paint. Perhaps she had been dropped at some point in the past, or perhaps other women had run their fingers down her nose, just so, in the hundreds of years since she was first made. Isabel liked to think that was what had happened, and that in this way her fingers touched their own, the doll a silent companion to them all.

She placed the doll in a packing box bound for Isabel's own home in London, beside her finely carved chair, and the doll gazed upwards, smiling her enigmatic smile.

'You have kept many secrets, I think,' she said to the doll. 'You can keep one more. And if – one day – you share it, I hope it will be with a kind reader.'

Epilogue

2025

THE HEAT OF THE JUNE day assailed Rebecca Francis as she climbed out of her Mini in the car park of the industrial estate outside Reading and made her way into the auction house to finalise preparations for the two-day specialist sale. Inside, it was blessedly cool, and she fetched a pair of white handling gloves, a scalpel, and plastic trays of various sizes to corral the lots that had arrived since her last visit. An assistant brought up the latest consignments, and looking over the paperwork, Rebecca saw that the third box was the one she had been waiting for with particular excitement. The assistant had already cut the tape and she scooped out polystyrene packing chips until she could free the contents – two wooden boxes originally made for whisky or wine, a baby- or doll-sized chair wrapped into a lumpy parcel of bubble wrap and tape, an old-fashioned document folder tied with string, and a letter addressed to her by hand.

Rebecca opened the smaller box first, delaying for now the pleasure of the larger. It revealed a small, late eighteenth- or early nineteenth-century wooden doll, in what she would list in its description as 'play-worn' condition. Its original wooden forearms and legs were gone, replaced by a small owner, or perhaps their parent, with stuffed cloth versions that gave the doll's body a sweetly comical plumpness under its frock. These repairs had clearly been made not long after the doll itself, the limbs constructed from the same early glazed cotton as the doll's frock, which was in the Regency style and wouldn't have looked out of place on an Austen heroine in a TV adaptation. The doll's original sparse wig was more or less complete and she had a little bonnet and a narrow ribbon around her neck. Her face was in good condition, with its dotted eyebrows, pupilless black enamel eyes and painted cheeks and lips. Under black light, Rebecca could see that there had been some minor restoration – it was common for the plaster layer on these dolls to 'pop' as the wood contracted and expanded underneath – but it was minimal and well done, a long time ago by the look of the paint.

Standing a little under a foot high, she wasn't the rarest, this little doll, although desirable enough with her early clothes and largely untouched paintwork. The absence of her original arms and legs was an issue, of course, but offset somewhat by the obviously early date of the replacements. Plenty of collectors would value a sense of connection with the little girl who had loved her so long ago, and Rebecca anticipated that she would fetch twelve hundred hammer price, possibly more. The market was strong for early woodens, and there were no signs of interest dropping off as their scarce stocks diminished ever further.

Once the little doll was safely stowed in a tray with her bonnet – luckily the cotton wool that had padded her in her box had not been bleached or otherwise treated with the sort of chemicals that attack organic materials – Rebecca turned to the letter again.

I enclose the items discussed on the phone, it read, *being an early C19th wooden doll in poor condition, and a Stuart doll with a chair I believe to be made for it, in extremely fine condition aside from two or three old wormholes in the chair. You ask for as much provenance as I can provide and I therefore enclose a number of photocopies of family wills in which the older doll is mentioned. It has been with us, as you will see, from the late C19th and was willed to me by my mother, and to my mother by her aunt, who had it in turn from a great-aunt of her own. That great-aunt put down in writing [enclosed] that the two dolls – the smaller is not mentioned thereafter in our family papers being thought, I imagine, to be of little value – were a gift to her from a friend, a Mrs Gardiner, who had no children of her own, and no nieces to leave them to. She had had the dolls from her aunt, a Mrs Booth née Baxter, whose family had been gifted the larger in the late 1700s. The gift was made to a valued servant, it seems, by the descendants of the original owners, a family of Girondists, who prior to the Revolution had been adherents of the Young Pretender during his exile in France. The family understood that the doll had been displayed at Holyrood Palace during the reign of Charles II or James VII and II, alongside a gentleman doll with which it formed a pair, and which was thereafter gifted to another family among the Stuart faithful. It was not a fashionable possession in Revolutionary France, but too good to destroy, and so back to Scotland it was dispatched.*

My mother never played with the dolls and neither did her aunt, as the larger doll was both understood to be a treasure, and sufficiently forbidding of countenance that children were not drawn to her. I have no idea whether she was ever handled by my great-great-aunt in her youth; certainly in later years she was kept from the light in a wall cupboard in a spare bedroom, along with the little doll who was always fancifully called her 'lady-in-waiting'. The grand doll was called 'Madame Pretender'. My mother had her on my aunt's death, and finding she reeked of mothballs, banished her to a cabinet in the dining room, which we never used. For my part, I was always more than half terrified of her and when I inherited her, I stuffed her in a box inside a trunk and put her in the attic. I kept the little doll out in my sewing room, and she greatly charmed visiting children, but you will be pleased to hear I didn't let them touch her but only make copies – after a fashion – from clothes pegs.

My husband and I are now at that stage of life where a smaller property appeals and my son and his wife live what they term a minimalistic lifestyle and have no interest in antique dolls. I send them, therefore, to you with such paperwork as I can gather. I have sought not to disturb them, for fear of damaging their clothes which seem to me in rather wonderful condition for their age, only rather faded.

One thing that may be of interest – by repute the Booths, who had the dolls before our family, were somehow connected to the philosopher William Godwin, father of the writer Mary Shelley. Not a familial link, as I understand it, but one of friendship.

Yours sincerely
Margery Kinniburgh

Rebecca opened the document folder and deposited its contents in another tray for later perusal, and then she turned to the lumpy bubble-wrapped parcel, carefully cutting the tape and lifting the wrapping away to reveal a perfect miniature of a Jacobean armchair. The frame was carved entirely in wood with a cane seat and back panel. The top rail had a crown in the centre and a cherub on both sides. The uprights were twisted, with a caryatid figure at each terminal, and the arms terminated in the heads of snakes. It was entirely regal, dated exactly as the provenance would imply, and would certainly not look out of place at the Palace of Holyroodhouse.

Then, at last, all that remained was the larger wooden box. With a thrill of excitement, she slid back the lid, first revealing an underskirt, palest blue in colour and fringed in metal brocade, then an overskirt trimmed with a different trim of the same manufacture. The lid slid back further and she saw carved wooden hands in kid leather gloves, sleeves spilling fine frothy lace, a tiny waist, tight bodice parting over it to reveal a stomacher made from yet more cloth of precious metal – it might be gold or tarnished silver – and then Rebecca closed her eyes and pulled the lid right off. Opening them again, she saw she was perfect, better than she could have imagined, her carved wooden face with its sardonic smile, all creamy paintwork present and correct as though done yesterday and not three hundred years ago and more. Her eyes were not glass, she was too early for that, but painted, with short, straight lashes and thin, arched brows. She had bright pink flushes sponged low on the cheeks and great black beauty spots dotted on her cheekbones and nose and forehead, the height of fashion when she was made. Rebecca would run the blacklight over her later but she knew it would show nothing, all was so clearly original. She had a wig of real human hair, pale blonde and sewn in tiny, sausage-like curls on her forehead, and over that she wore a great tall headdress of the type called a fontange, a fan of stiffened, folded gauze that made her a head taller again, with fine lace lappets hanging down her back. Holding her breath, Rebecca lifted her out and turned her over to see her gown retained more of its colour in the back, it had been a deep blue silk, which still glowed here and there among the complex pleats and panels that brought it in close to her waist and belled out the skirt so it appeared almost to have a train.

Rebecca laid the doll in a tray and fished out of her box a small envelope that contained a embroidered dolls' bag on ribbon handles – it looked to be of a one with the doll's clothes – and a miniature folder decorated with moonstones which she hoped might contain a letter, but on inspection was empty, as was the bag. These Rebecca placed in another tray.

A cup of herbal tea was next, to help steady her hands, before she returned to the doll to examine her further. Rebecca was not a conservator and had no intention of undressing her, but she carefully lifted the skirts to examine her legs, which were clad in linen stockings tied at the knee with ribbons, and fabric shoes. Gently she experimented and found the leg joints were good, although she was careful to avoid bending them too far. There were layers of underpinnings beneath the dress, beginning with a shift, a quilted petticoat and an underskirt which seemed to be stiffened inside with paper, densely written upon. She fetched a camera, and a lightbox, and took photographs as best she could without damaging the fragile paper, with a mind to sending the pictures off to a friend who was good with early writing.

Only once this was all done and the dolls safely stowed away, did Rebecca allow herself a moment's triumph. She had never handled a seventeenth-century English wooden – there were only perhaps thirty left in the whole world – and had never expected to sell one, let alone one with provenance in untouched and undamaged original condition. She made another cup of tea and picked up the phone to call Mrs

Kinniburgh and advise that she might expect her dolls to raise a very significant sum indeed.

* * *

The Jacobean doll was the cover star of the auction catalogue and, as anticipated, she caused quite a stir. The writing in her petticoat turned out to be something of a mystery, appearing to be an excerpt from the manuscript of a romance story of the late eighteenth or early nineteenth century, written in one hand, with some crossings-out and overwriting. The catalogue advised that this layer of her clothing was not original, but had been left in situ for her purchaser to retain or dispose of as they saw fit, as part of the doll's history. No mention was made of Godwin, because a family friendship with a famous philosopher a century after the doll's making hardly seemed relevant.

The dolls were sold separately, of course – even closely related collections were routinely split up for sale and this pair had no real connection at all. The little wooden went to a dealer in America, and was promptly dispatched to a restorer to have more appropriate legs and arms carved and fitted. The restorer was newly widowed and surprised himself with his reticence – every time he picked up the doll to detach the fabric legs and arms, he put her down again without touching her. In the end he made an offer to the dealer and the doll became his. He called her Bella and she lived in his workshop where he talked to her, sometimes, when he was at a loss as to how to tackle this task, or that, and oddly it seemed he knew the answer afterwards, and it was always the answer his late husband Bill would have given.

The Jacobean doll was sold with her chair, her bag and her folder. She was expected to go to a museum, but instead went to the wife of a hedge fund manager, also in the United States, whose enormous collection had been assembled with such care and exquisite taste that her home might as well have been a museum. 'Madame Pretender' achieved a record sum for a doll at auction in the UK and was swiftly dispatched to her new home. Although she was never reunited with her original partner – if such a doll ever existed – she looked very well alongside another rare wooden gentleman made in London around the same date by the craftsman whose dolls were known to aficionados as the 'Clapham Series'. A conservator of course undertook some minor work to stabilise her, including the removal of the inappropriate nineteenth-century paper-and-ink lining, which was stored in an archival box and never looked at again.

Author's Note

Poor Creatures is a work of fiction inspired by real-life individuals and events. It is set during a period which is unusual for its lack of documentation of the lives of specific members of a group of otherwise very well documented individuals. It takes some liberties in imagining the events of the undocumented time, and does not always follow in minute detail the documented events around. I hope this is forgivable in a fiction. To give some concrete examples of the ways it disregards the record for the sake of the narrative or the reader's ease: the Baxter daughters Elizabeth and Jessie were at The Cottage for some of Mary's sojourn there; Harriet Shelley called her husband Bysshe, not Percy as she does here; Mary Jane Godwin travelled to Dover with a male escort in pursuit of Percy and Mary, here omitted, and while Harriet and Mary did meet, the dinner in this novel is not based on any of their documented interactions.

Mary Wollstonecraft Shelley née Godwin wrote *Frankenstein* as a young woman of eighteen. We know that it was not her first work but nothing earlier survives, aside from a contested piece of writing called 'Mounseer Nongtongpaw' which she may have adapted from a song, in whole or in part, at the age of ten for her father's *Juvenile Library*. All other letters and writings she had saved from her girlhood were lost as she and Percy Bysshe Shelley ran off together to Europe in 1814.

Recalling her early work in the Preface to the 1831 edition of *Frankenstein*, Mary tells us, 'What I wrote was intended at least for one other eye—my childhood's companion and friend...' This friend may reasonably be identified as Isabel[la] Baxter, the third daughter of the Dundee family with whom Mary stayed for much of 1812–14. The relationship between Isabel and Mary and Isabel's marriage to David Booth have been addressed before in fiction, although I hope this book brings a different twist to the telling. I took as my starting point the meeting between the two women after Shelley's death, in London in 1823. They had not met since 1814, and Mary professed herself distressed by Isabel's state, telling James Henry Leigh Hunt (as relayed here by Robert) that she seemed 'disturbed in her reason'. Although she offered no further detail, Mary's comment has generally been taken at face value. Having some basic knowledge of Mary's life, and moreover having lived in the world myself for a good few years and met a number of people, I was inclined to wonder if there might be another side to the story. This was the starting point of *Poor Creatures*.

It is fashionable today to ask why we don't know a lot about Mary Shelley and blame misogyny for it. I wonder if this is entirely fair. An alternative take might be that the Wollstonecraft-Godwin/Shelley circle (I'll call them the WGSs for ease) were themselves quite invested in destroying and altering records to their own ends. The Godwins were hard up, the Shelleys were not, and in such circumstances it might seem prudent for the poorer family to forget or recast any less savoury episodes in their history. The Godwins had more than most families to brush over.

Biographies of Mary and of Shelley-featuring-Mary have not been entirely absent, and the oldest of these seem to me to follow something of a pattern of taking Mary's word for most things (see Isabel Baxter: mentally ill). For a long time I wondered if it was just me who tired of reading snide assertions that anyone the WGSs/Mary disliked was of 'the second order' or similar, thereby allowing for the dismissal of any of their concerns and an immediate guilty verdict in whatever matter Mary held against them. This reaches some pretty spectacular lows when it comes to actions of Percy Shelley's. Some biographers find his predation on underage girls to be evidence of his having been focused on *intellectual connection* (seriously). As I began reading in earnest, I was relieved to find that Mark Twain had had similar qualms regarding Shelley's 'soiled relations with Godwin's young daughter' and indeed with the Godwin household itself.

Twain writes that Fanny Imlay (Mary Wollstonecraft's first, illegitimate daughter) 'was a sweet and winning girl, but she presently wearied of the Godwin paradise, and poisoned herself'. Twain's essay is an impassioned defence of Harriet Shelley, whose suicide and later traducement is horribly sad. He jogs quickly past Fanny, who poisoned herself with laudanum in Swansea just three months before Harriet died. Rather as there is a theme of taking Mary's side in all things, there's a tendency in the biographies to accept that Fanny simply inherited Mary Wollstonecraft's tendency to depressive episodes and suicidal thoughts, and so killed herself, The End. There's occasionally some speculation that she might have fallen in love with Shelley and been depressed as a result, but that's about it. It seems to me to show an alarming lack of curiosity as to why a girl of not quite twenty might choose to travel two hundred miles from home to end her life in an inn.

I wonder if something – or more than one something – happened to Fanny that traumatised her. I wouldn't put it past Percy to have had one of his intellectual connections with her, and then there are all those other intellectual gentlemen we read of coming to dinner at the Godwins', and then the Godwin children are parcelled off hither and thither all the time, summering here and attending school there, and it's the early nineteenth century, so no one thinks of child safeguarding for an instant.

On this same note, I find it jarring that we know so little of Mary in this era but among the facts that are relayed are that she went through puberty young and had a figure that justified the wearing of stays by the time she travelled to Dundee at age fourteen. I have made an imaginative leap in the book which I think is just as plausible as the idea that Mary had to be sent away from home for a very long time because she had a mystery ailment that might have been shingles or psoriasis or eczema on one of her arms and didn't like her stepmother very much. Such letters as survive from her father to her or about her at this time are distinctly cool, and I couldn't quite work out why that would be the case if she just had something wrong with the skin of her arm and engaged in teenage sulks.

This gives 'my' Mary her (concealed) backstory when she comes to Dundee; the rest of the novel explores what was clearly an intense teenage female friendship that ended with both parties making questionable decisions. As in the novel, it was Mary's elopement that shattered the friendship, but Mary seems to have thought that Isabel would join her in her European travels with Shelley. Isabel's new husband had other ideas and, really, it's hard to blame him for that even if his taste in sisters half his own age and propensity for taking girls down mines against their will are distinct points against him.

Much of the Dundee/Fife action in the novel is pure fiction. For example, beyond that she died, we do not know what happened to Margaret Booth née Baxter. The sort of thoughts I was entertaining about Fanny and Mary's formative years led me to think of unhappiness and then of self-harm and specifically anorexia. Self-starvation was not unknown although little discussed – in just another thirty years or so, the fasting girls would come along, many of whom were members of Nonconformist churches like the Baxters (and Godwin, originally, although he later embraced atheism). That made me think in turn of social contagions affecting teenage girls, and that idea, together with the many gaps and imponderables in the stories of Isabel and Mary, gradually developed into the idea that the girls created a paracosm together, a shared fantasy universe. The most famous of these in literature is perhaps the Brontës' 'Glass Town' and 'Gondal', which were influenced, as it happens, by Mary's work.

Paracosms also play their parts in some extreme scenarios, including the Parker-Hulme murder case of 1950s New Zealand, when two teenage friends killed one of their mothers in hope of eliminating an obstacle to their continuing friendship. The girls had a shared history of ill health, which seems to be linked to paracosm creation (here, Isabel's childhood diphtheria is fictional but whatever the truth of Mary's arm, she certainly had a disrupted upbringing on some sort of health grounds). The Parker-Hulme case inspired the 1994 film *Heavenly Creatures* and, as a result of the publicity attracted, the bestselling writer Anne Perry was revealed to be the grown-up incarnation of Juliet Hulme, one of the two teenage perpetrators. It's a small world, and once upon a time I published some minor works by Anne Perry, who was kind and charming to deal with – she always seemed to be in a spa when we called

– and had by then given pleasure to millions of readers. She died in 2023.

While I hope it is plausibly written, Mary and Isabel's paracosm is fancy, as is the seventeenth-century wooden doll owned by Isabel's late mother which inspires it. The doll is based on the 'Old Pretender' in the collection of the V&A, which originated in the Stuart court at Holyrood. Its lost partner about whom Mrs Kinniburgh writes to the auctioneer has no equivalent in reality, although the roughly contemporaneous 'Lord and Lady Clapham' dolls, also in the V&A, are a pair, and it is not outwith the bounds of probability that there might have been a gentleman Pretender once upon a time (if you ever spot a candidate in a charity shop, please do get in touch). The writing-lined skirt is inspired by a different doll, of a slightly later date, sold at auction in 2024 and whose skirt stiffening turned out to be a broadside about the murderesses Elizabeth and Mary Branch from Taunton, Somerset, who killed a servant in 1740 and swung for it. The little moonstone folder is inspired by one in Liza Antrim's book *Family Dolls' Houses*, which contains a minute German love letter from which Christy's lover borrows a little inspiration.

Margaret Nicholson's attempt on the life of George III with a fruit knife is broadly based on reality, although I imagined her later work stitching in pursuit of abolition (such stitching did indeed happen). While Shelley and his friend Thomas Jefferson Hogg titled their 1812 work 'Posthumous Fragments of Margaret Nicholson', the real Margaret was alive in Bethlehem Hospital ('Bedlam') at the time of publication, and indeed outlived Shelley, dying in 1828.

I had a lot of fun in writing about Mary Jane Godwin née Vial aka 'Clairmont' (as far as I know, Mary never called her 'Mary Jane Vile' and I apologise to both for inventing that bit of childishness). In fact, Mary Jane relates to the only particular on which Mark Twain and I part company. Twain finds it wonderfully hypocritical that 'the colossal six' of Harriet Shelley's sins by the biographers' lights include her desire for a carriage and the fact that her walks with Hogg 'commonly conducted us to some fashionable bonnet-shop'. 'When Shelley ran away with another girl, by-and-by,' Twain writes, 'this girl persuaded him to pour the price of many carriages and many horses down the bottomless well of her father's debts.'

I agree it is hypocritical to find fault with Harriet for spending her husband's money when Mary spent Harriet's husband's money even more lavishly (as well as funds for Godwin, Mary was also partial to carriages and bonnets). I can't, though, quite despise Godwin and Mary Jane for not making money at the book business. There is an old joke – 'How do you make a small fortune in publishing? Start with a large fortune', and even today it remains a rich person's game. Mary Jane and Godwin were not in debt because they didn't publish decent books – *Tales from Shakespeare* is still in print over two hundred years after its first issue and they were the first to publish an English edition of *Swiss Family Robinson*, one of the most popular books of all time. I find Mary Jane interesting in her own right as an early woman publisher, translator and editor. She has, I think, also suffered from the biographers' attentions, that is, she is viewed only as Mary viewed her, and Mary found her an irritant. Perhaps, too, the fact that she valued books for children is a strike against her – the late Martin Amis once suggested writing for young readers was something he'd do only if he'd suffered a brain injury. Among her 'sins', I agree her green spectacles don't sound fetching but she wasn't alone in wearing them and they weren't necessarily an affectation. Samuel Pepys had a pair, believing that the tint would help with eye strain by reducing the contrast between white paper and black text, especially when working by candlelight. This is part of the theory behind tinted overlays for readers with dyslexia or visual perceptive disorders today, although it did nothing for poor Pepys.

Being a novel, this book touches on lots of events without offering a full account of any of the lives within it. For readers interested in the real-life characters, the following offers a brief account.

The Baxters/Booths

The Baxter/Booth families were living in London by the time of Isabel's 1823 meeting with Mary after the collapse of their interests in Dundee. Percy Shelley had understood them to be ruined as early as 1816 but this seems to have been a misapprehension. Isabel and David moved to Bloomsbury after he was appointed superintendent of the publishing branch of the Society for the Diffusion of Useful Knowledge (SDUK) in 1826. Booth continued to write and publish widely, including collaborative work with Godwin and others, and the Booth home played host to many literary greats. Booth continued to scandalise many acquaintances with his irreligious views and Isabel seems to have come to share many of these. The marriage was often troubled – they spent some time apart, they were beset by financial difficulties and Booth's later years were characterised by failing health. They returned to Scotland to live at The Cottages, Balgonie, with Isabel's brother Robert and his wife, later joined by their daughter Catherine, who had married Robert's business partner, and her children. We know much of what we know about the Booths and the Baxters through the *Reminiscences* published by Catherine's son James Stuart, an

MP and reformer, in 1912. Booth worked on his dictionary on and off with significant assistance from Isabel, leaving it unfinished at his death at the age of eighty in 1846.

The friendship between Isabel and Mary continued, although with long periods in abeyance. In the late 1820s there was even discussion of a trip abroad together, but this did not happen. Isabel offered to nurse Mary in her final illness in 1851, and on her deathbed Mary asked her son to pay Isabel an annuity of £50, a request he honoured.

William Thomas Baxter took a second wife twenty years his junior, and he too returned to Scotland, living by Robert at Balgonie until his death in 1842. Christy and her sister Elizabeth were set up in a shop nearby. In old age, Christy gave various interviews about her family and the Godwins, providing more of the little we know of Mary's time in Dundee.

For more, see: *Creatures of Fancy: Mary Shelley in Dundee* by Bannerman, Baxter, Cook and Jarron (Dundee; Abertay Historical Society; 2019).

The Godwins

Percy Bysshe Shelley died without reconciling with his father Sir Timothy, and Mary Wollstonecraft Shelley née Godwin lived in relatively poverty in London for the rest of the Baronet's life, producing editions of her husband's poetry and her own literary work. After her father's death she began a memoir and edition of his correspondence but abandoned the project two years later. She continued to have intense friendships (and possibly romantic relationships) with women, notably Jane Williams, a member of the Shelley circle whose partner drowned with Shelley and who latterly lived with Hogg. She aided numerous friends including Mary Diana Dodds/Walter Sholto Douglas and wife Isabel Robinson, Georgiana Paul and, latterly, Isabel. She turned down a proposal from actor John Howard Payne and possibly another from Washington Irving and generally seems to have been loath to enter into relationships with men. She moved to Harrow on the Hill to allow Percy Florence to attend Harrow and thereafter travelled with him in Europe, finally gaining financial independence when Sir Timothy died at the age of ninety in 1844 and Percy Florence inherited, Shelley and Harriet's son Charles having died around 1826. Percy Florence had married Jane Gibson St John, and Mary spent her last years living with the couple between Field Place, the Shelley home in Sussex, and Chester Square in London. She suffered from headaches and periods of paralysis and died at the age of fifty-three in 1851, most likely from a brain tumour. Percy Bysshe Shelley's 'heart' was found in her desk.

As well as *Frankenstein* (1818), Mary's works include the novels *The Last Man* (1826), *The Fortunes of Perkin Warbeck* (1830), *Lodore* (1835), and *Falkner* (1837). She was considered a literary talent in her own era and today is reckoned as a key figure of Gothic literature and a major feminist writer. Her reforming politics are a significant area of academic interest today.

The Godwin publishing business was eventually lost to bankruptcy. For a time, William and Mary Jane resided in the Palace of Westminster where Godwin had been made Office Keeper and Yeoman Usher of the Receipt of the Exchequer, but the palace was badly damaged in a fire in 1832. Their son William died in the same year. Increasingly, Godwin turned to Mary for support, and Mary helped maintain him until his death in 1836. Mary Jane died in 1841. They were both buried in St Pancras Churchyard alongside Mary Wollstonecraft. Ahead of the building of St Pancras Station, Wollstonecraft and Godwin's remains were removed to St Peter's churchyard in Bournemouth where Mary Shelley, her son Percy Florence and his wife Jane, Lady Shelley are also buried. Mary Jane was not moved.

Clara Mary Jane Clairmont, known in childhood as Jane and in adulthood as Claire, remained with Mary and Percy Shelley from the time of their elopement until Shelley's death. She was responsible for the association with Byron, having begun an affair with him prior to his departure from England in 1816. Her daughter with Byron, Alba (later changed to Allegra), was born in England in 1817. Byron took Allegra from Clairmont on the condition she would no longer see the child, and placed her in a convent in Italy, where she died at the age of five.

It is unclear whether Clairmont had a sexual relationship with Shelley. She may or may not have been the mother of the child named Elena who was registered as Shelley and Mary's child in Florence in 1818 and died in foster care in 1820. After Shelley's death, Clairmont spent a year with her brother in Vienna then travelled onwards to Russia where she worked as a governess. She returned to England briefly in 1828 before going to Dresden. From 1836 to 1841 she was in England, where she cared for her mother and then she lived in Paris, Pisa and Florence, where she died in 1897 at age eighty. Her relationship with Mary was fractious for the remainder of Mary's life and a legacy of £12,000 left to her by Shelley was unpaid for many years. Although she produced a small number of literary works, none of these survive, unless she is the author of 'The Pole' which was published in 1830 and credited to 'The Author of Frankenstein'. In recent years, her father has been established to have been John Lethbridge of Sandhill Park in Somerset, later Sir John, 1st Baronet.

Charles Clairmont became Chair of English at Vienna University and died in 1849. His father is thought to have been Swiss merchant Charles Gaulis as his mother claimed, although she described their liaison as a marriage and it was not.

See *Mary Shelley* by Miranda Seymour (London, John Murray; 2000), *Romantic Outlaws: the Extraordinary Lives of Mary Wollstonecraft & Mary Shelley* by Charlotte Gordon (London, Random House; 2016), *In Search of Mary Shelley* by Fiona Sampson (London, Profile; 2018), *Mary Shelley: Romance and Reality* by Emily W. Sunstein (Baltimore, Johns Hopkins; 1989)

Locations

None of the Polygon, the Godwins' shop in Holborn or The Cottage survive today. Although altered in various ways, Barns of Woodside still stands at the top of the brae in Newburgh, hidden behind high hedges and backed now by a railway line. Looking down from the gated wall to the great sweep of the Tay estuary, it is almost possible to feel one is standing where Mary once walked.

Acknowledgements

Books often start out lonely for the writer and end up a team game, but I was lucky in that *Poor Creatures* developed from conversations with Ali McBride at Black and White Publishing, to whom my first thanks are due. The rest of the team could not have been more supportive thereafter. Rachel, Thomas, Tonje, Lizzie, Hannah and Clem - thank you all. I know the book passed through many other hands at Bonnier during production, and thanks also to each and every one of them. I have been touched by many kindnesses from the Bonnier management and sales teams and especially appreciate the support of Sarah and Matt, Kevin and Arabella and all at team roadshow.

Spinning a narrative around real people has its challenges in terms of ensuring everyone can plausibly be where I want them, children all the right age, pregnancies lasting approximately the right duration etc, and I am so very grateful to Cari Rosen for a brilliantly attentive copyedit.

A thousand thanks to Emma Hargrave, who read the book first for me and then later for Black and White with all the skill and compassion she brings to all of her projects.

My mum and dad, Jim and Moira Kidd, are always a great help and support with historical fact-checking and with life in general. Thank you both, I love you and appreciate my great luck in the parent draw.

Thanks to all the friends who offered wise counsel and jollied me along, especially Viccy Adams, Harriet MacMillan, Lee Randall and Lucy Ribchester. Archer Thompson Adams was confused I thanked his mum in The Specimens while forgetting him, so I am putting that right now. I really appreciated the company of my fellow B&W author pals Coinneach MacLeod, Peter MacQueen and Alex Howard on many occasions. Particular thanks to Kendal Gater and Stephen Leonard who didn't complain when I had to cut a French holiday slightly short to make a book engagement back home, and got me to the TGV at Angoulême.

Last and greatest thanks as ever to Tom Morgan-Jones, for the gorgeous maps, for listening to endless rambling/grouching, being my events assistant/chauffeur, and for generally keeping body and soul together with all his customary kindness and cheer.